the house

of

wolves

the house of wolves

a novel

ROBERT B. McDIARMID

THE HOUSE OF WOLVES

ISBN-13: 978-1718930841 (CreateSpace-Assigned)
ISBN-10: 1718930844
BISAC: Fiction / Gay

This novel is a work of fiction. Names, characters, places, and
incidents either are the products of the author's imagination or are
used fictitiously, and any resemblance to actual persons, living or
dead, buildings or business establishments, clubs or organizations,
events, or locales is entirely coincidental.

Set in Goudy Old Style and Kelt.
Wolves Mandala: Yolanda Fundora.
Interior design: Alex Jeffers.
Cover Photo: John Cantwell, courtesy of Ray Cervantes Photography

We but half express ourselves, and are ashamed of that divine idea which each of us represents. It may be safely trusted as proportionate and of good issues, so it be faithfully imparted, but God will not have his work made manifest by cowards.

A man is relieved and gay when he has put his heart into his work and done his best; but what he has said or done otherwise, shall give him no peace. It is a deliverance which does not deliver. In the attempt his genius deserts him; no muse befriends; no invention, no hope.

—Ralph Waldo Emerson, *Self-Reliance*

1. Bowman Bay

IT WAS ALMOST AS if David appeared out of nowhere. We flashed a smile at one another as I was leaving the clinic. How sad is that, cruising someone on your way out of a therapy appointment?

He wore a tattered old black leather jacket, gray T-shirt, brand new Wranglers, and new blue jeans, as if he were trying to contrast his graying hair and middle age with something fresh and vibrant. His strong legs, muscular butt, and air of mysterious confidence drew me to him in a way that had never happened before. There I was, suddenly feeling sparks ignite in my heart as if I'd recognized a kindred spirit.

He wore his beard then, and it was bushy and wild with the tiniest traces of gray. His hair, tied in back in a ponytail, was frothing about under a red cloth ball cap. But the most amazing thing about that first moment (and I will always say this) was the momentary, childlike flash of baby browns that disarmed me from the very beginning.

For days afterward, between correcting math tests and grading reports on the latest childhood adventures, I found myself constantly daydreaming about him. I needed to be back at school that fall.

It was my classroom, Mr. Wallace's fifth-grade class. After my first partner died the previous year, my classroom and my young companions were my purest comfort zone. I dove into hanging fall decorations and reminding myself how to make long division exciting for my new group of youthful spirits. The walls were plastered with ten-year-olds' interpretations of pilgrims, Native Americans, and neon-colored horns o' plenty.

We were studying the early history of the Northwest, including Indian legends and how rugged life in North America had been, and learning about team building, loyalty, and each other. Fifth-graders are the perfect age where they really want to make a relationship with their teachers. They are starving for knowledge and have not yet learned the attitudes of their middle school counterparts.

It was just fifteen eager minds and I in a canoe on a sixteenth-century river in the middle of my classroom, searching for grizzly bears, bald eagles, and French Canadian trappers. They would shout out facts during interactive lessons and moan and laugh at my poor jokes. We were learning by doing—that was our motto. Interesting that, in the midst of all this enthusiasm, I kept denying what a nice distraction working with my kids was from having to really deal with what do past the death of Joe.

I don't do that dating, flirting crap very well. I was so used to being part of a partnership that when Joe died, I felt pretty lost outside of work for a long time.

Each of my kids keeps a journal. It's remarkable to watch the progression of these young people as the year progresses. My second day of daydreaming caught the attention of Marcel, my little writing star. In his journal, he wrote, "Mr. Wallace must have met someone, Robbie says he is going soft on us." I laughed out loud reading this observation; even little Marcel started to notice that I was ready for love again in my life.

I had spent lonely nights searching faces in bars, and had gone on dates that were clearly not ever going to turn into anything even remotely close to a relationship. I got lost in a few quick, lusty affairs that disintegrated when we discovered we had nothing in common but liking to fuck. I found myself in a very lonely place, wishing I could be back in the time, a few years earlier, when I had a partner and a life apart from work.

Then just like that, the man from the support group was show-ing up everywhere: at the grocery, at the gym, at the video store, at the coffee shop. That one moment, on a rainy October Sat-urday—when he reached out, held my hand to the counter and paid for my tea—changed my life completely.

With the unyielding Seattle rain as accompaniment, we sat in the booth at the coffeehouse and talked for hours. His name was David Moreau. A painter and woodworker, he was designing signature clocks and cabinets. This beast of a man spoke passion-ately about how he had found the work that made his spirit com-plete. It was completely natural to imagine this man surrounded by wood chips and the smell of linseed oil. He talked about artists he loved and how he would like to take me museum-hopping. We talked about art and paint and laughed about the things we had in common: a passion for eggnog, an undeniable need for dramatic romance, and fresh tulips.

Then his eyes changed tone entirely as he leaned in and said, "So, what is your story, young man?"

David knew when to touch me. From the first, this was like magic. He reached out with his callused hands, stroked the hair on top of my hands, and kept listening.

I was still grieving the death of my first partner in those days. The survivors' group and therapist were holding me together. I had kept this Hollywood romantic notion that Joseph would be with me forever. Even when both of us had tested HIV+ to-gether at the clinic, my dreams of forever were not dashed. Then the night sweats came, and then the slow, quiet wasting; my life seemed to fade along with the most important man I had ever met. I missed Joe's beautiful eyes and his infectious laughter.

There are times, these many years later, when my eyes still well up at the thought of those terrible few months after Joseph died. I told David about having to sell the house and how I kept even Joseph's smallest trinkets locked in a storage unit where they could not cause me further pain.

The last few months had been painfully lonely. I told David that I thought I was just now reaching the point where I yearned for something new. The struggle was that I was not sure what something new meant. Sitting there in the booth we learned that both of us lived with HIV and had a passion for alternatives, like herbs and relaxing with tai chi. The more we shared, the more intense our little hand game on the table became. While listening, he looked over at me with those glistening baby brown eyes, stroking my hand and forearm with real intent, pulling on the little hairs, manipulating them with his fingers.

When David touched me, it was like there was not a single care in the rest of the world. That was David's first lesson for me—that touch can heal.

He asked to walk me home, so we headed down Broadway holding hands beneath my umbrella. He had me laughing out loud, telling stories of abysmal dating catastrophes and his inability to conquer the country-western two-step.

"Some people have two left feet," he giggled, "but I have four."

Seattle's early winter rain usually made me feel maudlin; but there I was, walking down the street hand in hand with David as if it were a perfect summer day. He walked me to the doorstep of my 12th-Street bungalow.

Shadowed in oaks with crimson gold leaves, this had been my escape, my Fortress of Solitude. I had intentionally chosen a small home where only one person could live. No out-of-luck friends could suddenly become roommates; no transitory lovers could move in.

And here, on these steps, this bear of a man leaned forward and kissed me. It was an urgent, wet kiss, with purposeful intent. He pulled me to himself and slowly explored my lips for what felt like endless seconds. Then he gently ran his coarse mustache across my lips and nuzzled in against my neck.

That was the first time I remember the scent of pipe tobacco, his unique mix of vanilla and burley. It was definitely more of a scent than a perfume. We stood there for a long while, my arms wrapped over his shoulders as his short, stocky frame pressed me against my front door as if a cosmic jigsaw puzzle had finally found the missing piece.

He licked my neck and whispered, "I need to let you go, my sweet little man, but I will find you again."

He curiously took a deep breath from my neck and sniffed his way up to my ear, setting off goose bumps across my body.

"Believe that," he finished, as he withdrew and tapped my chin, a gentle smile on his face.

I watched him walk away down the cobblestone alley. It's still one of my dearest memories of David—his walking away, black boots clomping in his strong stride. At the end of the block, he paused, turned, smiled, waved, and then disappeared around the corner.

I sat on my doorstep for a moment, stunned by the encounter. Smiling, I put the key in my lock, entered the house, leaned against the door, and let out a large sigh.

"I could love this man," I thought to myself.

The rain continued well into the evening. I found myself totally distracted from any of my schoolwork. Trying to get back into my routine, I tried watching TV but just fidgeted, completely distracted. Finally, I retreated to my loft bedroom.

I sat in bed reading when the phone rang. It was David.

"Sorry, I just couldn't wait to find you again so I looked you up in the book. So, my dear Mr. Wallace, why don't I pick you up in the morning, and we'll go up into the islands together? The sun is supposed to shine tomorrow, and I am going out for an early morning 'get out of here.' I really want it to be with you," he said quietly.

"Sounds good to me, David. What time shall I be ready?"

"6 A.M., and dress warm. I don't need you getting a cold on me now, do I?"

It felt warm and gentle for this man to care so much about my welfare.

"Guess not. Thank you for today, David," I said, smiling into the telephone.

"That's a good little man. I'll be in a gray truck and, well, at 6:00 A.M., probably the only man coming down your alleyway," he said, laughing. "See you then?"

"Yes. Thank you!"

"You are very welcome, Mr. Wallace. See you tomorrow."

Click.

I hung up the phone, closed my book. David had me entranced. This man had, in the simple act of buying me a cup of coffee and coveting time with me, started me dreaming again. I honestly do not remember dreaming properly from the day Joseph died until that night.

This time it was all about dreams of David's vanilla and burley scent. Vivid dreams of waking with my face in the center of his chest and of wondering what mysteries hid behind his baby brown eyes.

I woke suddenly the next morning, bathed in the sunrise. It was just as David had promised. The dawn streamed in through the skylight above the bed. With the crystal sunrise dancing off the walls, I let out a large, contented sigh.

Stretching in my loft, I heard the coffee pot sputter and spit, filling the house with rich aroma.

I stumbled down the ladder to the bathroom, and the steam from the shower clouded the windows. The stereo played a local jazz station; Norah Jones crooned as I let the water run over me. My short brown beard dripped with water as I stood there. I'd never grown a beard before, and it had been the first thing David had complimented me on. I smiled to myself.

I've always loved the solitary power of a hot morning shower. Leaning up against the shower wall daydreaming, tracing my body with the soap, it made me smile; I made a singular dance out of making sure every inch of me was clean for my morning with David. I toweled off and headed for the kitchen, I poured myself a strong cup of coffee and read more of my novel as I waited for 6:00 A.M. to approach. The sound of the doorbell came right on time.

I opened the door and there was David, hair down around his shoulders. In his mouth was a small pipe—a very simple, black pipe. His eyes lit up when he saw me, like a child at a circus.

"Good morning, Mr. Wallace," he said, walking inside. "Ready to go?"

"Yes, my stuff is right here," I said. I grabbed my jeans jacket and baseball cap out of the closet and threw my pack over my shoulder.

I went to walk past him, and he pulled me to himself roughly, removed the pipe from his mouth, and kissed me. Unlike the romantic kiss of the day before, this kiss was hungry and urgent. The fresh pipe smoke in his moustache and the taste of the tobacco rushed into my senses as his tongue found its way into my mouth for the first time. Grunting, I reacted by running my arms into his leather jacket and around him and kissing back hard and deep, my pack falling to the floor.

He pushed me up against the kitchen counter, and we rubbed chests and bodies as we kissed. It was playful, frantic, and wild. When we came up for air, the Cheshire grin came to his face as he said, "I missed your green eyes, Mr. Wallace..."

I licked at his nose and said, "Good morning, David!"

I returned a warm, excited smile. With that momentary celebration, we headed out into the morning. The city streets on mornings like this are clean and fresh, and the morning air greets your lungs like a champagne toast.

"It's not pretty, but it'll get us where we are headed," David giggled as he proudly presented his beat-up Volkswagen pickup.

The vehicle looked as if it had survived a war, with spots of mismatched paint, no radio, and gauges broken on the dash. A Native American dream catcher was hanging off the mirror.

"I was hoping that you had most of the day," he said. "I'd like to take you up to the islands, but we can make a quickie out of it if you'd like."

I leaned in and licked his ear as he began to drive down the
road. "You can have me all day and night if you'd like."

"That, Mr. Wallace, is the correct answer," he said with a
chuckle.

We drove along enjoying the morning sun as he puffed away,
careful to keep the window open. I snuggled in next to him, my
hand on his thigh. We sat in a comfortable silence as he wound
his way down the hills of Seattle, to the freeway and then north.
When we finally started to break out of the city to the country-
side, the fall foliage of the northwest was displaying a brilliant
cascade of color.

"I thought I'd take you to Deception Pass and Whidbey Island.
I grew up near there; my pop would take me and my brother
and drop us off in the woods for the day. It was a great place for
hide-'n'-seek when I was a child—but it has also been a great
getaway for me as an adult. It's so beautiful there," he said, his
voice trailing off as he puffed on his pipe and the truck bolted
down the freeway.

A few minutes down the road we pulled off, and he said, "I
didn't get my cup of coffee this morning, so let's get me some.
Before I get grumbly. What do you think, Mr. Wallace?"

"Sounds good to me. I can always use a good cup of tea."

He smiled.

"How very old world," he said, laughing, "A cup o' tea, you say
(faking a really horrible English accent). Not any of that strong
American coffee for me, I say!" For such a brute of a man, out
of him came a childlike giggle. He had this sidesplitting snort
rather than an adult laugh. There wasn't a thing about him that
I wasn't completely falling in love with.

We wandered into the small-town coffee shop and ordered.
He sipped his latte. When the froth got all over his mustache,
David leaned forward, purposely smearing it in my face and kiss-
ing me.

"Can't let my mustache get all sticky, can we, now?"

He walked away, leaving me stunned in front of a group of rural folks, giggling his way out to the truck. I soon followed, chuckling to myself at this grown imp I found myself traveling with.

We turned off the freeway and were suddenly deep in the woods of the San Juan Islands. David explained that he'd always had a spiritual connection with them. The green forests of the islands, with their beds of ferns and plants, were like therapy for David. He called them his "ferny forests." He'd grown up surrounded by nature and the musk of the forest. As I sat listening to him, we entered the park.

The trees, unhampered by logging and the world, grew thicker and taller. The farther we drove, the deeper the mist and fog became. He told me about the days when the fog would come in quickly and quietly. You'd suddenly find yourself in so deep it would be easy to believe that the world had been swallowed and isolated away from everything else.

He pulled the truck off and down a winding, steep, single-lane road, heading toward the water. It was like descending into nothing as we headed down the hill. Through the shifting mists was revealed a small bay, lined with trees and rocks, and a small boat dock. The evergreens bent in the wind, showing that they'd long since given up fighting the ocean breezes. The air was thick with salt, and the fog moved through the inlet like a snake in the grass.

"This is our first stop."

With engine noise no longer invading the peace, we got out of the truck and started walking toward the water. He stopped for a moment and put his arms around me, peering over my shoulder. We sat down there taking it in. This scene was very alive. The fog danced with the shoreline while we listened to the ocean lap at the stone-covered beach.

"This is Bowman Bay, one of my favorite places. The last time I was here was with…well…" David's voice trailed off, hesitant to complete the thought.

He nuzzled my neck with his thick bushy beard. David wrapped his strong arms around me, shoving his hands into my coat pockets. We stood up and gazed out over the choppy waters of the bay. I felt great affection in David's warm embrace.

After a while, David released me. "C'mon." He led me along a path bordering the water, grabbing a belt loop on my jeans and pulling me closer to him as we followed the path deeper into the thick green forest.

After a few minutes, curiosity got the better of me. "Tell me about him?"

"Richard was my lover for three years. We met after a woodworking show." David's eyes grew radiant with memory. "I was at a home show with some of my work. He walked up." David laughed.

"It was springtime. Here was Richard in his trademark long coat and rainbow scarf, in May, hardly scarf weather. He loved my Saanich Indian work. He said he'd had childhood connections with them. They settled this area, you know."

David paused and moved his hand toward the scene around us. He told me about the Saanich, the tribe that had settled the very land we now slowly walked through, and of their artistic and spiritual traditions.

"I use a lot of their images in my own work. It…gives me strength." I sensed the tremendous pride David had for his work and the respect he had for the traditions of the Saanich.

He said that one day he'd take me to the Saanich Reservation and go "listening."

"You can only find true inspiration in art that believes in its integrity. So few artists understand that; they treat First Nations art like it's something to be copied and exploited. When I first encountered it, I decided I had to take the art to the next step. I had to honor its tradition and learn from the actual Indian artists, and find their stories behind their art. It's made my efforts more satisfying since I've tried very hard to make sure my work and my art are authentic to their practices, not some cheap dime-store imitation."

Returning to the story about Richard, he added, "After meeting me, Richard commissioned a large Saanich carving and installation.

"Richard was building a house and wanted the door to hold the sign of the wolf in Saanich tradition. He commissioned a beautiful original design of wolves with interconnecting tails. I really do try not to mix work and pleasure, but talking with Richard was unlike anything I'd ever experienced.

"He talked of ways to live authentically and was unapologetically masculine and sexual. So when he asked me to come stay with him at the new house the weekend we were installing the door, well, I jumped at it. I met Richard's housemates, and the house and Richard quickly became part of my life."

The tone he used when describing his home, "the house," was almost like he was describing a living being. On this comment David stopped, packed his pipe and lit it, staring at me for a moment contemplatively.

The sun started to peek through the fog as he continued his story.

"Honestly, there had been no dating as far as I was concerned; I was in love with Richard from that very first encounter."

Each time he talked of loving Richard, he held me tighter, closer. He deliberately made sure I was closer and closer to him.

David talked about Richard's incredibly soft voice, which had contrasted his lumberjack brawn. He described Richard as a man who had been in his late fifties, a longtime fitness buff, and tai chi instructor at the local YMCA. He described the first few times they were physical with one another, how Richard's beauty had shown David a whole new side of his own sexuality and his physical body.

His eyes softened from his reminiscing of Richard's life with him. He leaned into me, and I realized he was crying. It was at once uncomfortable and powerful.

Eventually David stopped, looked at me through tears, and said, "I lead a complicated life, Mr. Wallace, and I so want to show it to you. The house, the men I live with, the magic it has brought to my life."

I stopped walking and leaned into him, running my forehead along his beard. His hand naturally cupped my neck. My hand ran through his hair flowing onto his shoulders. He looked so rugged and yet so soft with his hair down, irresistible as he pulled me to himself with his other hand.

"You really are an interesting surprise, Mr. Wallace."

He continued his storytelling, his smoke swirling between us. Richard had been the headmaster of sorts in a cooperative house-hold of six other men. Since it started, they had kept adding special roommates, and Richard, as patriarch of the household, had decided that David would join them. He explained that "the house" and his brothers were now the center of his life, since Richard had died.

"I talked to my housemates about our coffee conversation, the things that we had in common. You know, I saw you watching me that day, leaving the therapist's office at the clinic. I had hoped we'd encounter each other again.

"The men of the house have been there for me since Richard left, and they've wanted me to find a new path, to move on. God, the last year has been a real struggle for happiness. It's just that getting out and meeting people doesn't come naturally. I don't do bars or parties, and most gay men have the shortest fucking attention span."

David giggled to himself. "I'd come to the conclusion that find-ing gay men where pretenses and shadows don't exist seemed im-possible. I have become frozen with fear at the same time, about being near or around my own kind. I feel paralyzed.

"I chose the isolation of the house, the busy chores, and my work to keep me happy, but then, yesterday happened, and, well, perhaps...perhaps..."

He looked at me softly and smiled. Tracing my mouth slowly with his hand, his eyes softened even further. I leaned in, removed the pipe from his mouth, and kissed him. He let out a little groan and started kissing me back, his tongue fresh with a thick, smoky taste, then nuzzling his beard and face into my neck and grinding against me.

He took the pipe from my hand and took a deep breath of it in and then fed it to me. I had no idea the head rush and spin it'd give me. The hot smoke filled my mouth and my throat. He breathed in again, and then slowly breathed it over my face.

His eyes taking on a sudden intensity, David took my right hand and held it to his crotch. My cock was so hard it gave away any doubt that he was turning me on; it ached at his touch.

He kissed me again with a mouthful of hot smoke and started grunting and sucking on my face. I pushed him up against a tree, and we slowly lowered ourselves to the ground. He sat back against the tree, and I kneeled between his legs.

Staring into my eyes, he worked his fingers in between each gap of the shirt as he unbuttoned it, swirling the hair on my chest purposefully and slowly. Once my shirt was open, he sniffed his way down while blowing warm smoke across the fur of my chest.

"Just as beautiful as I knew you'd be," he whispered.

He found my left nipple and the ring waiting there, took the pipe out of his mouth, stared into my eyes, and ran the bowl of the pipe across my nipple ring. I whimpered.

"That's good, pup. That's real good to see. I want to make love to you very soon. I plan to spend many nights up inside you and beside you. Believe that. But first we have today to kiss and explore, and then you'll meet the others. And the time will come when we'll have one another. I just know it."

David's eyes misted over. Lying on top of me, here was this beautiful man, almost crying, at the thought of knowing that one day we could be there for one another. It was a different tear in his eye than earlier, this one of happiness and dreams.

He blew another thick cloud of smoke across my neck and slowly, deliberately, buttoned my shirt. He paused for a moment, then reached down, combing my chest hairs with his hand.

"You are a beautiful man, Mr. Wallace. And you are captivating me."

He helped me up, and we continued on our hike, his hand installed on my belt loop.

We walked close as David gave me time to consider what he'd shared that morning. We continued to talk and laugh our way through those woods for the rest of the day, sharing more stories. His love for Richard had been strong, a feeling I knew so well after losing Joseph. I was captivated by his description of the household and the men he now cared for in Richard's absence. We didn't stop talking the entire day, not through dinner or when he dropped me off in the darkness of night.

I asked David up, but he said no, that he was tired, and that we'd have lots of time to keep learning about one another.

"One day at a time, Mr. Wallace, and you made this one day very special."

I kissed him and got out of the truck, smiled, and waved as he drove off. Isn't it interesting how life presents you with unexpected opportunities? David and I both had stopped looking for the right man in our lives. Now we had many things to think about.

He'd invited me to his house for dinner the following weekend, but now it was time to concentrate on a busy week with my kids. Later that evening, I realized his scent was in my mustache. David was part of me now; I was just beginning to understand how much that meant.

I sat there thinking how terribly long it had felt since Joseph had died, remembering how Joseph had always loved telling stories from his faith. He could tell stories until late in the night and make me smile with every word. Oh, how I missed those late nights up talking. There is one story in particular that I've always remembered.

Joseph woke me early in the morning and said he needed to talk. He was worried I'd never meet another man again or open myself up to true love. I've always thought it amazing that a man who was clearly dying had so much concern for my welfare after his departure. He laughed, coughed roughly, and told me that, of course, he had a story to tell me.

"The rabbis say that God created the universe by shattering vessels containing God's energy. These shards spread throughout the universe, spreading the divine spark, beginning all life. It is said that when strong, undeniable feelings happen between people it is because you are made from the same original ancient spark of this energy. This unique power recognizes itself within the other person and longs to be united again."

Strange, that he'd explained to me exactly the way I'd feel two years later, when I met David Moreau.

2. Of Blood, Wood and Stone

THE COLD WINTER WALK to work that next morning was contemplative and rich. I pulled my heavy coat on and ventured through the fog to school, briefcase in hand. I love early mornings—my time before the kids arrive, alone in my classroom getting materials ready and focusing on the day's tasks. I sipped my tea and enjoyed the bright sunshine bursting into the room.

This morning I caught myself distracted and dreaming of David, starting to wonder more and more of the household he described, a large collective that was home to six men, Richard making seven. I also wondered about the various personalities and the lives of the men I would soon meet. But first was the task of broadening the lives of fifteen young fifth-graders.

Monday mornings were my favorite because we started the day with a fun, high-energy discussion of history. I always found this to be the best way to get my kids back into the swing of things. History is a subject that's always fascinated me. Teaching fifth-graders Washington state history was one of my favorite activities of the year.

On Thursday, we talked about Lewis and Clark and the movement west, and how Washington had only been a state for about 110 years. We were much younger than much of the nation. Students gave reports, in teams, about different aspects of early Washington history, from logging to commerce to the little skirmishes between British and American settlers.

Robbie and Marcel got up and gave a report about the San Juan Islands and the different captains that discovered them. They told us about Captain Vancouver and his lieutenant, Jacob Whidbey, and described the very places David took me the day before.

We headed to lunch, and I wandered to the front office to check messages. There in my mail slot was an envelope. I opened it with a smile to find a beautiful card with bird feathers arranged on the cover: THANK YOU FOR BOWMAN BAY, SEE YOU TOMORROW FOR DINNER—LOVE DAVID. Even the card had the scent of his tobacco.

When I left work the next day, the two hours between work and dinner at David's seemed to last forever. I tore out my entire wardrobe, wanting to look my best for this date, finally settling on a cream-colored tab-collar shirt and a brand new pair of blue jeans, with cowboy boots. I stopped at the store and picked up some tulips in a bouquet and headed out to the house.

I followed David's instructions and came down a street along Discovery Park, by the water. The house number directed me up an inlaid stone driveway. There, nestled in the ancient trees, was a brick wall with an iron black gate. I opened the gate, walked up the path and, in the shadowy light, came to a door.

The porch light was on, highlighting the amazing design David had described on our trip. Carved in relief on the door were eight bright red wolves, painted in Native fashion, connected by their tails into a black circle in the center.

I reached out and ran my hand over the carving. The wood slid under my fingers, and I could feel the hand-carved ridges of the craftsman's knife. I stood there a moment, simply studying it. The imagery was powerful to me, partly because I knew this was David's work.

Then I knocked.

The door slowly opened, and an older man with a shaved head and a bright, white, close-cropped beard opened the door and allowed me into the room. He had a spectacular array of piercings in both ears and stared over his bifocals as he shook my hand, offering me a warm smile.

"I am Marlin. We are very excited that you are here. David has told 's eh lot 'bout you," he said in a thick English accent.

Marlin apparently didn't shower often; he had a strong scent. "David is still cleaning up from an afternoon working late in 'is studio, so he asked me to give you a tour of the house."

"Tulips," he said, noticing the bouquet. "David's favorite. Let me run and put these in water. I'll be right back."

He left me to admire the great room, the walls lined with wooden inlaid bookshelves and an old-fashioned ladder that ran on a track along the curved wall.

There was a spiral ladder up into a loft above it, and in the center of the room was the fireplace, where a fire roared. The floor was made of a silvery stone. In front of the fire were dark leather couches and chairs arranged around the firelight. The room's lighting was subtle and seemed to come from nowhere. I stood there a moment admiring the leather-bound books on the shelf, feeling as though I were in old English movie.

Marlin walked back into the room. "The library was the one room for which I had some input. Turned out right nice, if ya ask me. Come this way; let me show you the house, Roy."

From the living room we followed another curved hallway to a glass door that opened onto a patio. I finally got a good idea of the layout of the house. It was a collection of round structures, seven in total. Hallways connected the first three; then you had to step outside to reach the other four buildings in the complex.

From the stone paths between buildings to the adobe finish on the round buildings, it was clear that the complex was eclectic in style, combining English and New England architecture. The buildings were oversized and fortress-like, reminiscent of an English castle while also having a modern feel. The architecture was inspiring.

The buildings created an oval, and in the center was a raised bed garden surrounded by a fence. The garden had recently been turned in preparation for winter. Cobblestone paths led to each building. It really was an amazing piece of work.

"The main structure has the library, living room, kitchen and dining area. Them there are the outbuildings. Here's Tristan's design studio, our living quarters, the wet room, the gym, David's carvin' room, and Richard's greatest gift to the house, the meditation room."

Marlin's accent somehow belonged in this strange grouping of structures, adding to the experience, bringing the architecture to life. We entered into a large, empty, round room with a floor made of individually laid stones. Inlaid in the walls were mystic signs and scripts from various cultures, including Asian and Native American. There were square blocks with quotes from different scholars and historical figures. I was struck by a particular quote, and I smiled and ran my finger over its letters.

"What we take for the history of nature is only the very incomplete history of an instant."—DENIS DIDEROT.

"David was right. You are a wonderer, aren't you, Roy?" I felt Marlin step up behind me. "Richard completed 'is room just before he got sick the first time. David has always said it's like he waited for its completion before he allowed himself sickness."

Marlin's closeness felt nice but somehow inappropriate at the same time, and he seemed to sense my apprehension. "Don't worry, pup, I'm not here to corner ya, man—just to show yer 'round." He gave me a very strong hug and then leaned in on my ear and whispered, "Yer doin' fine, pup, jus' relax."

He led me into the center of the room and asked me to stand there for a second while he went to the wall, opened a panel, and started playing a CD. It was like the sound was coming from all around me as I stood there in the middle of the room: one of the Bach arias. Marlin and I shared a moment, eyes closed, enjoying the rich sounds in the perfectly acoustic chamber.

"Really is quite magical, isn't it, Roy? Classical music speaks a unique voice, doesn't it, without bein' hampered," he said as he let it play until finished. He looked at me over his glasses and smiled, then turned off the music, closed the compartment, and led me out and to the next building, which housed the living quarters.

"This is where most of us live, or should I say sleep," he said with a twinkle.

He explained it was polite to knock before entering the private quarters; Tristan especially insisted on this courtesy. While they were a cooperative household, some of the men preferred their own private spaces. Others, like Moose and Bear, can't sleep unless they hold a man in bed with them. He told me that I'd learn soon enough, winking at me, whether or not I felt comfortable staying there.

I was beginning to like this man, this leprechaun of a man. Even his strong aroma somehow felt comforting in these surroundings. This house was far more than David had suggested; it had a strong communal feeling like it belonged to all of them. Only a few places felt private.

"I sleep above the library in the loft. Just like the openness of it. And it keeps me close to ma books besides. Don't mind my solitude. Makes it a safe place to find yourself. Understand me, pup? Occasionally, one of 'em likes coming up and sleeping with me, though, and that's a treat."

The next building was the wet building. It included a laundry and a unique shower, like a shower from a high school gym, but with adult sensibilities.

There was a large community shower area but three well-equipped private stalls as well. A steam room, hot tub, Jacuzzi, and a lap pool were outside on a separate patio, surrounded by trees and fencing for privacy. The third building consisted of a large office with a spacious wooden desk for each member of the house and a large design table facing the patio. There was, curiously, one desk bare and facing the windows; I assumed it had been Richard's.

"That's Tristan's herbology practice up front there, and here is where the rest of us play on our computers," Marlin said, gesturing around the room, "Moose and Bear play lots of Internet games here—that blood and guts stuff." He guffawed.

"And it's where we get our e-mail and stuff. I personally find it too much, too impersonal, too much technology. I like my books. David prints me out what he thinks I'd like to read and leaves it in the library for me. Good man, that David is; but then you know that, don't you, Roy?" he said with a large, toothy smile, leading me out onto the central patio between the buildings.

On the way out, he pointed to a smaller, round building, off by itself, which had obviously been built after the other buildings. It had the same style of architecture, but it was constructed with rubble stone and had thick wisteria vines growing up its sides like something from Tolkien's The Hobbit.

"That, my dear Roy, is David's studio. Isn't that wisteria beautiful? Such a natural contrast, eh? In winter, a gnarly skeleton of vines and in summer, massive fragrant blooms and green leaves. I think David will show that to you, 'is room, in 'is own time, a very private man about his craft he is; and 'is work is one of a kind; but he often locks himself in there for hours with no company and simply is."

He explained that David would anguish over pieces of work and punish himself for not having instant creativity. He and Tristan often fought bitterly over the creative process. So bad, sometimes, that the rest of the collective's members would just leave the house to them.

"But perhaps I speak outta turn," Marlin finished.

We then re-entered the main building, and David was seated in one of the leather chairs by the fireplace. David grinned, pipe in his mouth, and muttered, "Brought him back in one piece, I see. Thank you, Marlin." His strong body was showing through a tight black T-shirt, and he had pulled his hair back with a tight braid.

"Hello, Mr. Wallace," he said. "No harm done…so far."

Marlin cackled and smiled back at David.

"You have a beautiful home," I said. "It is much more than you described."

David rose, walked up to me, and gave me a strong hug and a deep kiss.

"Tulips. You are quite the charmer, mister."

"OK, lovebirds, everyone else is waiting in the dining room." And with that, they led me deeper into the house. The stone library floor wound behind a curved wall into another great room that was a kitchen and dining room.

"This is Roy Wallace, gentlemen." Turning to me, David continued. "Mr. Wallace, this is William, Moose, Tristan, and Bear." Around the room were five men.

"These, Mr. Wallace, are my brothers," said David proudly. The friendliest and the first to come forward was a lumberjack of a man who had been cooking at the stove.

"Dinner will be ready in a jiffy." He turned, revealing an apron covered with spots of sauce and food. He had a huge red beard and sparkling blue eyes, and he extended a sauce-splattered hand. "I'm Moose."

Tristan sat at the bar. He was a small, muscular man with a trickle of a mustache on his lip like Genghis Khan; his deep black eyes concentrated on me.

David then introduced the two men at the table. Bear was clearly the eldest of the group, with black and white hair and a beard to his belly button. William almost towered over his compatriots and wore a bright blue tank top and a dark, mischievous, Vandyke beard.

"I'm ready," said Moose, and he started serving salads and soups as Tristan delivered them to the table. David sat at the head of the table and ushered me into a chair to his left. As each

of the men took their places at the table, I looked around rather
nervously.

"We're very happy to have you here, Roy," began William,
"and are delighted you've met our David. We hope you can relax
and just be yourself. We know that we can be a little, how you
say, overbearing. At first."

Marlin chimed in, "But dunna worry, pup, we don't bite. Unless
you ask real nicely, anyhow."

The table of men giggled. William said they needed to say
grace, and they bowed their heads. David spoke, "For food in
a world where many walk in hunger; for faith in a world where
many walk in fear; for friends in a world where many walk alone;
we give you thanks, O Lord. Amen."

The dinner conversation quickly drew me in and started answering my unspoken questions. I watched and listened as each
contributed. They allowed me to participate in silence. Tristan
then explained how each member of the household had different chores and distinct roles, but that they learned from one
another.

He explained that being a member of the house meant that you
were open to learning from each discipline that others brought
to the collective, and explained that each member of the household had specific duties. Each member, upon arrival, had seemed
naturally suited for inclusion.

William then spoke up: "Why doesn't everyone go around and
explain your role and where you've fit into the house?" William
pointed out that he was responsible for making sure the group
had activities and cultural events to attend, such as theater and
community lecture series.

He explained that community service was an important core responsibility of each member or the house, and that each member
was expected to volunteer time with a community organization
outside the household.

Tristan was the gardener and the lover of things that grow. He made sure that, when possible, the household used natural homegrown items, from food to soaps to incense.

Marlin was the teacher, but he also had the reputation as an attentive student. Marlin added, winking at me, that teachers tend to be the best students. He was the one who looked after the library and chose books for them to read.

Moose was the cook and the man in charge of making sure laundry and other domestic chores got done. He made sure everyone picked up after himself, that the house remained a haven without clutter.

Bear was a personal trainer of body and soul. His job was to make sure everyone kept physically fit with gym trips and meditations of sorts. He also helped the men in the house that were HIV+ by coordinating their various medications and regimens, and made sure the men kept to their schedules and plans.

Finally, I learned that David had inherited the patriarchal duties of overseeing everyone else's chores and responsibilities; he also mediated disputes.

William smiled, leaned back on Marlin, and said in a deep baritone voice, "We are so very glad that you liked it, Roy. Our David here has told us a lot about you; you are just as charming and smart looking as he told us. We are happy you are here. Perhaps —"

Tristan interrupted abruptly. "But to know one member of the house is to know all of us. That's the way Richard always wanted it. So, while David is the man who brought you here, we'd like time with you; to get to know you."

"All in good time," said William. "Let's not overwhelm Roy on his first visit, gentlemen." His voice was very quiet but intense and final. When he spoke, his eyes lit up, and he seemed to stare completely into you, making you feel that you were the only focus. His commanding presence was just beginning to show.

William continued. "Since you two met at the coffee shop, he's been unable to talk about anything else, and we took that as a good sign. Then, when we encouraged his trip to Bowman Bay with you, that sealed his first impression."

So, as you continue to get to know David, we'll be interested in who you are, who you've been, and where you think you are headed. We haven't had a teacher in the house for years since Marlin retired," he said as he looked over at Marlin, who huffed under his breath.

"There are many things to learn about us, as we're a varied and complex lot. So we'd like you to consider, while you continue to see and date and romance our David, that you spend some time with each of us and let us share and show you what this arrangement does for each of us. Let us learn about you. It should be pretty clear that to date one of us means, in some shape or fashion, to date all of us. We're not looking for an answer this evening, we're just very happy you've met our David. We want to know more about you and see if joining David here would be something you'd like; that you'd want."

The men around the table seemed to beam at the mention of our romance, with David blushing a deep red. I found myself swimming in a swirl of ideas and questions.

"So, Roy, why don't you tell us a little of your journey, a little about yourself?" said Tristan.

"I didn't know what to expect when I came here today. I know that I am falling in love with David. But I've never been around a group like you clearly represent. Honestly, I'm finding it rather overwhelming. I'm looking forward to getting to know you, because anyone important to David has to be worth investigating. But, gosh, it's going to take me time to digest this and see where it goes."

My mind swirled with the images of the house and the group of men I sat there with. What a unique blend of personalities this group represented, from Marlin's playfulness to Tristan's obvious discipline to David's soft touch.

"Where have I been before here? What is my journey?" I smiled. "My life for the last year has been career, career, career.

And therapy." I flashed a grin at David. "I love my kids at school, and I'm having a spectacular year. Kids are so smart these days, and I love making them think in new ways.

"When my partner died two years ago, I was convinced part of me had died with him. And I guess I've been denying myself for a long time. I mean, I dated and stuff, took my turn at the baths. But how long can that be fulfilling, eh? It's been lonely, but for the most part purposely so. I didn't want to share my grief and struggle with anyone. So I have few friends these days and have lived the life of a loner. I'd seen David here and there and wondered what it would be like to be with him. He wanders into the coffee shop, and then it happened so quickly.

Then to meet you through David, men that I could be friends with and learn from. It's a great offer of change; but, gosh, you are...pretty intimidating...and, honestly, the thought of ya'll being sexual with one another...well, it's over the top."

William smiled and said, "We love each other. That makes for ways to enrich each other's lives some of us never found elsewhere. And that means physical love as well as camaraderie. We are a brotherhood of men who know we have needs, emotional and physical, and we are here to make sure those are met. We celebrate our bodies, minds, and spirits. It's important in our collective here, to celebrate every part of ourselves.

"But I don't want the physical to interfere with you getting to knowing us, so let's leave the physical till we know you. We'd each like to spend some time outside the home or on the grounds being with you, and we'll worry about demonstrating that physically later. When we share physically, it's a statement of long-standing love and commitment to one another.

"We hug and kiss but each of us knows the respectful boundary of this time of getting to know one another, and we'll ask you to respect that as well, particularly with David.

"And that goes for you, too," as he looked at David and smiled. "He's told us that he's eager to 'go there' with you; but we've decided as a group that it, too, can wait until you've had a chance to absorb the reality of our home and our collective. Roy, that's all in good time," William repeated.

Tristan rose dutifully and cleared dishes. William suggested that David and I go for a walk and spend some time together.

Each of the men hugged me 'good night' as we left. It was overwhelming but very warm and comfortable at the same time. Marlin gave me a kiss on the cheek, and Moose hugged me so hard it made my bones crackle, much to the amusement of the rest of the men.

They left and allowed David and me to be alone.

He walked me out to the living room, helped me on with my jacket, and led me down the driveway. We held hands as we walked through the neighborhood.

"So, what do you think?" David asked.

I let out a deep, relaxed sigh.

"Marlin is certainly a piece of work." We both laughed. "You can tell they care about you very much. That is very clear. But wow, I mean, I've never considered a setup like that, with everyone sharing everything and each other."

I stopped, and traced my hand along his face. "I think, quite frankly, that I'm falling in love with you and want to be with you."

David whispered, "Yes, Mr. Wallace; I am sure that we should…" He leaned forward and rubbed his beard on mine and growled under his breath. "I think, very soon, I shall need you in a way I haven't needed someone in a very long time. You make me so happy, and I am delighted that the house feels comfortable."

He kissed me, softly and romantically. "You are so beautiful, Roy."

David kissed me again, but this time lifting me against him. He growled and kept kissing, and I relaxed into his embrace. By the time he let me go, I was utterly breathless, and stared deep into his soft eyes.

We walked for a great while in quiet. The cool autumn evening seemed calmer than any I could remember. David puffed away on his pipe, and we held our hands tight. David had a unique talent for making even the slightest event terribly romantic. We walked through the evergreens, our breath showing, holding each other close.

"I should get you back, Roy. It's a school night and we can't have you tired for your kids now, can we?"

On our walk back to the house, I told him how amazed I was by the offer of friendship in the house. He gave me another wet, inviting kiss before opening my car door for me. "Sleep well, Mr. Wallace." He stopped, looking me straight in the eye. "Know that we are patient, understanding men, and there is no pressure to go anywhere you don't want to, but I do want to see you again soon." He ran his hand down my chest, then sniffed his way up my neck in his trademark fashion. I kissed him again before leaving him for the night.

I pulled down the driveway and made my way home, listening to the classical station and breathing it in. For weeks prior, I'd been feeling terribly isolated, and now I was facing my love for David. I also pondered the larger decision of the collective of men he was so clearly part of something greater with.

I smiled as I remembered Marlin's remarks to me in the meditation room: "Yer doin' fine, pup, just relax."

I got home and took some time to think it through. There was so much to consider after my evening with the men of David's home. That night I dreamed again of David, myself, and the round rooms of the House of Wolves.

3. Treetops and Totems

THE NEXT FEW DAYS were a busy blur between classroom work and keeping up with correcting papers. I spent my evenings working at a table in my apartment, on papers and lesson plans. I've always had a fascination for the organization that education takes, and am one of those sick people who get a charge out of it.

At a very early age, I decided I wanted to be a teacher; I don't know whether that was from a love of learning or the crush I had on a seventh-grade social studies teacher, Mr. Dickson, who rode a Harley-Davidson and was an impressively masculine man. He was a master at the art of making even the most boring topic pure magic.

Years later, I'd met up with Mr. Dickson after I finished school, and he said that the trick to being a good teacher was exhaustive preparation, being ready to take the lecture in a different direction if necessary. My fifth graders learn the value of team building, the value of diplomacy, and early personal management skills. Kids that age are learning to think for themselves in many situations.

Because many of them walk to school unaccompanied and come home to empty houses as their mothers are returning to work after raising them to this point, I love having the opportunity to a stable force in their lives as a teacher.

Fifth-graders at Clover Valley Elementary are at the top of the school because, in sixth grade, they move on to middle school.

They feel like the big folks on campus. My kids get to go on their first field trip. I was in the middle of planning the annual fifth-graders' trek to the zoo.

We'd go in the spring, along with hundreds of fifth-graders from around the city. The planning for a safari theme began early. With this huge project in front of me, I tried my best to keep to task and not let my daydreams of the men of the house take over.

It was difficult. Despite the complex situation that was presented me, I found I was even more taken with David, and found myself dreaming of other men in the household as well: William's curiously alluring darkness and intensity, Marlin's laughter and warmth. My fantasies and dreams had become menageries of ideas and concepts.

I wrote David an email suggesting that we get together for breakfast on Saturday, at my home. Before bed, he answered me.

"Dearest Mr. Wallace: Breakfast 9:00 AM is perfect. Marlin is insisting on coming along with me; he's impatient and ornery about you. Can you blame him? See you then. He likes his toast burnt. Don't ask me why; I think he's batty."

I wrote back saying I was excited to see them both on Saturday and that I needed to get busy working on my zoo project. So I guess that's how it began: me learning about the house and it learning about me.

I found myself up at dawn on that Saturday, cleaning like a madman. My little apartment sparkled and was full of the smell of fresh coffee and burnt toast as 9:00 AM arrived and my doorbell rang.

I stuck my head out of my second-story window and looked down on David and Marlin at my doorstep. It was fun to spy on them for a moment. David wore his hair in the same tight braid. Marlin was in a black leather jacket, his white hair contrasting brilliantly, his earrings shining in the morning sun's reflection.

"Let me buzz you up," I said, revealing my perch above them. They peered up at me, each with a pleasant smile. I left my door open and could hear them talking on the way up the stairs.

"Can't you put da damn thing out even to eat breakfast, ya tart?" said Marlin, obviously talking about David's pipe. Particularly when he gets angry, Marlin's speech gets lost in his heavy cockney accent.

They entered my apartment. Marlin ushered David to the sink in my little kitchen and said, "Be a good one and just tap that shit out while we eat, eh?"

David sheepishly did as he was told, tapped his tobacco out, and rinsed it down the sink. All the while, I watched with great amusement as the two continued to playfully bicker.

I soon had three plates of eggs, potatoes, and toast ready to go, one black as the earth.

"Think we're funny, do you?" said David, approaching me and kissing me good morning.'

"You bicker like a pair of my schoolgirls," I said, giggling.

"Always have," said Marlin, taking off his coat and leaning forward and kissing me.

We giggled through breakfast. David insisted on cleaning up; Marlin and I kept talking while I showed him my little home. My small, 12th-Street bungalow really was an architectural treat. It had a small, five–hundred square foot living area with a row of barstools by the kitchen just inside the door. All the appliances were out of an old travel trailer and were smaller to fit the scale of the apartment. The ladder out of the living space up to my bed loft suited Marlin very much, and he commented on how nice and spartan everything seemed.

I explained how hard it had been moving into this space after sharing a home with Joseph. I talked briefly about how small it seemed at first but how much the place had come to feel like home to me. Marlin asked to see the loft and its windows so I led him up; we sat on my futon staring out the bay windows. The winter snow was fresh in the mountains, and the clouds whipped around the bay.

The view from that loft was worth the high downtown rent. Marlin was delighted.

"You can see the whole world from here, Mr. Wallace," Marlin said, smiling ear to ear. He reached forward and cranked the windows open, letting in the moist winter air. "Truly a special place." He leaned over, set his body against mine, and leaned into me. David's face popped up the ladder, and he scooted up onto the bed and shared our view. We sat there sipping coffee, looking out at the busy city and just simply enjoying it all. It just seemed natural to nuzzle into David arms while holding Marlin across my lap as we watched clouds flow by my window, enjoying the softness of David's arms and chest and realizing for the first time how truly muscular Marlin was. His slender frame stealthily hid an amazing physique.

Sitting there in my loft sipping coffee and chatting, I hugged him and held him and discovered his muscular back under his tight-netted black shirt. I sat there while we talked, gently stroking the muscles of his back. I've always hoped that if I reached my fifties I'd have the drive to keep myself in that kind of shape. I was beginning to admire Marlin. It was clear that he treasured all kinds of strength:, mental as well as physical. Marlin told us his idea for the day, suggesting that we drive up into the hills.

"It's a quick drive up there; we could stop in on the Salish Indian reservation. I've been meaning to get a look at some new art pieces the tribe has on exhibition. There's an artist there who is working on a totem pole for the house—you'll adore her, Roy."

Marlin paused for a moment, obviously thinking out his next words. "When people are bonded, they form an emotional totem. A spiritual version of the physical totems you see here in the northwest, if you will. It is considered an intrinsic bond that is honored between two people. At the house, we each have

received Salish tattoos—marking ourselves as bonded to one another."

"Show him yours," Marlin said to David.

David stared at me for a moment with such longing, then
undid his shirt dutifully. It was the first time I'd seen David's
chest. It was strong, muscular, well defined, and covered with
thick black hair. Through the hair he revealed a dark red tattoo
across and including his left nipple. It was the design from the
front door of the house: eight red wolves connected by their tails
to a dark black circle.

The circle at the center of the design enclosing the nipple. The
black coloring made his nipple look dark and menacing.

Then I noticed a miniature ornament in the ring through
David's nipple, a killer whale, carved in bone. It was tiny but
painted with incredible detail. "May I touch it?" I asked.

Before David could answer, Marlin blurted out, "Yes, you can
touch. But don't ya go playin' with it or we'll have ta let the old
man have his way with ya, and you know we can't have that;
besides, we have a schedule to keep."

He laughed and David blushed a deep red. I ran my finger over
the design, then touched the outline of the killer whale totem
in David's nipple ring. David let out a sigh and pushed himself
against me gently, then moved my hand away and closed his
shirt.

"Each of us has that totem somewhere on our body, with our
own personal animal sign involved, like my killer whale here,"
said David, tapping his left chest.

"When we first met David," said Marlin, "We were out on
the beach, and as a group we saw a pod of killer whales playing
offshore. We saw one leap from the water over 'n' over, splashin'
'n' playin." David's always had a connection with the ocean and
its places of beauty, so Richard decided his totem would be the
very same killer whale.

"Mine is the owl, and my totem is inscribed on the small of
my back at my waistline, with the owl in the center of the circle.

Everyone will share their totems in time, Mr. Wallace, and when the time is right we'll show you yours; it'll come naturally. They always do."

"Our totems come from the Salish, 'cuz Richard always felt we had become a tribe of men; iff'n we'd all chosen to live near the ocean, a water people should serve as our example. This tribe ought to learn the legends and adopt the imagery and icons of the Saanich. That special relationship made the members of the house somehow part of our community's deeper relationship with nature, as it were, originally told to Richard as a child," Marlin said, pausing, "but I'm got ahead of myself. We better get going before we get late."

"And we're drivin' my truck;, not that deathtrap David calls a truck. Roy, ma boy, help me out here," Marlin said, looking for me to chime in on his argument.

Holding my hand up like swearing an oath, I said, "I have to plead the fifth here."

"Pshaw, you just don't have any backbone where this one is concerned," he said, motioning at David.

So we got on the road, and on our drive Marlin explained Salish artwork and his connection with it.

"The Saanich are part of what was the greater Salish Nation; it had once stretched from Wyoming to the ocean in Washington. The Saanich Indians—Salish tongue for "canoe people"—now live along the Skykomish River north of Seattle.

"The First Nations peoples of Saanich have always used the canoe as a means of transportation. The cedar tree, from which the canoe is made, is very sacred to First Nations people, as it is also used for housing, medicine, and spiritual needs. Every aspect of their relationship with the canoe was considered a sacred act.

"Before the cedar tree is taken down, a special ceremony is performed so that there would always be a relationship between the cedar canoe and the First Nations people of Saanich. The water, on which the canoe travels, is cared for and talked to. The Saanich believe that newborn children must be introduced to the water at the very beginning, so that the tribe would not be strangers to the water. The people and the water will always look after each other.

"It was legend, and perhaps even fact, that the Saanich tribes were among the first settlers of the North American continent."

Marlin felt that the reason their art is so incredible is that it was bigger than just art; it was a representation of eternity. Despite the hardships, the Indian Nation had endured since being conquered by the Americans, after Lewis and Clark, and they remained a totem to strength and respect of nature.

"The legacy and inspiration of the Saanich Indians was a major part of the bonds the men held with each other in the house. Richard had grown up near the reservation and had a childhood friend who was full-blooded Salish. When Richard and I met, he brought me here and trained me in the powers and the rituals of the Saanich people."

Listening to Marlin describe Richard echoed the admiration that David had used at Bowman Bay when telling me about Richard, who had been powerfully loved by all of these men. Marlin pulled off the highway, and we wound our way through the woods, coming out by the river and a small town. "Welcome to the Saanich Reservation," said the sign.

The town was very simple: a post office, a grocery, a community center, homes, and other businesses. Marlin pulled through town, drove a couple of miles, and then pulled up in front of a small home.

A large Indian man came out of the house at a trot and greeted Marlin with a hug. He was a strong man with jet-black hair to his shoulders, beaded in colorful patterns. He grasped and shook David's hands.

"It is good to see you, too, Set-Ho-Tid," the man said, talking to David. "It has been too long, much too long."

The man paused for a long moment, looked over at me, and studied me.

Smiling, he continued, "So, this is the teacher you've told me about."

"Ben Paul, Roy Wallace." David gestured at me, smiling his adorable, childish grin.

"Roy, it is great to meet you; please come inside."

"What is the name you used for David?" I asked Ben as we walked toward the house.

"Roy," answered Ben as he stopped to face me, "Seehotid is the Native tongue for Second Mountain. Richard's totem with me was always Se-Hee-Ah-Hi or Strong Mountain. So when Richard left us for the spirits and David was naturally chosen to lead the tribe of wolves, I named him Seehotid, the second mountain."

David had a sullen look on his face, as if the mention of these names hurt him. Marlin stroked his beard gently, making him break out of the moment and smile.

There was a moment's pause and Ben said, "Come now, Jean is eager to see you!"

We entered the home. It was small and humble with the feeling of a deep woods hunting cabin. At the main table sat an Indian woman in her fifties, with long, graying hair beaded identically to Ben Paul's. She lit up as she saw us enter her home.

"Marlin! David!," she said.

Rising and walking toward us, she enthusiastically hugged both David and Marlin. While hugging David, she looked at me over his shoulder and winked.

"Welcome. We are honored to have you in our home," she said, extending her hand.

"My name is Roy," I said to her timidly.

She traced my face with her finger and took hold of my ear.

Leaning in and letting me feel her breath against my cheek, she said, "Yes, I know. You are the teacher. You are the final totem Richard knew would come."

Staying for a long moment, she then moved to David, taking him by the hand. Speaking to David in a lower, almost murmuring voice, she said, "He is the son-man Se-Hee-Ah-Hi searched for. How is it that he comes now? How is it that the son-man comes to Se-Ho-Tid? It is not the way Se-Hee-Ah-Hi saw it. But he is living around these ones still…As his totem is finished." Speaking to Ben but looking solemnly into David's eyes, she added, "He's still grieving and fighting…our dear Se-Ho-Tid."

She let go of David's hand and said, "Come, follow me."

Jean led us into a larger room, obviously a painter's studio with canvases and brushes strewn about. There, in the middle of the room, lying on its side, was a strikingly large wooden totem pole, obviously hand carved and showing eight distinct characters. There was an eerie silence in the room.

"Se-Ho-Tid started this carving before See-Hee-Ah-Hi left."

"Yes," said Marlin.

David's face grew mournful as he moved toward the totem pole.

"We all miss the See-Hee-Ah-Hi. We were all brought to his table."

He kneeled down and touched the carvings.

"I just couldn't finish it. It was very much like a part of me died along with him; each time I'd work on this, I'd remember."

The silence in the room was palpable.

Jean said softly, "See-Ho-Tid has yet to realize how much he honors the spirits by leading the house and looking after the wolves in your tribe."

Jean then took my hand and led me to the totem pole. Kneeling, she held my hand in hers and traced the totem's features.

David explained how the totem pole was created. "The first three totems were the bear (Bear), the owl (Marlin), and the eagle (Richard); the others, in order of their arrival at the house: my killer whale, the moon (William), the moose (Moose), and the hummingbird (Tristan)."

Kneeling close I could see that the totem was connected to the black, solid base, which was carved so it almost looked like maps of blood vessels running collectively down the back of a living being.

"Ben Paul knew Richard from childhood. They met when they were four years old, playing in the very woods you drove through to arrive here. They became attached almost immediately, and he stood at the foot of Richard's bed as he moved on into the spirit world," said Jean.

Ben spoke from behind them. "Of course, at four I didn't know Richard's two-spiritedness, his special qualities. Our bond was and continues to be strong. I talk with Richard in my dreams, and he worries for you, David, and for his men at the house."

Turning to Roy, Ben added, "He knew you were coming, though, even before he left us. He told me to expect the teacher.

"When we were teenagers and had been friends already for a decade, Richard showed the signs of the two-spirited soul."

"Two-spirited?" I inquired.

"The Saanich people have always believed that the two-spirited person was one who had received a gift from the creator, that gift being the privilege to house both male and female spirits in their bodies. We see it as a conscious choice by the creator to create gays, lesbians, bisexuals, and transgender persons of Native origins. The gift of two spirits means that these individuals have the ability to see the world from two perspectives at the same time. This greater vision was a gift to be shared with all, and, as such, two-spirited beings are revered as leaders, mediators, teachers, artists, seers, and spiritual guides.

"They are treated with the greatest respect and hold important spiritual and ceremonial responsibilities. It was a responsibility Richard took very seriously.

"My father, who was the tyee, or chief of the Saanich people, treasured Richard in a unique way. A deeply spiritual man, my father felt that Richard and I were spirit descendants, each of Peace and Brotherhood. One would foster peace, and one would create a unique brotherhood of knowledge and reverence.

"He believed we are the spirit brothers told to us in the legend of the two sisters."

He asked us all to sit a while at the foot of the totem. David, Marlin, Jean, and I sat as he told us of the magical man his father had been, the great tyee.

4. Many Thousands of Years Ago

BEN SPOKE OF HIS father in detail. "The legend was intensely fascinating as it left my father's lips in his quaint, broken English," started Ben. "Words come out differently, dulcet as when they slip from an Indian tongue. My father's inimitable gestures—strong, graceful, comprehensive—were like a perfectly chosen frame embracing a delicate painting, and his brooding eyes were as the light in which the picture hung."

As he began to speak of his father's legends, I witnessed the transformation of this man into a spiritual storyteller. He spoke with an almost inhuman voice. As if a magical force had entered the room, he became trancelike, using exaggerated gestures, and his eyes focused in an intense manner.

"Many thousands of years ago, there were no twin peaks like sentinels guarding the outposts of this sunset coast. They were placed there long after the first creation, when the tyee Sagahlie molded the mountains and patterned the mighty rivers where the salmon run because of his love for his Indian children and his wisdom for their necessities. In those times, there were many and mighty Indian tribes along the Pacific—in the mountain range, at the shores and sources of the great Fraser River. Our law ruled the land. Our customs prevailed. Our beliefs were regarded.

"Those were the legend-making ages when great things occurred to make the traditions we repeat to our children today. Perhaps the greatest of these traditions is the story of the two sisters, whom we know as Chief's Daughters, and to them we owe the great peace in which we live and have lived for many countless moons.

"There is an ancient custom amongst the coast tribes that, when our daughters step from childhood into the great world of womanhood, the occasion must be made one of extreme rejoicing. The being who possesses the possibility of someday mothering a man-child, a warrior, a brave, receives much consideration in most nations; but to us, the coastal tribes, she is honored above all people.

"The parents usually give a great potlatch and a feast that lasts many days. The entire tribe and the surrounding tribes are bidden to this festival. More than that, sometimes, when a great tyee celebrates for his daughter, the tribes from far up the coast, from the distant north, from inland, from the island, from the Caribou country, are gathered as guests to the feast.

"During these days of rejoicing, the girl is placed in a high seat, an exalted position, for is she not marriageable? And does not marriage mean motherhood? And does not motherhood mean a greater nation of brave sons and of gentle daughters, who, in their turn, will give us sons and daughters of their own?

"But it was many thousands of years ago that a great tyee had two daughters who grew to womanhood at the same springtime, when the first run of salmon thronged the rivers, and the ollalie bushes were heavy with blossoms.

"These two daughters were young, lovable and, oh, quite beautiful. Their father, the great tyee, prepared to make a feast such as the coast had never seen. There were to be days and days of rejoicing. The people were to come from many leagues. They were to bring gifts to the girls and to receive gifts of great value from the chief. Hospitality was to reign as long as pleasuring feet could dance, enjoying lips could laugh, and mouths could partake of the excellence of the chief's fish, game, and ollalie.

"The only shadow on the joy of it all was war, for the tribe of the great tyee was at war with the upper coast Indians, those who lived north, near what the tybos named Vancouver." Ben

explained that tybos is the Native American name for the Euro-
peans who settled on their lands.

He continued. "Giant war canoes slipped along the entire
coast, war parties paddled up and down, and war songs broke the
silence of the nights. Hatred, vengeance, strife, horror festered
everywhere, like sores on the surface of the earth.

"But the great tyee, after warring for weeks, turned and laughed
at the battle and the bloodshed, for he had been victor in every
encounter, and he could well afford to leave the strife for a brief
time and feast in his daughters' honor. He would not permit any
mere enemy to come between him and the traditions of his race
and household. So he turned insultingly deaf ears to their war
cries; he ignored with arrogant indifference their paddle-dips
that encroached within his own coastal water; and he prepared,
as a great tyee should, to royally entertain his tribesmen in honor
of his daughters.

"But seven suns before the great feast, these two maidens came
before him, hand clasped in hand. 'Oh, our father,' they said.
'May we speak?'

"'Speak, my daughters, my girls with the eyes of early spring,
the hearts of early summer.'

"'Someday, oh our father, we may mother a man-child, who
may grow to be just such a powerful tyee as you are, and for this
honor that may someday be ours, we have come to ask a favor
of you.'

"'It is your privilege at this celebration to receive any favor
your hearts may wish,' he replied graciously, placing his fingers
beneath their girlish chins. 'The favor is yours before you ask it,
my daughters.'

"'Will you, for our sakes, invite the great northern hostile
tribe—the tribe you war upon—to this, our feast?' they asked
fearlessly.

"'To a peaceful feast, a feast in the honor of women!' he exclaimed, incredulously.

"'So we desire it,' they answered.

"'And so shall it be,' he declared. 'I can deny you nothing this day, and sometime you may bear sons to bless this peace you have asked, and to bless their mother's sire for granting it.' Then he turned to all the young men of the tribe and commanded: 'Build fires at sunset on all the coastal headlands—fires of welcome.

Man your canoes and face the north, greet the enemy, and tell them that I, the tyee of the Saanich, ask—no—command that they join me for a great feast in honor of my two daughters.'

"And when the northern tribe got this invitation, the warriors flocked down the coast to this feast of a great peace. They traveled with their women and their children. They brought game and fish, gold and white stone beads, baskets and carven ladles, and wonderful woven blankets to lay at the feet of their now acknowledged ruler, the great tyee. He, in turn, gave such a potlatch that nothing but tradition could vie with it. There were long, glad days of joyousness; long, pleasurable nights of dancing and campfires; and vast quantities of food.

"The war canoes were emptied of their deadly weapons and filled with the daily catch of salmon. The hostile war songs ceased, and in their place was heard the soft shuffle of dancing feet, the singing voices of women, the play games of the children of two powerful tribes that had been, until now, ancient enemies, for a great and lasting brotherhood was sealed between them—their war songs were ended forever.

"Then the Sagahlie tyee smiled on his Indian children: 'I will make these young-eyed maidens immortal,' he said. In the cup of his hands he lifted the chief's two daughters and set them forever in a high place, for they had borne two offspring—Peace and Brotherhood—each of which is now a great tyee ruling this land.

"And on the mountain crest the chief's daughters can be seen wrapped in the suns, the snows, the stars of all seasons, for they have stood in this high place for thousands of years, and will stand for thousands of years to come, guarding the peace of the Pacific Coast and the quiet of the coastal forests."

The tribe embraced Ben's father's explanation of the bond between Ben and Richard and how, as they'd grown closer, the
other children on the reservation considered Richard, a non-
Indian but blessed by the tyee, an equal.

As they grew older, it became clear that Ben was not two-spirited and that he and Richard were destined for different paths.
Ben's father told them that while Ben would become a teacher
of peace and understanding, Richard would be the man to create
a unique brotherhood. It was this basic truth that was the forma-
tion of the house that Richard began with Marlin and Bear.

Ben told me how delighted he was that I was opening my soul
to the experiences of the men in the House of Wolves, and that
he and Jean would see me soon, when they would bring the finished totem to the house in the city.

As we were leaving, Jean handed me a small bag. It was a tightly bound leather patch with symbols and writing on it.

"It is your medicine bag. I have given you the sign of knowledge. I ask that you keep it close to you and see what it chooses
to reveal to you. The spirits that will revolve around you are
attracted to the energy within your bundle, so you must keep
it tightly closed. Rest well, son-man, your path is going to be
changing. You will need your strength."

I tried not to let the intensity of the visit to Ben and Jean
affect me, but it drove me into a deep silence. It was a silence
that David and Marlin respected as we drove back to the city.
In fact, I simply leaned into David, and we listened to the wind
on the truck.

Marlin stopped the truck out front of my apartment. I sat up
and surprised Marlin with an honest masculine kiss.

"Thank you, Marlin."

Quite bewildered and blushing a deep red, he gently kissed me
back. As I got out of the truck, I leaned through the window of
the truck and kissed him. He tapped my chin and told me he'd
call later and see if we wanted to have dinner together.

The sun shone through my windows, and it was just a beautiful, peaceful day. It was peaceful to find myself in my home with time to think. I began to seriously consider the tribe of men I'd been introduced to. It really had never occurred to me that men of any type, particularly gay men, could form groups like this.

It was all so overwhelming! I fretted over my real need to be physical with David. The honest physical lust between us was building with each encounter. I considered, though, that the members of the house had asked us to not be physical beyond kissing and hugging. The thought that, while he wanted me, there were these other folks to consider in my actions, stopped me.

If I wanted to move forward with David, I needed to take the initiative to be with other members of the household. I needed to know them and learn their relationships with David, with each other, and, honestly, with me. This scared and thrilled me at the same time. I was certain, however, that I belonged with David and would accept whatever other emotional and physical risks came along as part of that goal.

5. Believe What I Reveal To You

I SAT IN MY apartment taking in all that had happened to me in the last two weeks since meeting David, Marlin, and the rest of the men of the house. I also realized that I had not stopped tracing the symbols on the medicine bag that Jean had given me. It had me totally distracted. What spirits would revolve around me? What did that mean?

I decided that I needed to shake the uneasy feeling and try to find a quiet break from it all. So I brewed some tea, grabbed my book and new medicine bag, and headed up to my sleeping loft to read in the sunlight. Leaning back into the pillows, warmed by the afternoon sun, it wasn't long before my feelings of drowsiness replaced any interest in the book.

I was awake one moment and, the next, lost in a suddenly dark dreamscape.

Eventually, I emerged from the darkness into the light of the dream, in which I am back walking the trails at Bowman Bay. Immortal evergreen trees jut out of gray stone at the water's edge, leaving eerie ghostlike reflections. Like a moment out of a Hitchcock movie, it is almost too quiet. It is foggy and cold. I have on a thick winter coat and my burgundy baseball cap.

There is a bench out in a clearing, alone facing the water. A man is sitting on the bench, staring into the fog. I spy on him quietly, watching him stare into the swirling mist as if he is searching for the horizon. He is bald with a closely trimmed beard, wearing nondescript attire except for a flamboyant scarf around his neck that drapes behind him on the bench. I see him cough a few times. He sings in a raspy voice,

"'Tis the gift to be simple, 'tis the gift to be free, 'tis the gift to come down where we ought to be."

The man coughs violently. Recovering, he laughs and keeps watching the dark gray waters of the inlet. I walk out into the clearing by the water. My feet crunch on the gravelly northwest beach, and my footsteps on the path startle him, making him jump.

He looks back at me. "Sorry, I didn't mean to startle."

"It's a small park. I can hardly be expected not to share it," says the man.

"I hope the fog will clear," I reply. "It's supposed to be a pretty day; instead, we got all this gray."

"Winter days here on the ocean are special, aren't they?" the man responds.

"Yes." I stop and look past him, noticing the view from the vantage point of his bench. The inlet seems to dissolve into nowhere, the thick fog swirling about. An invisible bird is somewhere cawing, like a person crooning from a minaret at noon. No sign of sunshine through the fog whatsoever.

"You are welcome to join me if you'd like," he says, motioning as he scoots over on the bench.

I sit next to him. He takes a small, black pipe and burlap bag... economy of words out of his jacket, fingers out a small pinch of tobacco, and taps it into the pipe. A slight smile of contentment flashes across his face as he prepares to smoke.

I watch his aged hands hold the pipe and tremble as he lights it. He takes a draft and seems to enjoy the moment, although he coughs out a cloud of smoke.

"Did your smoke go down wrong?"

"No. And I really shouldn't be down here. When my brothers find me here, I'll be in great trouble. You see, I have been sick."

"Winter is not necessarily the best outdoor time for someone who is sick," I say.

"Perhaps not, but iff'n your days are numbered, you just go seek the things that you cherish, one last time. My lover isn't handling this very well. He's brooding, angry that my death will come sooner than later. He feels powerless," the man says, letting out a deep sigh.

"He doesn't understand the spirituality, the depth of this experience. He's fighting to keep it all physical and real. He knows he's loved and will always be loved, and his brothers will take care of him. I never thought I would see him so angry."

"As long as he knows he's loved. That is what's important, right?" I ask, trying to reassure him.

"His fear is so great. I worry for him. It makes my heart heavy that he may choose to be alone so long after I'm gone. He doesn't trust that the future will provide him new love. His brothers are concerned he'll leave them when I move on…and move on I will." He coughs violently.

My dream returns to its original swirling darkness. Suddenly I'm back on the same beach in brilliant sunshine. It's a springtime day; the forest is green and vibrant. The bench is gone, and that is when I look up and notice there is a man in the water. His head is shaved, and his back is to me. He is holding a small canvas bag.

The dream zooms, swings around so I face the man.

Suddenly, I recognize the man in the water. It is David!

He's cleanly shaven, his eyes are red and weary. David slowly takes handfuls of ash from a burlap bag and lowers them into the water, letting the ocean claim each offering with the lapping of the gentle tide.

I watch him lower handful after handful of ash into the water.

"If I was weak," he whispers, "forgive me; I was terrified."

His hand is coated with ashes, as is his wet chest. Ash coats his face. He is careful to slowly lower his hand so the ocean water has to lap at his hand to claim the mournful prize. It seemed like I was there forever watching this ritual take place.

Suddenly he stops and, after a moment of silence, softly sings,

"'Tis the gift to be simple, 'tis the gift to be free, 'tis the gift to come down where we ought to be." David sobs and bows his head. His body begins to shiver from standing in the cold ocean water. He holds the bag underwater suddenly and rinses it finally clean.

"What am I to do?" he whispers. "Tell me, what I am to do? What I am to do, See-Hee-Ah-Hi, what am I to do?"

He seems to be whispering into thin air, as if it could return his conversation.

He cries a single tear. Seeing him like this is overwhelming.

I want to touch him but cannot. I want to cry out to him but cannot.

A man joins him in the water and puts his arms around David, holding him tight from behind. "All in good time," the man says. "All in good time."

I realize it is William. Once held, David collapses in emotion and cries as William holds him in the cold ocean water. Sobbing and helpless, David sinks in against William's body.

My dream fades to black. Through the sudden darkness, a raspy, menacing voice speaks to me in the dark: "Aquohiyu Wachdalehna."

All at once, the voice is soothing but unsettling. It comes from all around me.

"Aquohiyu—believe what I reveal. My wonderful Wachdalehna—my wonderful culmination. You are the man I thought David was."

I can hear him but not see him.

"You are the completion of the circle of wolves."

The voice scares me. It seems to come from all around me. I want to wake up to keep away from the voice, but it continues.

"You are loved; do not be afraid."

I feel a hand trace my face. I flinch and tremble. "Your spirit is so beautiful, Wachdalehna. It is beautiful how David already so needs you, after such a short time. I know you want to speak to me, Wachdalehna, and find answers; but your voice is not heard here—and answers come with time.

"He is frightened right now. He is thinking that, in reaching out to you, he risks letting go of me completely. He is confused and is fighting his soul. He is not ready for you yet; but your arrival comes with no schedule.

"My terribly beautiful son, David, is now a man worth loving.

"I was his father, where you will be his peer, Wachdalehna. You will return him his balance, his confidence and bring all of his strengths to the surface.

"He has inherited my sense of brotherhood, our brotherhood. You must bring him a sense of peace for the circle to be completed.

"Quiet your thoughts, Wachdalehna.

"Just be here, with me in this moment."

I feel his arms wrap around me.

I am suddenly held in an affectionate embrace and fall deeper into darkness.

I hear a voice singing. It is a single tenor voice, high and alone.

"Sleep now. Sleep now. O, sleep now. O, you unquiet heart! The voice of the winter is heard at the door. O sleep, for the winter is crying to you to sleep no more. My kiss will give peace now and quiet to your heart. Sleep on in peace now."

The fear I feel is growing palpable. The darkness feels like a prison I cannot escape.

I want to speak.

I want to ask questions but am mute.

I feel a body come up behind me and the arms around me again.

"Aquohiyu Wachdalehna. You of the unquiet heart."

I feel breath on my ear.

I feel lips kissing the back of my neck.

I feel a strong body pressed against my back.

"Shhh."

Fear. It is true fear now. I am trembling; I cannot awaken. I am trapped in this confusing darkness and feel lost. I am crying in the dark, no sound, just solitary tears. His breath returns to my neck and ears. I feel a kiss on my neck that sends chills down my body. Hands surround my middle and pull me against the man in the dark.

"Inescapable," he whispers into my ear.

Suddenly, I lurched upward and found myself sitting awake in my loft, sweat soaking my clothes. The brightness of sunset was shining in my face. I had never experienced anything like that. The dream was tactile; I could feel and hear everything clearly. I caught my breath and sat there for a few minutes when a knock came to my door.

I climbed down the ladder into the living room and went to the door. I was surprised that, when I opened the door, there stood William. His eyes were red, and his strong body looked exhausted. He beat his hand against the doorframe.

"Where have you been? How did you get there?" he said with his deep bass voice. He stormed past me into my apartment, knocking me sideways.

"I was in the dream room house meditating, and the vision of David and me at Bowman Bay entered my dream, and there standing on the beach was you," I told William.

"How could that happen? You were not there," William replied.

He was clearly shaking. Continuing, William said, "You were not there.

Nobody knows about that day at Bowman Bay. How were you there?"

I stood speechless. I barely knew William and to have him in my home in such a state was a little unnerving. William picked up the medicine bag on the kitchen counter.

"I should have known," he said, quietly smiling.

I said, "I was just...dreaming."

"Yes. You were just dreaming," he said, running his fingers over the leather sack in his fingers. His face suddenly relaxed, as if he'd figured out the puzzle. William smiled. "Marlin and David didn't tell me you had the Saanich medicine bag," he said, reaching into his pocket and picking out a somewhat tattered and aged version of my new possession. "An ingenious trick, finding a way to connect us through our dreams."

"'Aquohiyu' is what the voice said to me, William," tears welling in my eyes.

"It's pronounced A-goo-oh-hi-yuh." William paused, smiled, and said softly, "Believe what I reveal to you."

I flinched. William came forward to me and wrapped his arms around me in a strong hug. Suddenly and overwhelmingly, I sobbed.

His arms held me tight, and I totally let go all of the feelings of the past week: meeting David, meeting the men of the house, meeting Ben and Jean, the totem, the house, seeing David and William in my dream.

"Yes, Roy, let it out; that's a good man." William was crying too.

We stood there for a long while in each other's arms. My sobbing let up, but William held me in his strong embrace. Unlike David, who always smelled of vanilla and burley, or Marlin, who smelled of sweat and musk, William was scentless but for the slightest hint of eucalyptus. When he realized my emotions had subsided, he let me go.

"We've all dreamed since we moved into the house, Roy. It's the first time someone not in the house has had such a dream. Today, in my meditation, when you appeared standing on the beach watching David and me in the past, it scared me. Nobody in the house has ever visited another man's vision."

I explained to him how it had started, sitting on the bench with the sick man and how the dream had suddenly become the scene with David and then finally shifted to darkness and the voice. He saw me trembling again. He reached out for my hand as I continued to explain.

"The voice touched me, William. I felt him kiss me and hold me; he said it was inescapable."

"We've all had different experiences but never heard from an disembodied spirit; it's all very interesting, actually, but we'll figure it out in good time, all in good time."

We sat in silence for a while, then William looked up at me. "Understand, I was such a lost person before Marlin found me and invited me into his life and the lives of the men of the house. All of us have always needed saving from parts of our lives that are broken. You come to the house after losing your Joe, and grieving and understanding loss and loneliness.

"David is becoming impatient for us all to let you come be with him at the house. I've been guarding David as he's started reaching out and, honestly, have been skeptical of you. But in my vision today, I saw your goodness, saw your rich spirit; I saw you cry on the beach in Bowman Bay. David has left his journey alongside Richard go unfinished, and now it's creating such conflict."

"Look, I told Marlin and David I'd only be a while and look at us...like we have all night here. They are waiting at the restaurant. I figured we'd walk. You're OK with that, right?"

I told him I needed to take a shower first. He said he understood, but to be quick about it. I quickly showered and dressed.

"All better now, yes?" he said, combing my beard with his hand. "Good. Shall we?" He motioned at the door.

It was a warm twilight as we walked to dinner. William walked beside me with his wide, strong strides, reminding me of the bad guy from an old western, brooding black hair and beard along with deep brown eyes. He also had an old-fashioned swagger to him, as if he were ready to start a fight at any moment.

"It took most of us weeks before we noticed the dreaming; for you to have them the same day confirms many suspicions I've had about you," William continued.

"What does it all mean?" I asked.

"All in good time, sweet Roy, all in sweet time. You know that our David has been despondent, restless, and angry since Richard left us. Nobody has reached him. I have tried with patience and reason; Marlin has tried with passion and deep love; nothing. Yet, you, in the span of a few weeks, have him thinking in new ways, have him considering that he might love again.

"He's whistling happy songs around the house. You simply cannot imagine the difference, and now you dream of him at Bowman Bay. That is exactly as it happened," said William, turning toward me. "It was a spring day, warm. The breeze that Richard always adored. David didn't want to let his ashes go, but I drove him up there and insisted. I made him face it.

"He grieved so hard, and the permanence of the act of giving Richard to the ocean—well, it almost destroyed David. It was a powerful moment. We didn't share with the others in the house. Me holding him in the water and letting his grief come out in the open for the first time.

"You are such a strong spirit, Roy. Do you know that? Such a strong will and a confidence. It's nothing like the house has seen since Richard." I felt uncomfortable with the comparison. "Well, it appears to me that Richard was far more than simply a leader; he was inspirational and innovative in such extraordinary ways.

I'm at a foggy time in my life—where I don't have much direction, so very unlike a leader. I can hardly be compared to Richard."

"And how do you know that you are not also?" said William, giving me one of his deep, penetrating looks. "Come. Let's discuss this more over dinner." We walked up to the restaurant door, and there were David and Marlin, waiting at a booth. The restaurant they chose was tucked away in an unassuming neighborhood of older homes and was not well marked. It was a treasure to be found—if you noticed it.

While we talked and read the menu, David stared over the table at me. I was struggling not to react emotionally after seeing him in my dream that afternoon, so touched and vulnerable. He reached out and held my hand on the table.

Then he gave me a reassuring, beaming grin.

"OK, you lovebirds. Cut it out," said Marlin, slapping David's hand and placing it back on the table. David shot me a childlike grin, as if he'd just got caught with his hand stuck in the cookie jar. I felt David's foot gently land on top of mine under the table. He held it there, rubbing its sole against my ankle slowly.

Then William took David's hand in his and placed it back on top of mine.

"He's started dreaming, David," said William.

David's look suddenly became one of concern. Marlin leaned in and said, "So you've been dreaming, eh, pup? Damn dreams. They render me sullen for days when they come on. I know they are part of the house and that I wouldn't trade for anything, but they can be my curse often. Those dreams put me in fits."

"My dreams are often of when I was a boy," offered David, "but in different settings. Everyone dreams of me as a boy. It's like the dreams of everyone in the household are connected somehow, and we each are seen as we want to be."

"I am a pup and teaching still," said Marlin. "I dream of simple things. Writing exams and lecturing and of passionate debates. I've had David here as a student several times; and the others have been peers and debate partners. It's always on subjects I find troubling like war and conflict; on death," said Marlin.

"My dreams are usually about special times I create in my mind for each of the members of the house," William said, looking at me. "I've taken a younger Marlin on long hikes in the mountains, done craft projects with the boyhood David, and so forth. But today, I was dreaming of walking at Bowman Bay with David, and suddenly I was reliving that difficult day with David there two years ago; and then I saw you on the beach watching."

David gasped and looked at me. "What do you mean, you saw him at Bowman Bay?"

"Roy," said William, with a fatherly, paternal tone, "tell David about your dream, please."

William's request was simple enough, but I found it hard to speak. I sat silent for a moment, staring at David uncomfortably. His eyes began to quiver, and he stared away.

"It's all so hard to understand. It's just the most vivid dream I've ever had."

Sensing David's discomfort, I said, "I don't want to hurt you, David, please, please look at me."

David looked away, growing more and more agitated. I reached my hand out to him and spoke, in a quick rushing summary, of my dream.

"I was at Bowman Bay. In deep winter, and on the beach was a bench, and I spoke to a man who said he was dying, and he kept looking out into the fog, like it was concealing something…then suddenly I was watching you, David. In the bright sunlight of winter day, there putting Richard's ashes in the water. You said, "'if I was weak, forgive me. I was terrified," and you cried as you put the ashes in the water.

Then you said, "What must I do?" and William joined you in the water and held you as you cried, "I said, as my eyes glossed up. David became visibly upset and pulled back from the table.

"I wanted to talk to you. I wanted to help you." I realized I began trembling, as I had been when I suddenly woke earlier. "Then the voice came, and it scared me. It called me Wach-dalehna," I said, remembering the name from my dream.

David's hand formed a fist, and he shot an angry look at William.

"Where have you heard that word before, Mr. Wallace?" shot Marlin.

"I have never heard that word used till today. What is it?"

"Well, Roy, it's a special name in our household," said William. "It means roughly 'ultimate completion,' or a culmination. It is the Saanich name Richard always used for the man who would complete our circle. He said that one day a man would come into our midst and complete us. The search for spirits at the house would end. This would end the circle and make us a whole house.

"He'd heard the name from Ben's father. And always assumed that he was Wachdalehna; well, until he was sick. He told David that he'd find the 'wonderful Wachdalehna.' Oh, Roy, this is most interesting."

"I felt…I felt arms hold me." I stopped, tears welling up and tracing down my face. I reached out and touched David's hand on the table. "What is wrong, David?"

He remained silent and looked over at me, trembling with glassy eyes.

Marlin looked at me and said, "David has always doubted Richard's mysticism at the end. He thought Richard was only telling us those things to give us hope; that the mysticism had died with Richard."

"This is not right," David said, tears in his eyes. "It's just not right."

With that comment, David got up from the table and rushed off, leaving us at the table staring at each other silently. I rose to follow him, but William held me back.

William scooted over in the booth and put his arm around me. It was clearly one of the strongest hugs I'd ever experienced. I let out another burst of tears and emotion.

"What did I do wrong?" I said.

"He fights it, Roy. And it's his own fight; leave him to it," said William.

"He's right, pup, leave 'im be," said Marlin

"What is he fighting?" I said through my tears.

"I have never seen a love as fierce as Richard and David's, Roy. Ever!" said Marlin. "Even when Richard was dying, David fought next to him, as if the cancer that killed Richard could be cured simply by the power of strong love.

"Richard had become a father figure and mentor for David, beyond anything that anyone else had with him. Richard was the leader of the household, of the life that David had completely embraced. But Richard's death was inevitable at a certain point.

"'David has been sulking ever since he saw the finished totem up on the reservation this morning and is simply not ready to let Richard go. He was already hurting because he loves you; but now he sees a connection between you and Richard and is feeling torn, feeling drawn backward and forward at the same time."

William added, "The dreams are different for each of us. Each of us sees different things at times. As each person has joined our tribe, all of our dreams change accordingly.

"I will have to ponder this for a while to try to decipher all its meanings. All of our dreams are personal, of ourselves in different times, and now we add the voice in your dreams, the spirit that is visiting you in your dreams. And now, David knows that the only spirit that would come to you and embrace you as Wachdalehna is, of course, his...our...Richard."

6. Visible Ghosts

WILLIAM TOUCHED MY HAND and said, "I don't know what to say, Roy, and this is certainly a unique set of circumstances."

"That is the understatement of the goddamned century, William," barked Marlin. "Dm'it, just when we had the old boy all settled down. This is just like Richard—to stick his nose in where it don't belong."

The discussion of my vision quest was certainly bringing out interesting responses from all my new friends.

William smiled and then laughed. "Yes, it is."

"Always was a danged control queen, that one," continued Marlin, "always making sure he gets the last word on all things. Why should this be an exception?" William and Marlin laughed but, quite frankly, I didn't see that anything was funny. David had just walked out on dinner. I sat at the table stunned by William's revelation. How could I have known that my comments would upset David so much? I sat there speechless for several minutes and had trouble understanding why William and Marlin seemed to not be in the same state of mind.

It was all very complicated. What kind of group of mystics had I let myself become involved with? What was this medicine bag, and what was it doing to my subconscious? How did it make me dream such personal intimate things about these men? William and Marlin looked over and took notice of my discomfort.

"David's a fiery, passionate man," said William, calmly. "But, in our five years with him, we've never seen him react so. It'll take time to sort it all out."

Somehow his tone was comforting, but it wasn't convincing. I felt he was holding back and perhaps even manipulating me. I was losing patience.

"Sort what out? What the fuck is all this about?" I snapped at William.

"Now, pup, calm down a bit," said Marlin.

I couldn't stop the flow of my brain and spat the words out of my mouth, hoping that somewhere in the noise they made sense.

"How do these dreams work? You could have told me that my dream would hurt David; I mean, I could see, as I retold the dream, that I was literally hurting him with ever word. I like you both; but, dammit, I am in love with David, not you. And now I've chased him off. Calm down? Let's see, first you let that woman give me a bag of spells, which immediately brought on this vision of Richard and all the hurt in David. Then you led me here to discuss it, as if this happens every day, and I've now lost David."

Marlin sank in his chair. William took my hand and, turning to me, said, "Jean would not have given the mahalet bag to you if she didn't think it was the right time. You are right; the medicine bag is a bag of spells, if you want to call it that. It helps the men of the house to be closer and share spirituality on a root level. You are the first man she's given the medicine bag to—before living at the house. But I'm sure she had a reason."

"Did you know that revealing my dream would anger him so much?" I asked.

"I had an idea but thought that enough time had passed and that he was ready for someone or something new. His mind remains closed to the idea that the mysticism is still alive in the house and its inhabitants, as well as (motioning toward me) those it cares for. Whether this makes any sense at all, you are part of the house, even if you are not a member."

"YOU had an IDEA and you're, what, using me to draw him out?" I said, getting angrier. "What do I do? How do I repair the damage?"

"How do we repair the damage," said Marlin. "You'll learn that a man or a brother is never alone in his quest, when the house is involved—and so it shall be for David and for you."

This had an instant, calming effect on me, somewhat comforting. William went on: "David has been unhappy for so long, and you represent a chance for him to move on. I mean, we all saw the way he looked at you when you arrived this evening.

"David is falling in love with you; but considering the house and all of its collectiveness, the situation is far more complicated than even I'd thought it ever could be."

They both saw the anger and fear drain from my face, and my flushed skin returned to its normal color.

"How do we uncomplicate it, then?"

Laughing, Marlin answered me: "Well, there, my dear friend Roy, is the problem. Nobody has ever uncomplicated David, including Richard. He's just a bugger when it comes to dealin' emotionally. Richard was the first person to come into his life who unconditionally loved him for who he was. No idea was substandard, no idea was 'stupid' or not worth considering."

Marlin paused before adding, "That wasn't to mean that Richard would blindly go after anything David came up with. Richard would consider all his ideas as absolutely worthy of consideration and bring them into the light.

"Just five years ago, Richard invited David to carve the door for the house that he, Bear, and Marlin were building up in the evergreens. When David joined our household, we all knew that Richard had finally found someone to be his lover, someone he could mentor and bring into the collective. The house was growing. Richard's dream of a brotherhood of loving men became, with David, a reality.

His dream of men loving one another without barriers was happening.

"When all of us began the mystical household of men, we always thought others would naturally feel right to be included in the magic that was the House of Wolves. Richard brought David to meet them. David was initially jealous of Bear and Marlin and their special bond with Richard. It took David time to understand the deeper currents of the collective."

William interrupted. "Marlin, he doesn't need a résumé of David's life. He wants to know what happens now. The things you are telling him are for David's voice."

"You're right," Marlin responded, and he turned to me and asked what I would like to do.

Even with all this new information, I found David's reaction and departure still hard to deal with. I needed to go find him and discover a way to work this through with him. I told Marlin and William that I wanted to come back to the house with them in the hope that David had returned there. Marlin told me David could be very stubborn, and I should not have high expectations that David would respond if he truly was angry and hurt. I said that if David really thought I was the man for him, he'd have to communicate with me.

We then drove to the House of Wolves where, in the driveway, sat David's beat-up gray truck. Bear met us at the door and informed us that David had come home crying and angry. David had said to leave him alone, and then retreated to his carving studio. Bear turned and motioned for me to be seated.

Around the fireplace in the library were Tristan, Bear, and Moose. I realized that the others had been in discussion before I arrived.

"Care to tell us what happened? What did you pull off at the restaurant to send David home in such a state? He wouldn't speak a word," Bear said, looking at Marlin rather sternly.

Marlin and William filled the others in on the conversations we'd had at the restaurant. Every time emotions got testy, Bear simply sighed and glanced over at me.

"Clearly, Jean gave Roy the medicine bag for a reason. We all know her judgment and know that, if the timing was wrong, she wouldn't have presented the gift. We all have had personal visions, and Roy's are unique and powerful, as all of ours are."

Tristan interrupted. "But isn't it clear to anyone but me that David is not ready for Roy?"

Marlin shot Tristan an angry look but remained silent.

"He'd rather pout than embrace the love that has finally come his way,"

Tristan passionately continued. "How long do we let his behavior continue? How long do David's needs and emotions rule the direction of this house? Albeit reluctantly, I have respected Richard's request that David lead our household.

"But how long do we remain stagnant? How long do we let David grieve and keep the rest of us on hold? And Marlin, don't tell me till he's ready.' Richard has been gone two years. We've been waiting two years to continue our journey together."

Tristan stopped speaking, and the room filled with an intense silence. I could see each man reacting individually to Tristan's questions. Until that moment, I had not realized that the men in the room were basically strangers to me but for brief encounters.

"We are well aware of your feelings regarding David, Tristan," Bear said calmly. "And I do think that very soon we will have to address David more directly. But for now, let's concentrate on this moment. David is in great pain. Roy has been drawn into our midst, and these are all things we need to address before larger issues are confronted."

Turning to me, Tristan continued. "Please, Roy, don't get the idea that I am not in love with David." He looked at the others. "Our David. It hurts me to see him always in pain and not seeing the need to move on and be the strength he was when he first arrived."

Moose broke his rhythm and the room's focus.

"I think Roy should go to him. Let's see if David will talk to him," said Moose, sitting with his arm around Tristan. "If he'll talk to anyone, he'll talk to Roy. Love rules that man's heart."

Bear chewed on his cigar, and Marlin remained silent.

William spoke to me in a quiet, small voice, "I've been here the least amount of time, Roy, so I know some of what you are going through. Even without the intense emotions, all of this can seem too much. I arrived two months before Richard died. I barely knew David and Richard as a couple. I never knew them when sickness and death were not with them. David has come back to life these last few weeks. He's carving again, he's engaging all of us at evening supper and in the meditation room, showing me all sides of himself I've never seen. I've never seen a man grieve so heavily. And your arrival has been the first sure sign that his spirit was lifting. I agree with Bear; you should go to him."

My eyes were tearing up at William's words. Marlin rose, sat next to me, and held me. "Now, pup, you know he's right. Just go out there and be gentle; get David to open up to you."

"OK," I said meekly, wiping a tear from eye.

Tristan moved forward and hugged me. Soon, each of the group was touching and hugging me. We all sat there for a moment in a swarm of gentleness and contemplation.

"Then come back here afterward, and we'll talk together a bit more. OK, pup?" said Marlin, winking at me.

All the men in the room sat silently for a short moment, and then I walked out onto the patio and looked back on the compound to David's studio. In the early evening darkness, the complex seemed to glow. Lights hidden behind glass on the walls gave the illusion of torches, lighting the path back to David's small studio. I stood there for a moment looking over the wisteria-covered walls and watched the smoke curl from the chimney.

I've always been truly nonconfrontational but I was so certain David and I were meant for something, I forced myself to knock on his door.

David yelled from inside, "Go away, William, I don't want to talk to right now."

I spoke evenly and said, "David, it's Roy. Please let me in."

There was silence, and I feared he had decided not to see me, but the latch on the door clicked and the door opened. David stood there with tears in his eyes, shirtless and in a pair of sweats. All at once I was truly distracted by the muscular, hairy beauty of his chest and the similarity between his red eyes at this moment and his eyes in the dream vision at Bowman Bay. I reached out and touched the center of his chest. He came at me in an embrace, held me, and burst into tears.

This strong man I'd been admiring was suddenly broken and sobbing in my arms. I stroked his hair as he buried his face in my shoulder. His whole body shook from his sobs.

We stood there for a long while.

David started sniffing on my neck, then kissing it. He wiped his eyes and asked me inside.

As we entered his studio and closed the door behind us, my first glimpse of the surroundings was astounding. First of all, the room was in total disarray. Piles of tools and paintbrushes in different places and several half-finished carving projects on the counter in the corner—one was of a man's chest, in great detail, that suddenly stopped unfinished in mid-air; the other two were Native designs, a bear and a heron. The carving on each looked completed, but the painting was barely started.

In back of the room was an adobe fireplace. Next to it, a futon bed, which was covered with black sheets and an enormous, overstuffed, black comforter, probably thicker than the futon. There were also custom cabinets and storage units curved into the walls. And above the bed, on the wall, an oil painting of the man from the bench and my dream vision, a picture of Richard.

He was shirtless and wearing a leather harness and chaps revealing his hard cock and balls.

This was not the sick Richard I'd met in my dream but the healthy Richard that David had originally known.

David saw me looking at the picture of Richard, and he spoke in a small, quiet voice. "He died right here in that bed, and now it is mine alone. He was so beautiful."

"I am so sorry, David. I never meant to hurt you."

"I know you didn't, Mr. Wallace," he sighed heavily. "I don't know what to make of your dream, and it has me totally outside myself. Do you know how many nights I've hoped that I'd close my eyes and talk with Richard? How many times that I hoped he'd stay close to me in my dreams? That day…that day at Bowman Bay allowed him to rest, giving him back to nature. So, if he's resting, why does he choose to speak to you?

"Dammit, Mr. Wallace, it's unfair." His eyes suddenly flared as they had in the restaurant. "I think you know why I am going to need time to figure this out and why that means you won't see me again for a while. I know I got you into this mess by introducing you to Jean and Ben and to my complicated fucking life.

But, Mr. Wallace, my dearest Roybear, as much as I want you here, I am going to need space on my own to figure this out."

I leaned forward and kissed him madly, running my hands up his muscular back and holding him. He responded by turning me around and laying me down on the futon. I could taste the salty tears in his beard and returned his powerful kisses with purposeful, deep passion. His weight on top of me, and the feeling of his naked torso for the first time, was, frankly, overwhelming. My hands traced his muscular back and shoulders. I felt his nipple ring and chest hair rub against me. We shared our hardness with one another and each began moaning and grunting as we kissed and licked one another.

David nibbled on my neck, grabbing my hands and holding them to my sides. He then sat up on my stomach suddenly, still holding my hands to my side, and studied me. I felt his balls and hardness against me through his sweatpants, and I saw that he had leaked precum clear through them. I tried to move my hands, but he held them more firmly and simply studied, looking down at me. His beard was all ruffled from my kisses, and his chest rose above me in a maze of black body hair and tribal piercing.

"Do you understand, my dear Mr. Wallace? This is a path that I must take alone," he said, remaining painfully close. His scent and sweat were distracting.

"I don't understand this all either, David," I said, catching my breath. "But I'll respect your need for privacy. You know that, when you are ready to find me again, I'll be here for you just as you were there for me at the coffee shop. I am confused, horny, hard, and all fucked up."

David then flashed me one of those boyhood smiles, all teeth and charm. I looked up at him as the fireplace light danced on his body. "I do love you, David."

"I know you do, Roy," he said, "and I treasure your trust in me to do this for me, and for you. I need to find clarity." He climbed off me and helped me up.

With that I said, "Well, I am going to go now. I will miss you, David. Call me soon, OK?"

I stood, tucked myself in, and straightened up. Tears came to his eyes, and he kissed me slowly, whimpering a little as he did so.

He then let me go, showing me to the door. I didn't look back as I heard the door close and the latches click.

I stood in the courtyard for a long time. The evening lights made the scene seem surreal. I realized how, from David's home at the end of the courtyard, the house made a small oval and created a sanctuary.

I decided to see where the others had gone. I entered the library and there, sitting by the fire, were all of David's brothers—Marlin and Bear, William and Moose and Tristan—all sharing the light of the fireplace.

Marlin gestured to the empty spot next to him and Bear and said, "Come here, pup, join us." I sat on the couch next to Marlin; he put his arm around me and held me close.

Bear spoke in a deep baritone voice: "That was very brave of you, Roy. It shows us that you are genuinely attached to David, and his welfare is as important to you as it is to us. He's going to hurt for a while, and he's going to spend a lot of time meditating, hoping to find a vision to help him figure all this out."

I let out a deep sigh and described my conversation with David, how I'd agreed to give him space.

"When Marlin and I met Richard," Bear continued, "we knew he was going to change our lives in incredible ways. We built this complex and have created our brotherhood here. When our Richard fell in love with David, we celebrated their connection: the father and son in our midst. It's strange, sometimes how naturally men can live with one another when they are authentic. We are astounded at your authenticity, Roy, and it reminds us all of a bit of Richard. "But hear it from a different perspective; we've always wondered what the house would have continued to evolve into, had Richard lived and stayed. When we met you last week, we saw so many parallels. And, of course, I adored you because you remind me so much of Marlin when I first met this bugger," he said, reaching out and pulling on Marlin's ear.

"You've such passions for teaching and for life; and you've dealt with adversities with honor. You are making yourself open to our experiences and what we might experience with you."

William looked over. "Even though David is withdrawing for a bit, we'd all like to continue getting to know you, Roy. As it appears, more than ever, you are going to be with us for a long while, whether as simply a friend of ours or as David's partner. We've all decided that we want to continue to get to know you and share our lives with you."

"I'd like that, too, William. Even you," I said poking Marlin in the ribs.

"But I think, considering all that's gone on today, I need to head home and just be with myself."

With that, Marlin stood and walked me to my car. "You going to be all right, pup?"

"Yeah, I think so. Until I get to sleep later on. Who knows who or what'll visit me then."

Marlin hugged me. "Welcome to the House of Wolves, pup; it'll all be fine."

I got in my truck and drove home. Never had one of my days featured as many highs and lows: waking from the dream, upsetting David, visiting his studio, feeling his body, and realizing I wouldn't see him for a while. As I drove home, I realized how exhausted this ordeal had made me, and I looked forward to reaching home and my bed.

I finally arrived at my apartment, poured myself a glass of port, and sat in my loft in my nightshirt. I felt myself sliding off into sleep and realized that the dreams would come again, but I was tired and needed to sleep.

Darkness, then a voice. It is not Richard's; it is not David's. It is a woman's voice, strangely calming.

"What color do you get if you blend black, brown, white, yellow, and red? Do you get clay-colored mud on a mossy riverbed?"

I am standing on a riverbed. The water at my feet is teeming with rainbow trout fighting upstream to spawn. I am alone. I kneel where a small stream enters the river. The water is frigid to the touch. The dirt in the water is like the blood of the world as it flows over my hand, filtering out remnants of mountains between my fingers.

"How many bones does it take to build a house? A dream? A story?"

The moss on the trees is thick like frosting on a cake. The rain forest is dense; yet the isolation fills me with a greater sense of peace and purity.

"Do you wish you were on a star instead of Earth? Is Earth glad you are here or sorry? How does it feel to be one with everything?"

"How do I keep the feeling here? How do I hold it back but sometimes let it near?"

"In the woods, it occurs to me that these are the mysteries worth seeking. That nature, once stared into, has never let me go."

"The sun, the moon, and stars all shine with lamplike glow; the faintest trace of music carries through the endless miles of space. I wonder, does the universe cry or laugh to see us journey strangely through this place, our world, our earth. I know now why I have come."

I see a canoe on the river moving slowly downstream. In it is a pair of Indian women decorated in bright costumes. They seem to move very slowly, their aged and tired eyes scanning the wilderness. They spot me on the shore but simply float by, staring at me. I wonder what they see.

"To drum and play away and think a thousand thoughts a minute while I spin through the sun's daily whim to sweetly dance awhile—in good company, to leap upon the earth."

I look at my reflection in the water. My beard is long and full of dirt and blood, and I am naked. My eyes reflect their tired natures.

Then the voice booms.

"Be always true to self, true to destiny, true to time. To each other we look, as night follows day, here and the cycle never ends: but life goes on the best it can, and the worst follows unforbidden! Oh, humanity! Need to know what is possible to do, in this one short life span, and whether we have time and heart and skill to love in dazzling beauty, or shrug and fall away like hot ash.

"We are like so many sleeping, dreaming beauties, you and I, my love children, waiting for the kiss to set us free. I long to dream yet lie awake—someone has leaned over and kissed me and then disappeared and left me to discover.

"I am mortal among earth's creatures, vulnerable, yet curiously strong; the odor of flower and dust and dread hangs ominous like smoke upon my bed."

Rising up, I walk beside the chocolate river; my mind is thrumming, and my heart beats loudly in my head, the path before me strewn with petals and thorns.

I cry out as the thorns cut into my feet.

"Oh, such beauty and such pain!"

I sing softly to myself, "'Tis a gift to be simple..."

I walk into the night alone and see the first star of the evening shyly fading into view as if reluctant to take her eternal post. I sing softly to myself. The star sparkles in the night sky as if it is winking at me.

I am forgetting how difficult the path is to climb as the dark valley echoes back my song with its hollow voice.

I think how beautiful and mournful. But mostly, I feel how precious is life.

Then, on the trail in front of me are two Indian women. One in blue and one in green. They welcome me and we join hands. Silently, we walk together in the woods. Time fades, and with my companions I walk on into the night, seeking the mystic.

7. The Meaning of the Mahalet

I WOKE THE NEXT morning, and Seattle's trademark rain had replaced the sunshine, the raindrops beating the vertical windows of my loft like a Caribbean steel drum. I lay there in the calm of a Sunday morning as the click of the timer on the coffee pot set loose the smell of French roast coffee throughout my apartment.

Considering the previous day of unsettling, yet exciting events, I expected to feel spent and exhausted; instead, I found myself rested and recharged. My dream of the mountains had not been accompanied by the fear of my dream the afternoon before. I climbed down the ladder from my loft and poured myself a hot cup of coffee. Wearing only my robe, I walked downstairs to get my morning paper.

The coolness of the Seattle day reminded me of my nakedness under my robe as I opened the door to the front step. I returned upstairs and sat in reassuring silence, reading about the day's news and rolling my eyes at the comics. Then I headed for the shower and soon found myself sitting, rather than standing, in my tub under a warm downpour.

The previous evening, holding David had been so powerful for me. It had been much too long since a man had effortlessly brought out a physical reaction in me. Since Joe's death, the morning shower was my only true physical release.

I found myself this morning, with the first real hard-on that didn't feel like a repetitive morning task. It was a demonstration of pure pleasure. A primal reaction to my feelings for David and my growing attachment to him. As the water beat down upon me, I stroked my cock while dreaming of the night before, of David on top of me. His taste and smell and masculinity were overwhelming. As it rained outside, I lay in the tub, letting my imagination float with dreams of David. Gently playing with my nipples with one hand while stroking myself with the other, I was soon very hard, and the water beaded up in my hair.

I'd sat here frequently, beating off about a fantasy man who would come to me and claim my body. Now, I dreamed of him on top of me at Bowman Bay, holding his pipe to my nipple. I dreamed of his smell on that first day in the coffee shop.

Since David had arrived in my life, these sessions had become dreams of our nakedness and him, staring me in the eyes deeply as he discovered the joy of slowly fucking me.

Slowly, as I increased pace, I started whimpering "please" under my breath as the cum erupted from my cock, causing me to kick the tub wall. Dream and fantasy came together in my release. I moved my cum-covered hand to my face and smeared my beard and mouth, licking the fresh cum from my fingers as I continued to tremble in the steamy shower.

I lay there for a long while, letting the water run over me as the feeling of release sank in. Started with the soap tracing every inch of my body with suds and cleanliness, then I covered my entire body with a deep layer of white suds and rinsed off slowly. Turning off the water, I stood silently as my body dripped and steamed in the cool morning air. I grabbed the thick towel and dried off my body, continuing the sensual rub I had started earlier.

I walked out into the living room naked and sat in the middle of the rug, wondering to myself. Had I let my feelings simply get out of control? Had I, in my loneliness, leapt too quickly to want David? With all the extra issues surrounding him and the household of men, I began to question the sanity of it all.

The men had made me feel bonded to them the night before in the group embrace. Still, I had not spent any time around four of them. They were strangers, for all sakes and purposes. I released a deep sigh and wondered what I'd gotten myself into and whether I was truly walking a positive path. The medicine bag sat on the counter where I'd left it when I got home from the reservation. That's when it occurred to me that, if I wanted answers to a lot of what I was seeking, I had to go back to the reservation and see Ben and Jean. The magic or spiritual energy flowing from this gift to me was altering my sleep and my subconscious; hell, it was altering me and who I thought I was. For the first time, I realized the overwhelming change approaching my life, and it brought a smile to my face.

I finished my coffee and dressed. The day now had purpose.

I went down to the garage, got in my car, and turned it toward the mountains that had welcomed me the day before. I drove up into them with the silent noise of that encounter still banging in my head, along with all the other influences of the day. The medicine bag was my companion as it lay on the seat next to me.

Seattle is one of those remarkable cities where one minute you are surrounded by skyscrapers and the sound of the urban area, and twenty minutes later you are engulfed by evergreen trees and mountainsides, with no real proof of civilization anywhere but the road before you. This Sunday morning, I drove into the mountains trying to remember the route Marlin had taken the day before.

I was soon driving along the Skykomish River and into the deep forests of the Saanich Indian reservation. I had intended to head straight for Ben and Jean's, but somehow it felt right to stop and walk through the town. After I parked my car and got out, I noticed the powerful smell of the forest and the deep wetness as soon as I took my first breath.

Tall evergreens with shrouds of thick green moss surrounded the small village. The freshness of the rain made the forest almost glow. It, too, dripped and steamed as the shower had, something I might not have noticed just the day before. The dirt roads a muddy mess in the fall rains. These were the woods where Richard and Ben had met as children, where Ben's father had declared them the descendants of Peace and Brotherhood.

These woods were immortal, and I found myself entranced by their beauty. I walked into the village, gathering courage to continue my odyssey. The buildings looked as if they were out of an old western: post office, grocery, and barber shop. Tucked away at the end of the row of buildings, I discovered a small museum.

A woman was just flipping the "Open" sign on the window as I walked up. She greeted me, and we talked about the rain and the coming winter as she invited me into the building. As I walked through the small building and its exhibits, she told me about her work at the museum.

She said that the Saanich people have lived in the northwest for a thousand years. The Saanich were now six or seven enclaves stretching from Portland to the northern parts of British Columbia in Canada. She said I was lucky because I'd come in time to see their exhibit on death rituals.

"The world view of Saanich Nation," she continued, "is quite different from that of those who are raised around the Christian Molo ways. Saanich Indian people perceive the world as an intimately interrelated phenomenon in which the living and the dead, animals and humans, all things, are intimately connected and belong together in this place and do not leave it.

"The Saanich people have long held solemn food–burning ceremonies, which they called the mahalet. The function of burning food for the dead is to carry on the mutual responsibilities and respect that Indian people here try to accord to all of the other parts of the world as they see it. One of the things that always seems to be incomprehensible to Indian people is how the rest of us can pick ourselves up from one part of the world and move to another and abandon and cut ourselves off from our dead relatives, because they perceive of themselves as being in continuous association with and having ongoing responsibilities to the dead. This is a very ancient traditional practice among all our people, and the essence of the ceremony is to provide food for deceased relatives by burning it, and the essence of the food is transmitted through the smoke to the essence of the deceased person."

"So, " I asked, "Saanich Indian tradition is that those who are deceased continue to be an important part of ongoing life?"

"Yes, exactly. The spirits of our elders live on in the environment around us, and if we allow ourselves to be sensitive enough to it, we can continue to learn from them. When one dies, the remains are cremated, and then each member of the family receives a mahalet bag. The mahalet bag is customized by the shaman for each family; it includes ashes from the burning ceremony, actual remains of the burned animal and honored loved one, runes and special objects."

I was astounded when she showed me, under glass, several small leather bags almost identical to the medicine bag Jean had given me. "The mahalet bag serves as the spiritual medium to keep our loved ones close. As each generation moves on, the remains are disseminated in the same fashion, and the mahalet bag receives a place of honor in each individual's home."

I asked her to tell me about the markings on the bag under the glass. She showed me a marking on the side of one bag that was a series of written words.

"The words are in Sencoien, the ancient language of the Saanich."

That is when I showed her my mahalet bag, which Jean had given me. I explained to her that I had just gotten it and that I did not know what it was when it was given to me. I asked her to decipher the words and symbols for me.

She studied the bag momentarily. "Jean gave this to you, didn't she? You are a member of the House of Wolves, aren't you?" she said, with a smile on her face.

I was astounded. How did this woman know about the house? Did she also know about Richard?

"Jean is a wise shaman and my friend. Richard's time as See-hotid among us Saanich was widely honored after he was blessed by the great tyee,"

"If you have questions, she will know the path to set you upon for answers. The bag keeps spirits close to us. Did you know Richard?" She said all of this in an altogether different tone, reminiscent of the tone Ben used when reciting the legend to me the day before.

"No. I only know of Richard from what others tell me, and I've seen pictures," I said, trailing off.

"He's spoken to you, hasn't he?" she said, with great excitement and sudden wonder.

"What do you mean, spoken to me?"

"In your dibaajimowin," she paused and thought for a moment, "What is the molo word for it—in your dreams, your visions."

"Am I to expect to be spoken to?"

"Most mahalet bags are marked with the existing relationships, and it's rarer for existing relations to have communications from spirits; but your bag is unique. I have never actually seen one marked like this," she said, showing me a pair of claw-mark drawings. "These mean 'to come,' or 'for the future.' So, your bag was designed without an existing relationship; the spirit will work to establish one. Your bag reads for Wachdalehna, meaning "for the teacher who will come after me."

Richard made this bag before his transition, knowing you would come. Knowing that the relationship between you and House of Wolves would come to pass. And if Jean gave this bag to you, she is sure you are Wachdalehna. Are you the teacher that Richard spoke of, with Jean?"

"Yes, I teach elementary school."

"Then you already know that I am the wrong person to discuss this with; I can see on your face that you have questions." She paused.

"You need to go to Jean and to Ben. They are just past the end of town, down the final road. Don't be afraid; our spirituality is not about angry ghosts or fear. It is about love. I knew Richard when he played in these woods with Ben, and I know that Richard was about love." She led me to the door and pointed down the street. "It's that last stop sign down the lane, on the right."

"Thank you. I am Roy," I said, extending my hand to shake.

She embraced me in a hug.

"I am Jane. Be well, Roy, and take the path slowly; and again, don't fear."

That was easy for her to say. I was the one with the mixture of dead animals and Richard's ashes tied to my hip in the mahalet bag. I knew now that my dream of Richard was not a mistake, that it had been purposeful.

I got back out in the rain and walked down the street toward Ben and Jean's home. I turned at the stop sign and walked down the lane, letting the forest swallow me. Soon, I was at their doorstep. Taking a deep breath, I knocked.

The door opened to a small little boy; in a Disney-like voice, he said, "Hello. How can I help you?"

Sometimes I am more at ease with children than with adults. I smiled and asked, "Are Ben or Jean home?"

"Yes," he said, turning his back to me and then screaming, "Poppa, it's for you."

Soon Ben's familiar face appeared behind the young man, and he was quick to smile. "Hello. Come in, come in."

The young boy had me momentarily stunned, but I soon found my manners.

"What's your name, young man?" I asked the boy.

"Richard, sir," he said, very shyly, nuzzling his head into his father's belly, in contrast to the confident little boy who had answered the door.

"I hope you don't mind my showing up unannounced."

"Our home is your home, Roy, don't worry. Let me go get Jean. Richard, keep our friend company.

The young boy had the dark features of his Indian heritage and was already strong for a boy his age. I guessed little Richard to be six or seven years old. He sat at a small table in the room, playing with Legos.

"You are the teacher, aren't you?" the boy said casually, as if the question made complete sense.

Stopping for a second, I said, "Yes, Richard, I am a teacher."

He got up from his table and sat himself down next to me on the couch, and that is when I noticed, tied to his belt, a small version of the mahalet bag.

"Mother tells me you are the teacher that my uncle knew would come into our lives one day."

"Your uncle, yes. He predicted many things, and they confuse me a bit."

"Uncle likes you! He says you are the perfection, the completed cycle."

I tried not to show fear or discomfort, but the adult words coming from such a small child were very disconcerting.

"How do you know Uncle likes me?"

"When we walk the woods at night, he has spoken of you. When he shows me the woods in my night visions. He and I walk and talk while hiking in the woods by the river. He likes the tree fort I've built there. He says that, when he was a child, he and my father built similar tree forts together. He says that the smell of the woods is what he misses about being physical."

He spoke like a grown adult, with deep thought in his voice; then, suddenly, his voice changed, reverting to the child he was. "I see you have your mahalet bag; I just got mine, also."

"May I see your mahalet bag?" I said.

"Yes, here; let's trade," he said excitedly.

We undid the bags and handed our mahalet bags to one another. His was very small and felt as if it contained a hard marble. The markings were very similar to mine but drawn in a childlike fashion. Almost as if, for the bag to speak to a child, they had to be drawn in a manner that a child would understand.

There were drawings of wolves, a rendering of the carving from the door at the house, and a drawing of a waterfall.

"Uncle says that the waterfall is a powerful sign of nature. It is natural energy, he says," said the boy. "Have you asked him to explain yours to you yet?"

The boy's eyes were full of excitement, as if he knew I was the only other person who might be visited by Richard's spirit. "No," I said, "the first time I spoke with Richard, it frightened me."

"He knew that and is sad for it."

I was grateful when the boy's parents interrupted his train of thought. Ben reappeared in the room with Jean.

"Richard, leave us alone with Roy for a while."

Handing me back my mahalet bag, the little boy said, "It is very nice to meet you, Wachdalehna. I hope we can talk more another time."

He leaned over, kissed my cheek, then got up and left the room.

"Quite the boy you have there."

"He is growing nicely and will start grade school this year. He is part of the family that Richard and I started in these woods so many years ago," said Ben.

"I see he wears a mahalet bag," I responded.

"Yes, he received it for his sixth birthday. And he has had unique visions and magic along with it."

"Well, we were both just discussing that. It seems that Richard spoke to me yesterday in a dream just hours after you gave this to me."

Telling them about the dream of Richard and David, blurting everything out at incredible speed, I shared with them how Jane had explained to me the history of the mahalet bag—wondering aloud about the symbols reading "for the teacher who will come after me."

"This could only mean one thing, that the bag wasn't designed by either of you but by Richard," I surmised.

Ben read the mix of fear and excitement on my face.

"You are right. Richard gave it to us before he moved on and told us that, when David met a new love, we should immediately give him the mahalet bag, to share with him the dreams and the power of the mahalet."

"The dreams the mahalet brings to its owner are never to be taken literally. They are more reflections of your own mind along with the ancestral magic of the mahalet. When you were here yesterday, we discussed that my father thought Richard and I were reincarnations of the sons of the two Indian women who gave birth to brotherhood and peace. All the mahalet in the House of Wolves are a gift of our people."

"Why does Richard contact me instead of David? Doesn't it make sense he'd want to be in contact with David?" I asked.

"That is because David refuses to wear his mahalet bag," Jean answered, "David won't honor Richard's faith and beliefs. He seeks answers in the physical world and wishes for answers from a spirit world he does not believe in. We've watched him fight and struggle so hard since Richard left us.

All the others readily accepted the new gift, but David is stubborn, as you know, and seeks his own answers in the past. Getting David to wear his mahalet bag? We hope it will bring him peace with his future."

"But the way to the Seehotid heart is to learn the men See-He-Ahi surrounded him with," said Jean.

"Only then will you be able to reach out to Seehotid with true strength." She came and sat next to me, taking my hand, and continued. "When he came into See-He-Ahi's world, he embraced the physical man."

Reading the confusion on my face, she explained: "My apology. Let me use their molo names. When David came into Richard's life, he struggled with the idea of connecting with a man in both the physical and the spiritual manner. Richard tried to teach him the Saanich tradition of death and transformation. David resisted, wanting to fight harder to keep Richard in the physical and not allow the transformation. He still fights it, the troubled spirit that he has become.

Richard knew you'd come, though; his sights showed him a teacher. A strong man who would embrace the spiritual first and the physical second. In his grief for Richard, David has lost faith in the magic of the House of Wolves.

"You see, each man is endowed with a unique ktahtaw, or divine fire. Richard understood that. For the House of Wolves to be at peace, there could be nobody within the circle who had shame or felt they could not live up to their uniqueness. He knew that, if someone would get lost and find shame in his life, the circle would be incomplete. He knew that the teacher would come when the circle started faltering; when David needed to be reminded of his divine fire, the teacher would come. He knew that this person, Wachdalehna, would be able to rekindle the collective light of the whole household and make it shine into their souls again, revealing a new, unique magic for the house, without Richard's presence. Then, the house could make a new step forward on its own and find its own path."

All of this was now starting to make sense. It was as if the fog was starting to lift from my brain. New emotions and thoughts came pouring in, replacing confusion with strength. I realized that the choice of celibacy toward me by the men in the house was another one of Richard's requests. Everything, including the trip to the reservation, had been orchestrated by Richard.

Jean continued: "Richard knew that, in order for David to find peace, Wachdalehna would have to come. He would complete the circle where Richard could not. He could be David's peer where Richard was more of a father figure to David."

I said, "That is what he told me in the dream when he spoke to me. Oh, Jean, that is what he told me; I can hear it as if it happened a moment ago. Richard said, 'My terribly beautiful son David is now a man worth loving. He is no longer weak and has found his stride. I was his father, where you will be his peer, Wachdalehna. You will show him parity and bring all of his strengths to the surface. He has inherited my sense of brotherhood—our brotherhood. You must bring him a sense of peace for the circle to be completed.'"

"Richard attracted six different spirits to the house," Jean explained, "then, when he found out that the plague was going to bring his transition sooner than he'd expected, his plans changed. He spent the last year of his life planning for the future of the house without his physical presence. There is one thing that he underestimated: David's grieving. He underestimated how David would miss Richard's physical being—and never thought that, in his grief, David would turn his back on the teachings he'd held so dear to his heart.

"So it means for you, Roy, that you must complete the path, get to know the other men in the House of Wolves," Jean added. "You are the man to bring David peace. And you will; but first you must get to know his brothers.

"You've spent time with Marlin and with William. But the bear, the moose, and the hummingbird remain. Each brother in the House of Wolves is there for a reason. You cannot begin to imagine the completion of the circle without knowing what the circle contains.

"But I am seeing you lost in the thought of losing David in the journey; you are afraid of losing him in spite of the path you've been set upon by Richard. Richard is so proud of David and sees in you a key. A spiritual key. He sees an opportunity to unlock a part of David that he could not reach."

"Trust in Richard," Ben added. "I still do."

"How does he see? How does Richard see?" I asked.

Jean continued. "He has gone through the transformation to spirit. To living, yet not living, to being one with the Great Spirit. He lives with the two daughters of our ancestors and all that have gone before, guiding us. But he is not gone. He sought to comfort you, not scare you. Tell me, how did you envision Richard? How did he appear to you?"

I told her about the first part of the dream. I was sitting with Richard on the ocean as if I were sitting with my father in the park, feeding ducks. How serene it had felt. But then, how suddenly he spoke to me from darkness and how he frightened me with touch and darkness.

"The next time Richard visits you, Roy, relax and let the conversation happen."

"It wasn't a conversation, though. Richard said, 'I know you want to speak to me, Wachdalehna, and find answers; but your voice is not heard here—and answers come with time.' I've never had a dream I could recall word for word.

"Never a dream where all the senses were so overwhelming—the smell, the sounds, the touch and the taste…my dreams overnight were out in the wilderness, naked and feeling breezes in my hair and the sun on my nakedness; it was raw and felt peaceful."

"Yet you awakened this morning refreshed and in touch with yourself, no?

That is the magic of the mahalet working to heighten your journey when traveling in sleep, when reaching out for other places. He knew your dreams would be vivid and strong, like your character," Jean said, with a smile.

Ben and Jean and I spoke for a while longer about their lives with Richard and David. Jean was sure to repeat many times what would become my new goal. I must know all the men in the House of Wolves. I was still uneasy with her assertion that I was somehow the final piece in a puzzle, that somehow I'd reach David in a way Richard could not.

Ben, Jean and their young son, Richard, walked me back to my truck. The rain had stopped, but the forest swelled with the moisture which still dripped on our heads as we walked through town.

"We are so glad that you came to visit us," said the young Richard. "Perhaps Uncle will invite you to go walking in the woods together some night."

"I think I'd like that very much, Richard, thank you. You know that I teach kids just a few years older than you. Perhaps I'll bring my class up here to meet you then. To meet a Saanich boy and trade stories."

Richard smiled shyly and Ben said, "You are welcome anytime, Wachdalehna. You are family here."

With that, I got in my truck and drove back toward the city. Today's odyssey was surely something I would not forget to write in my journal: starting my great day in the shower and feeling the same release of emotions as I drove off the mountain. I couldn't wait to get home.

This was the pivotal moment when I realized that I could either sit and watch the magic of the House of Wolves happen or become a player. It was then I decided I'd do whatever it would take to bring David back in the circle and see if that meant I'd have a place there, too.

It was clear, now, that the only way to reach David was to join his brothers in awakening him back to the path that Richard had originally had in mind. But I had three more men to meet and understand before I could turn my energy back toward David.

I got back to my apartment and, letting the momentum carry me, I called the house. Marlin answered. "Hello, pup! How are you?"

I explained how I had gone up to visit Ben, Jean, and their son, Richard. Considering yesterday, it felt like the right place to go to try to figure some of this out.

"Jean told me that I won't be able to reach David until I know all of the rest of you at the house. Talk to the men and let them know I am ready."

"It's been a hard week for you, pup. You've been through a lot of hard stuff. I am so thrilled you got guidance from Jean. She's a smart woman, and that child, wise beyond his years. Much like his father.

"I was hoping I'd hear from you. Gotta tell you, you impressed the boys here yesterday. Particularly that Tristan; he does not handle drama well, and even that bugger felt OK with how things were left. I will let the boys contact you as they will and tell them you are waiting."

Marlin assured me that he'd let the others know about the trip to visit Ben and Jean. I asked for an update on David.

Marlin told me David had remained in his cottage except for working out and coming to meals; but he was well. He reassured me and said patience would prevail. He was sure of it.

I settled in for the night and watched a little television, thinking to myself it would be good to get back to a routine with the kids after my wild weekend with the House of Wolves. The hour was late, and I was just about ready to go to bed when the phone rang.

"Hello?"

"Good evening. Is Roy there?" said Tristan's familiar voice. He was being so formal!

"This is."

"Hello, Roy, this is Tristan."

"Hello."

Right to the point, he asked, "Do you exercise out at the Y? Right? You go and work out after teaching each day? David said that you did. I am unsure; is he correct?"

"Yes, I do, Tristan. I work out at the YMCA after school each day, on Fourth Avenue."

"I work downtown. Can I meet you after your workout? Say for some sushi or dinner?"

"Yes, I'd like that, Tristan. Say, six o'clock outside the Y, tomorrow?"

"That is good for me as long as it is no inconvenience."

"It is no inconvenience, Tristan; in fact, it's my pleasure."

After a polite silence, acknowledging that the appointment was accepted by me, "Good, then; 6:00 PM tomorrow. See you then." Tristan hung up.

He communicated so differently from the others. His manner was so formal, so strict, and so perfect. Sushi with Tristan would surely be an experience.

I realized that what Jean had asked me. I would continue to keep thinking of ways to reach out to David. Already missing my pipe-smoking man, I wondered how he was spending his first day trying to figure out the weekend. I was sure that Jean was right, though, that the path back to David led to the lives of Tristan, Moose, Bear, and the rest of the men in the House of Wolves.

I climbed up into the loft. The rain had not stopped all day long, and the same rhythmic rain on my roof that had welcomed me that morning slowly set me to sleep. I dreamt deeply.

As I walked into the coffee shop, water dripped from my short haircut, and I wiped my brow. I set down my book bag and ordered a latte. The barista winked at me and delivered a hot, frothy cup in no time at all. I picked up my book bag and walked to my usual booth. The day was very dark out, with low clouds, so the normally bright coffee shop was dimmer with the wintry rainstorm. I broke out essays to grade and disappeared into my student work.

I heard the bell ring on the door of the coffee shop and a raspy voice order a cappuccino. Change rattled on the counter, and as he walked toward me he whistled and then sang softly, "'Tis a gift to be simple."

I looked up into Richard's bearded face. He wore the same outfit I'd seen him in at Bowman Bay, a long leather coat with a flamboyant, loud scarf. Taking the coat off and settling into the booth across from me, he wore a black-and-red flannel shirt, a brand new pair of blue jeans, and black, flat-toed boots. He sat there very much as David had in the real world just a few weeks beforehand.

"Hello, Richard," I said, as if I'd expected his entrance.

"Wachdalehna. It is good to see you."

8. Diving Kites

I FOUND MYSELF WALKING to work the next morning in the fog of autumn, reflecting on the new path on which I'd ventured. Richard had set before me a household of men with minds and spirits toward which I found myself drawn more strongly than ever. The brilliant colors of fall were fading, and it was time for a classic Seattle winter of gray skies and rain.

I missed David—his smell, his pipe, his voice, his calming manner and the way he simply disarmed me. But I also missed laughing with Marlin. It was then that I realized I was becoming attached to all the men in the house and that the House of Wolves called to me, now, stronger than ever. I was confident that my place was with David and this new way of living.

At school, I picked up my mail and found my classroom. "Mr. Wallace" was the sign by my door. I walked to my desk at the back of the room, set down my briefcase, and looked through my mail.

In my mail was a brown envelope. Looking at it closer, I saw the envelope was covered with hand drawn colored leaves. It had a red wax seal that was suddenly recognizable—the wolves from the door of the house. I opened the envelope to find a simple manila card that read:

Dearest Mr. Wallace,
    I am going to go away for a while. I have accepted my mahalet—and am off to Bowman Bay for a retreat of quiet

contemplation. I'll take my books and write in my diary. Please know that I have you in my heart—and know that all of these emotions from me are sometimes hard to handle. I'm not sure what it all means. I know that I belong with you, Roy. No matter what happens while I'm away, the first thing I'll do upon my return is come find you.—Your David.

I sat at my desk and realized a tear had come to my eye. It had been so long since another man had coveted me, that someone honestly had loved me. Considering my experience with the mahalet over the last few days, I could only imagine the journey David was beginning. I did love this man and was amazed at the courage of the house of men to ask David to accomplish such a great task.

David's brothers were starting to give to me, as well. The men in the house were more than a simple collective of men. They were interconnected spiritually and sexually in a way I'd never experienced. David's task was also mine. I had my date with Tristan that afternoon, and I was going to be sure he understood my appreciation for the great reconnection with David that I was sure he'd engineered.

The students started arriving in my classroom, so I put the note from David into my backpack and started my day. My kids wandered into the classroom in their energetic morning routine, giggling, chatting about the latest topics that would only interest fifth-graders. The morning bell rang, and announcements came over the loudspeaker.

I started the morning with a casual discussion of what Thanksgiving meant to each of my kids. I got the normal responses about being thankful for what we have and commemorating the Pilgrims' first dinner with Indians.

One of my kids said that Thanksgiving for her meant hope. She thought that Thanksgiving should be about hope. I furthered the discussion by considering, with the kids, the topics of hope and brotherhood; after all, the relationship with the Indians had gotten the Pilgrims through the cold winter.

Discussions with my students often lead to points of view being expressed you never see coming. While discussing the holiday, Pam, probably one of the shyest students in class, suddenly interrupted and said, "Thanksgiving should remind us that, even at the worst time, we can have the hope of the Pilgrims on that fall day when they feasted with the Indians."

The rest of the kids fell quiet—like they'd heard a special pearl of wisdom. It was clear this year's class had some magic all its own.

It occurred to me that Ben and the spirituality of the Saanich had provided hope to Richard and to his vision of the House of Wolves. It was clear that the integration of Indian spirituality had helped Richard and his brothers through a spiritual winter. The presence of Saanich culture in their lives had fortified the men of the house and strengthened them. Perhaps David would share in that hope, once he'd let himself be open to the magic of the mahalet and the spirituality that had originally drawn him to the house.

My students and I spent the day on various Thanksgiving crafts and assignments, and the time flew by. I saw my last kid to his bus and then slung my backpack on my shoulder and headed for the gym.

The sun was setting as I walked in the doors of the YMCA. I always loved this time of the day, folks coming from their stressful jobs to work out. My workouts these days consisted of some serious treadmilling and rotating of weight sets. Today was upper body day, and I got changed and went right to it. Soon I was sweating hard on the treadmill. I put on a CD of dance music and bounced into an entirely other world. After a few minutes, I shut off the music and went to step off the machine when a pair of strong, furry arms wrapped around me and lifted me off the treadmill and to the floor.

The strong man let go of me, and I turned around to be greeted by Bear. His long white-and-black beard matted with sweat, he was smiling ear to ear.

"Roy! Tristan told us you worked out here. How are you?"

I told him I'd had a great day. This was the first time I'd seen Bear since I'd been at the house. He was extremely handsome. His body was covered with a thick mix of black and white body hair, and two very large nipple piercings showed through his T-shirt.

He wore a bone nose ring and smelled very much like David, earthy and masculine. His presence caught me quite off guard, and I stuttered as I told him that I'd had a good, busy day, and that I was headed for the free weights. He said Moose was already working out with the weights and suggested we spot one another. I stepped ahead of him toward the free-weight area, and he slapped my butt, making me jump. I heard him giggle softly as we walked toward Moose.

Moose was working at the bench press station and was dressed in a similarly revealing tank top and short workout pants. His red body hair and pirate-like beard made him appear to be the larger man. He was incredibly defined, with bulging arms as large around as my thighs. I felt as if I were working out with two giants.

"Roy," said Moose in a huff, between reps, "how the heck are ya?"

He finished his routine, set the bar back into its starting position, and reached out his large hand, which covered mine in an enthusiastic shake. Bear told him that we should work out together, unable to hide his grin under his beard. Both of them were covered in sweat, and I'm afraid my attraction to them was hard to hide. Moose smiled like a good friend and suggested that we get started.

Since they were at the bench, we started there. I lay down as Moose and Bear removed weights from the bar. Bear stepped up at the head of the bench and stood over me.

"We'll start you out light, Roy. David would kill us if we broke ya," said Moose, smiling.

I stared at his furry body as he pressed up against the bench. These were two of the furriest men I'd ever seen. Bear's body hair almost hid his skin. His long beard met his belly, and he stared down at me with a whimsical smile, the hair sneaking into his shorts.

"Ready?" he said, and he lifted the bar with me and we began lifting the weight. The reps started, and Bear and Moose stared down at me as we lifted together. My arms arched, and I started huffing and grunting at the weight they'd put on, a bit more than I was used to.

I started to slow as I got close to my fifteen reps, and Moose spoke softly:

"Come on, boy, that's it, push."

Bear reached down and helped me gently with the last two reps. He and Moose added considerable weight to the bar and did their reps while I looked on.

"God, it's going to be fun to have another muscle bear around," said Bear, with a big smile, squeezing my bicep with his full hand.

We continued to work out together, lifting on separate stations. The two men gave off an air of familiarity that was astounding, considering they'd briefly met me just twice. They were genuinely affectionate throughout the workout, and I caught myself flirting back at the two of them.

There has always been something authentic about men when they are working out. These two were wet with sweat, and each of them made a unique sound as every man does when he's trying his hardest. Add that these were two hairy, muscular men with eager hands, and it was turning into the most erotic workout I'd ever experienced. We exchanged soft smiles as each of us positioned himself with his crotch over a man's face as he lay down to lift weights.

As the workout came to a close, Moose suggested we take a steam before hitting the shower. We walked to the locker room and stripped down. I was very comfortable being naked around these guys. I wasn't sure why. My usual shyness seemed to evaporate. I chuckled at myself as we entered the steam room.

"What's so funny, Roy?" asked Bear.

"Well, it's just that I haven't even seen David naked, and here I am heading for the steam room with you two," I said, smiling.

"Well," Moose quickly responded, "only because David didn't think of meeting you here."

As we stepped into the fog of the steam room I noticed Moose's totem. The moose tattoo on his shoulder with the antlers wrapping around and up his neck. It was clearly the most dramatic and most visible of the house tattoos I'd seen. His chest and arms were truly massive and strong, and his uncut cock hung with a zero–gauge PA.

Bear was simply covered in black hair, his bear tattoo across his inner thigh and wrapping around his massive legs. Drawing attention was his cock standing out against his mat of body hair, half hard with at least eight different ladder piercings and ending with a matching PA.

"Everyone stares at Bear's cock, Roy, don't worry," Moose said, making me realize I was gawking.

"That's a lot of piercing; did all that hurt?" I asked Bear.

"No more than that did," Bear laughed, reaching out and tugging at my nipple rings. He explained that he'd always been a piercing fetishist, and one night, after some long play, with lots of temporary piercings to his cock, he'd decided to make it permanent.

I asked them how the body placement of their tattoos had been decided. Moose said he'd asked Tristan to put it somewhere untraditional, that it has meant more to him having it placed there. He added that its placement gave the tattoo a purpose for him beyond adornment.

Unlike the others, Bear's and Moose's names had been given them well before they joined the group, so their totems were clear. They were the large bear and the towering moose of the group of men from the very start.

We sat and laughed our way through conversation for a long while. I realized it was getting on in time, and I'd better shower and get ready for dinner with Tristan. I started to say good-bye when Bear stepped across the steam room and threw his arms around me, delivering a hot, wet kiss. He held me to him for a moment, pressing his pierced cock against my thigh.

"See you soon," he whispered in my ear as he let me go.

Moose said good-bye in the same manner, moving in for a hug, running his hands down my back, letting one finger rest on the crack of my butt. The chemistry I'd felt during the workout was real. These two men were going to follow through someday on some real, honest intimacy. The three hard-ons we now shared in the steam room made that clear. I blushed.

"I need to go. I'm going to be late meeting Tristan," I said, quickly searching for words.

"Don't worry, you'll make it on time," snarled Bear, as Moose looked on with a coy smile. "There will be plenty of other times to discover one another. We are so glad David has brought you to us; you're a beautiful one," and again his large fingers gently cusped one of my nipple rings, squeezing the flesh with the metal.

I gave out a soft moan, which was greeted by both men with a satisfied smile. I looked around the otherwise empty steam room and at the door, nervous that someone might catch us in the act of exploration.

"That's enough for now," said Moose, reading my comfort and simultaneous conflict. "I think Roy knows that we'll find a more suitable place one day to explore these hard-ons and feelings. I think he knows it real well."

Moose slapped me on the butt and turned me to the door, "Now, get goin'—before Bear has you for dinner instead of Tristan."

With that, I said good-bye and rushed to the shower. There I stood in the shower with a hard-on, and I found myself shaking. Here I was with two men who obviously found me attractive. It was like something out of a tawdry porn movie fantasy.

This was my first confirmation that the house was polyamorous, that they shared physical as well as emotional intimacy. I felt thrilled as I remembered my attraction to Marlin earlier and the thought of actually being able to act on that attraction. Such thoughts spiraled around in my head. There was a time in my life when such arrangements would have been out of the question, but this household of men presented such uniqueness.

So many gay men spend their lives trying to reflect the heterosexual norm of relationships, but this group of men was living authentically as a group. The House of Wolves actively disregarded the norms others strive for and sought their own comfort levels in their choices.

This situation lent itself to thinking differently. The openness of the group didn't seem to take on the same flavor as the predatory types who head out to bars to pick up tricks. It felt deeply fraternal. I had to get out of the shower, but my erection was refusing to go down. I was thankful that this particular Y had private shower stalls. With a blast of cold water, I shocked my body back into submission. Yet, even in the cold, my excitement fought the brave battle…but lost. Again, I gave thanks and moved before I could give it a chance to surge back.

I walked by the steam room, back to my locker, and Bear and Moose waved to me. I got myself dressed and headed out to meet Tristan. I'd been very careful to write down Tristan's directions to the sushi restaurant he had picked out. And just as Bear said, I would get there with plenty of time to spare.

Although I had only met Tristan, it was clear to me that, after just two meetings, I could make some guesses about the man and his role in the present situation in the house. Always the first to speak out, Tristan was clear about his displeasure with David. He vented about how long it was taking David to grieve.

I was sure he was behind the latest confrontation that had sent David off to Bowman Bay with his mahalet. So, while at the same time interested in who he was, I also worried that Tristan was the one person in the house whom I might never learn to love or be close to.

The restaurant was unassuming from the street; but upon stepping inside, I saw it was a Zen-like escape from the outside world. Small tables lined the outer edges of the room, with stark oriental writing on the walls in large, broad-brushed calligraphy. It seemed to me the perfect restaurant for Tristan, artistic and powerful, yet stark. The air had the musk of incense burning somewhere and the sting of ginger. I leaned against the wall near the counter, waiting for Tristan to arrive, trying to clear my brain of naked images from my workout.

The tinkle of the tiny bell signaled the opening of the door. Framed by the outside light was Tristan's sleek shadow. Tristan was a short but muscular man whose first impression was of someone impeccably groomed. His pencil-thin mustache was unusually long and hung off his upper lip like a modern Genghis Khan. He wore a perfectly ironed green silk shirt, the kind of shirt that most men see in the Undergear catalog but would not wear because the style only works on the models; Tristan looked? perfectly natural in the green shirt, fit for a Caribbean island. He was coming in from a Seattle winter, but he looked perfect.

"Hello, Roy," Tristan greeted me, matter-of-factly. "Let me settle some business, and I'll be right with you."

He set a little case, much like an old-time lunchbox, on the counter as the woman behind the counter approached. They exchanged some fast-paced words, and he opened the case and handed her two small envelopes that were sitting among bottles and envelopes. Each gave a slight bow to the other, and she proceeded to show Tristan to a table. I duly followed. Our table was in back with a magnificent window overlooking the waters of Puget Sound. Tristan sat, clasping his hands together in front of him, staring directly into my eyes.

"Hello, Roy. Thank you for meeting me here. The owner is one of my customers. I am an herbalist. She enjoys baths with eucalyptus, which has great healing powers for stress in the body, and my source has a unique tree that she is quite fond of." Tristan added, in his thick Thai accent, "Let's have tea."

He motioned to the waiter, who quickly brought us a steaming pot of tea as Tristan said, "This is gyokuro, or jade dew, and is the highest-quality green tea. It is picked from ancient bushes when the leaves are young and tender. In early spring, when buds first appear, each old bush is enclosed in a slatted bamboo blind so that the sun's rays are shut out. About two weeks later, when the leaves are two centimeters long, they are picked. It is the traditional tea to serve with sushi."

It was clear that I was there to learn from Tristan, that this was less of a conversation than his time to teach me his passions and his knowledge. Another server approached our table, and Tristan looked at me and said, "I will order for us. Nasu, maguro, shiro maguro and amaebi, and more tea, thank you," he said to the waiter, who took down our order and scurried away.

"Nasu is eggplant in a garlic glaze; it feeds your immune system with lots of vitamin E and plenty of protein. As positive men, we'll be looking after ways to boost your immune system. Maguro is red tuna; it has strong astringent qualities. Shiro maguro is white tuna, for strength. I chose amaebi, the sweet shrimp, because it's my favorite," he said with a satisfied and sudden smile.

I was startled by his manner and the care he took considering me when planning the menu. I wasn't sure if that was a good thing or not, but I was quickly learning that HIV didn't even begin to scare Tristan, and he wanted me to know that. I was touched by his protective manner and found myself quickly relaxing with him.

He shot me a grin as he poured us both tea and spoke again.

"I am very glad to have this time with you, to share myself and have you see me for me, without the loudness of Marlin or the allure of our David distracting us. It really is the best way, I think.

"When I first met William and he became involved in the house…" He saw me react. "You did not know that William was my love? He's so shy about calling me that, but that he is. We are inescapable to one another. But I rush myself.

"I first came to be in the House of Wolves after meeting Richard, through his tai chi. He was a marvelous master of the art. I called Richard that. Master Richard showed me how to find the inner power that I'd been denying myself, and I began studying with him. Richard was training me in his meditations and use of herbs.

"In my time studying with Richard, I learned of the lives of the other men of the house. I came into the house as the odd man, the man without love. Bear had Moose, and Richard was with Marlin. Yes, before David arrived, Marlin and Richard were together. Our lives moved forward, Richard teaching us new skills, sometimes without our even realizing it.

"I arrived as the construction of the house was close to complete: the one room I helped Richard finish was the meditation and group meeting building. Richard imported jade tiles from the East, and we worked long hours making the room ready. Richard had me work with Marlin to research the imagery we'd use. Each totem from the household, as well as a few particular runes and markings Richard had insisted upon. He said that these runes would guard the room and seal it for use by the brotherhood. Marlin had the music system installed. I was really astounded by his contribution. One can listen to music in that room in an entirely new, invigorating way. Music seems to flow around you in that room—you actually experience the music.

"You must know, Roy, that despite my obvious issue with his hygiene, I do love Marlin. It is simply that Marlin often says a lot, without saying much."

Tristan laughed again and continued: "He's like the bad television show sometimes, a lot of talk about nothing."

Even at that comment, I had to laugh. Marlin did tend to ramble on sometimes.

"Now, mind you, I was weak and young when I entered the house. I asked Richard once, while studying with him, 'Why does life not present me a love of my own, rather than surrounding me with men I love but do not covet as I would my own love?' He answered that life presents things like events on the breeze, and the breeze would one day bring me love.

"You know that difference, don't you, Roy? The difference between loving a man and the powerful coveting of a man, feeling incomplete without him? I know you do, as you showed me when you came to the house to let David know you'd be there when he was ready.

"David and I have always been argumentative. He is such a free spirit. At first, I wondered what Richard saw in him, until the day he delivered the door, bringing order and completeness to the house. Yet I was still alone, and here was David, who was clearly captivating the master and bringing new energy to a household I had only just begun to understand myself. I withdrew into myself and resented that even more love, unavailable to me, was being demonstrated in the house.

"I was distrustful of David, sure he was not the right choice for the sixth man. He was not mine; he was the master's! But the master had already loved Bear, Moose, and Marlin, and now he loved this new man with more passion and energy than any before. I grew resentful of the lack of power left for me in the house.

"I was emotional and grew withdrawn. David felt that from me from the beginning, and I have kept up boundaries where he is concerned.

"Six months before Richard became sick, the breeze came to me in the form of William. My love. We were all out in the park by the house, flying this bright kite that David had made

Richard. Kites had always captivated Richard. When the spring winds come, we design a kite as a group and take it to Discovery Park for flying. That year it was a kite based on nature, an old-fashioned paper kite on which David had drawn a total eclipse of the sun, with planets trailing off the kite onto the tail.

"He asked each of us to write a quote on the kite before it flew. I meditated long on what to write. Richard stood over me as I wrote my quote that morning; strangely enough, I used a quote from a book that Marlin had left on my pillow a few weeks earlier. The words were from Ray Bradbury's foreword to Heinlein's *Stranger in a Strange Land*:

'We are cups, constantly and quietly being filled. The trick is, knowing how to tip ourselves over and let the beautiful stuff out.'

"Richard said to me, softly, 'Excellent choice, catechumen.'

"He always called me that, explaining that it meant 'a student learning a great subject.' He always told me he'd seen great things from me and that I was learning new ways to channel the energies of my culture; he saw me one day becoming a great teacher of herbs and meditation arts.

"So, it was with a real sense of having impressed the master, and finally feeling like my place in the house had been established, that we headed out to the bluff to fly that year's kite. The trip always transports us back to our childhoods, the great joy that comes when the kite leaps for the heavens and soars in the springtime winds. This particular kite shot like a rocket into the sky, nearly pulling the roll of string from Richard's hands. All of us laughed and hooted like small children.

"Marlin was being his normal childlike, smelly self and danced the kite over the meadow, when suddenly the kite lost the wind and dove onto a man sitting on a blanket. The poor fellow was just trying to find some peace and quiet, looking over the bluff at the whitecaps in the sea. The day was windy, and I could see the breeze off the ocean blowing through his black hair. Only after he stood up did his tall, dark body come into full view.

"The stranger walked up to our group, tattered kite under his arm, and introduced himself in a friendly way. He effortlessly giggled with Richard and David over the kite's interrupting his day. Then he turned to me, his startling blue eyes radiating at me: 'Hello, I am William.'

"Just like the total eclipse David had drawn in watercolors on the parchment on the kite, his visage eclipsed me. His soft darkness has always captivated me."

Tristan suddenly came to life with the story of his brush with the breeze, that had brought William into his life. I knew exactly what he meant. I sat there, momentarily lost in my reactions to his story. It reminded me of days laughing with Joseph, and I recognized that Tristan had experienced the kind of powerful loneliness I'd felt after Joseph died, only to have it replaced with his love for William. Simultaneously, I knew that David was at this moment on his way to Bowman Bay, hoping to find fresh perspective. It was all so much to digest and understand.

"William and I were almost instantly inseparable. As he and I grew closer and our spirits danced in the moonlight of our bedroom each evening, he was very soon living at the house. But our new love, our new bond, was soon overshadowed by the failing of Richard's health—and David."

Tristan saw me frown a little. He reached out and touched my hand on the table, his face softening up considerably, and he continued.

"I know you hear me being critical of your...our, David. Only recently have I realized that my alignment of feelings toward him was hurting the household. I am sorry and angry that I have allowed this to enter my life. Let me use a verse of the Tao as an example of my point:

"The Tao existed before its name, and from its name, the opposites evolved, giving rise to three divisions, and then to names abundant. These things embrace receptively, achieving inner harmony, and by their unity create the inner world of man. No man wishes to be seen as worthless in another's eyes, but the wise leader describes himself this way, for he knows that one may lose by gaining and gain by losing.

"You see, Roy, it took the death transformation of Richard for me to see the powerful love between them. In this proverb, it says that, for all things to have inner harmony, powerful opposites must exist to receive balance. In regarding David as not worthy of respect, I had lost the opportunity to celebrate their bond.

"I failed both the master and David when I failed to see the great power and pride from which David grieves. It has kept me in turmoil, knowing that I could not approve his energy until the man who'd drawn him into the house was dead. But my treatment of David had darkened his attitude toward me, another misfortune of mine."

Tristan was baring himself to me, confessing how he struggled with David. I now realized what William and the rest of these brothers saw in the man. On one hand, the educated voice of reason, of balance; but on the other hand, a unique person with his own struggles that have caused him complex pain and open conflict.

I found myself immersed in him and, all at once, changing my preconceived notions.

"The next few months were a blur," continued Tristan. "Meeting William, his amazingly quick inclusion in the household, and then a great sadness as it became clear that Richard's health would not return, that the master was dying."

Tristan's whole demeanor changed as if the moment of Richard's death had just occurred. His grief was now showing, probably more than he wanted, and he looked into the table for the first time, not wanting to see my reaction. Tristan seemed somewhat embarrassed that he had expressed too much; but, with a breath, he looked up and continued, through glassy eyes.

"Then came the terrible night when I went to David and Richard's house. William and I sat with David as Richard made the death transformation. His passing was calm and as peaceful as one could imagine. David was silent, but his anger was just beneath the surface. It was a great loss for all of us, and we are ashamed we didn't see more clearly how to help David through it all.

"Jean and Ben arrived the next day and removed Richard's empty body. From that day, David started avoiding group meals and activities. He mourned late into the night. I remember lying in William's arms, hearing him wail and grieve in the darkness.

"We all grieved in our own way and meant to give David space to respect his love for Richard. Looking back, perhaps we didn't include him enough, didn't reach out with enough group love to keep him.

"A month later, Ben and Jean returned and asked us all into the meditation room. We sat in a circle as Jean started a small incense fire in the middle of the room and let the smoke dance around. She came with words from See-He-Ahi, she said. He had made the spiritual transformation that is death.

"I watched David. He was barely able to compose himself, his grief still raw and uncontrollable. The simple mention of Richard's spiritual name created intensity in the room that was palpable.

"She said that, in the tradition of the Saanich, he'd prepared for each of them a mahalet bag. She told us the legend of the mahalet, how they'd sent Richard's body to ashes with a buck they'd killed on the hunt, and that she had Richard's final gift for each of us in these bags: the remains of his body and the proud buck that walked with him now in the spirit world.

"She also announced that Richard wanted me to design a tattoo for each of the members of the house and that, in his absence, we must mark each other to remember our bonds to the house, no matter the way the spirits led us to follow in his absence.

"Doing her duty, she set the mahalets in the center of the room, each inscribed with a totem, the totems Richard had chosen for each of us. She told us the story he'd given her for each of them and explained that Richard felt Bear and Moose had been born into their names.

"This was the night that changed us all. We didn't realize until the next morning that David had not taken his mahalet. When William and I went to clean the meditation room during chores, we found it lying there, solitary by a now dead set of incense ashes. I urged William to let me take it to him and inquire why he'd left it.

"William, in his great softness, said to me, 'Tell me, catechumen'—having adopted Richard's nickname for me—'my sweet, how would you react in your life if I were to leave in death?' His question struck me like a sword; I was speechless.

"'See, my love,' William continued, "David has lost his Richard. He was ours, too, yes, but he was bonded far deeper to David. David is so alone; you remember describing for me your despair before I came. Give Seehotid time. Give him time.'

"With that, William picked up David's mahalet and said that we'd keep it until David was ready. Only when David wanted the mahalet voluntarily would it do him any good.

"I found it hard to tolerate that David, one so powerfully coveted by the master, could openly disrespect the master's wishes; he and I exchanged words over the next few months, words that I am hoping he and I both regret. The two of us have been apart emotionally for some time. Then, Roy, he met you.

"I was sitting in the library as he came home and told Marlin about meeting you at the AIDS Foundation. How childlike his voice. How he wanted to know more of you, needed to find you. Then I was alone in the library again, reading by the fire the night he returned from the coffee shop and his first significant time with you.

"David came into the house all wet, his black hair frayed in his face. He greeted me in our accustomed cursory fashion and, quite uncharacteristically, I spoke to him openly. I told him that I'd been in his path, alone, hungry for coveting love. In his artistic way, he cried, came to me, and held me. His spirit is unconditional, and he said he'd been redirecting anger toward me but was uncomfortable with the curtness. He admitted he had been rude in not celebrating the joy of seeing William and me in a special bond, like the one he had shared with Richard.

"We collapsed on the couch and talked for a while before my William came into the room. He was overjoyed to see us together, David and me, like the brothers we had meant to be. Marlin rustled out of the loft above the library to come sit with us. David then described the entire time with you in the coffee shop—including your scent! David is so tactile. William and the rest of us quickly assured him that it was important for him to find you again, and that led to your venture to Bowman Bay."

He stopped talking suddenly as if I had learned enough for one sitting. Tristan blurted all this out in a solid, constant stream of thought, no pauses, no stopping to discuss. It was clear that I'd greatly misjudged him. His story and contribution to the house were obvious. Richard had been drawn to the sense of honor and order hiding under his youth. He was the spiritual opposite of David, which made me wonder even more what Richard had been like as a man in the house when he was still walking with them on the grounds, teaching each member.

"Richard becomes more and more complex the more I hear of him," I said to Tristan. "He knew instinctively to bring this group of men together, from moments like David's delivering the carved door to Marlin's diving a kite at William."

"Your sense of order and style shows on William. I should have guessed that you two were connected in a special way," I said with a smile.

"William is an amazing blend of the bear in the rest of the house and the meticulous man I have always dreamed of," said Tristan. "He completes me. So this is why, Roy, where David is concerned, I grew impatient of his choices. I wanted him to let go of Richard, re-embrace the spiritual, and find his place with you, to find a new path. I grew impatient for the order that Richard had intended David to take over, for David to assume his place back in the circle. He's been struggling and fighting."

Suddenly, Tristan stopped talking and a giant smile crossed his face. I heard the telltale ring of the restaurant entrance, and in walked William with his normal confidence. Almost as if it were choreographed, the waiter added a chair to our table, and William sat down.

"Hello, Tristan," he said, caressing Tristan's ear and hair.

"Roy and I are getting to know one another. He is a good listener."

"And you, Roy. Has my intense little man here been good listener as well?"

"As matter of fact, yes, he has; it's been a very nice dinner."

"Good. I hear you were almost the entrée for Bear and Moose at the gym earlier," he said, winking. Tristan shot me a look of interest.

"Oh, dear," I said, as I felt myself blushing.

"Those two are incorrigible," said Tristan. "I think, even if the house burned to the ground, it'd turn them on. I keep wishing they'd get some control of it all."

William chimed in: "They are who they are, catechumen; as you are unique, so are they."

"Yes, my love," Tristan said softly.

"Do you guys share everything you do with one another?" I asked, referring to his knowledge of my encounter with Bear and Moose at the gym.

"Pretty much. You get used to a certain lack of privacy with this group, but I promise my teasing is all meant in fun," said William.

William changed his tone and added, "I also wanted to make sure you felt good about David leaving with the mahalet at the urging of the rest of us."

"I am worried for him but excited at the same time," I admitted.

"Indeed," said William. "I am delighted he was finally ready to make that step. No matter what magic the mahalet reveals to him, it was finally time."

He could see me tensing up at the subject and quickly segued. "The others are waiting for us at the Eagle for a beer. Get your stuff together, pay the bill, and let's go join them."

We paid the bill as Tristan said his good-byes to the staff in brilliantly fast Chinese. William's truck was parked out front; with Tristan in the middle, we drove uptown to the bar, Tristan in his green silk and I in my teacher drag. We hardly looked like the types who would head for the Eagle.

The bar was busy for a weeknight but not crowded. On the patio, Bear and Moose were discussing something with Marlin, whose normally braided white hair was down in a spectacular sheen of beauty. We entered, and everyone loudly greeted us.

I'd learned much about these men, these loyal dedicated men of the House of Wolves. We had a few beers and enjoyed each other's company, laughing and discussing the topics of the day, each of us silently wondering what was happening to David.

He'd now been out with the mahalet in Bowman Bay for two days, and nobody was sure what he'd be experiencing. I reflected on my first frightening interaction with the mahalet and the dream that led me back to that secluded bay in the sea to watch David bid good-bye to his love.

I wondered where the magic of the mahalet would lead him; but before I could get lost in thought, one of his brothers would touch me and bring me back into the conversation. It was a cool early winter evening, and here on the patio of the bar was my new family.

9. Deception Pass

     I SPENT THE NEXT few days falling back into the same work and gym routine that had been my life before encountering the House of Wolves. Mid-term writing projects from my creative fifth graders were piling up before the Thanksgiving break. I was spending late nights staying up, grading papers.

     I'd occasionally found myself drifting away and staring off into space, worrying about David. He'd left four days earlier to visit the woods with the mahalet tied to his belt. Interesting, though, with David's absence, how the other men in the house deliberately took up the emotional slack left by his absence. Every day, one or more would call with some kind of false pretense; but I knew they were checking up on me. It was nice to feel supported but better to feel loved by all of them.

     Bear and Moose had figured out my gym schedule, and soon we were a trio of sweaty lifters. They would discuss sculpting my body in front of me, as if I were not there, then laugh as they put me through the new, more intense regimen of weight training. Their pretend squabbles over my physique were starting to get stares from the other members of the club, but I was truly enjoying our time together. If these two muscular guys wanted to mold me, who was I to argue?

     Tristan and I exchanged e-mails. His questions and dedication to my health and well-being were intuitive, and he was clearly breaking down any barrier between us with his patient and caring manner. We talked about herbal additions to my pill regimen for HIV and how we could monitor my health naturopathically.

Marlin called one evening and asked how things were going in school. He and I talked for what seemed like hours. It had been a long time since someone other than a fellow teacher took interest in the work that I do or appreciated the effort involved in doing it.

He told me he would love to meet my kids and, if I wanted help, just give him a call. He was quick to accept my instant offer on my upcoming Thanksgiving project.

We had my annual Thanksgiving mother's gift project coming up. Each year I'd send my kids home with gifts for their mothers, for which, we could all agree, they were thankful. This year's project would be as simple as it was charming: each student would fill a small glass terrarium with miniature palms and other assorted green plants. In each terrarium, we would place a porcelain mouse and, crouching over the edge, a porcelain cat that was reaching into the tank after the mouse.

Marlin met me at the nursery. The two of us selected the twenty terrariums and boxed up miniature palms and some beautiful jade plants. This was the first time we'd spent alone since I'd taken the tour of the house with him weeks earlier.

Watching Marlin get involved in my project , I saw an entirely new side of him. Gone was his trademark smart-ass attitude, and he seemed driven to make this, our project, the best it could be.

"You know," he said, "this is the kind of project David would have loved to be involved with."

With the mention of David's name, he knew that he had said the wrong thing, reminding me of the reality of David's absence. He smiled at me with incredible warmth as he saw the signs of worry on my face.

"Ah, now, pup, don't be down. You know that he's fine. He's our David, after all. You have been so good giving him space. Letting him find his way back to us, on his own terms. And come back to us he will, pup...he will."

He quickly got our focus back to the task at hand, which put me at ease as we continued our shopping. Dropping him off at the house, I said I'd see him at the school on Friday. Marlin kissed me gently.

Talking to me through the window of the truck, he said, "Ya know, that William is right. You are such a strong little man, pup. It'll all be fine." He tapped my chin and walked into the house. I drove back home.

The next few days crawled by. David's absence from my life seemed to last forever. I wanted David to be here to see the relationships grow and develop with the other men in the House of Wolves. Friday arrived, and Marlin came in to meet my class and help us with our final project. Marlin had called me the night before, just to see if everything was ready for the project. I could hear his anticipation of the event and the prospect of getting back into a real classroom.

It was a great joy to watch Marlin, who had been a teacher of literature for many years, interact with my younger students. To Tristan's delight, Marlin had meticulously chosen to shower and braid his hair for the event. Marlin even showed up in pressed Dockers and a bright white dress shirt, almost matching his beard. I was touched by his dedication to my project.

He was an almost instantaneous hit with my kids, feigning anger and frowning deeply when one of the students compared his Welsh accent to Robin Leach's on Lifestyles of the Rich and Famous. The children saw right through him, and he returned a smile. He quickly won them over though with his ability to laugh and tell silly little jokes.

One of my students was having a difficult time because she did not want to get her hands dirty working on the project. I was about to step in and help when Marlin provided the perfect solution. As if he were a magician, he produced a pair of kid-sized latex gloves from his pocket and helped her put them on. Marlin explained that now she could get as dirty as ever and "pop them off and be all clean."

Her young face lit up with new enthusiasm. She dug right in, planting her terrarium with a sixty-year-old friend looking over her shoulder. When the project was finished, I don't know who was prouder, Marlin or my kids. The students beamed as they headed home, each with a terrarium-in-a-box, packed carefully so the gifts would reach their destinations safely.

Marlin and I cleaned up my room.

"I always hate breaks in the middle of the year. The kids get away and lose routine, and I end up spending two weeks after the holiday whipping them back into habit," I said.

"You've got a good crew, Mr. Wallace. Ya sure do. Particularly that little lass with the dirt issues," he chuckled, using his fingers like quotation marks. Reminds me of Tristan."

We both laughed and turned out the lights. I stared into the quiet room for a moment and then closed the door. Marlin watched as I locked the door, and then, in a tender gesture, ran his fingers across the nameplate on the wall.

"Mr. Wallace, a fine young teacher of young minds," he said, and let the fingers drift over to my chin for another tap. I blushed. I was starting to enjoy his boxing with my chin. I walked him to his truck in the parking lot and gave him a strong hug.

"Need a ride, pup"?

"No, no thanks," I said, with some luster lost in my spirit.

He stopped us in our tracks.

"No, pup, we haven't heard from him yet; but don't worry at all. He'll come around. You can be sure of it."

He looked back at me with the kindest look, as if he understood my increasing moodiness and need to be alone. He gave me another strong hug, hopped in his truck, and drove off.

I headed up the hill toward home. It struck me how the brothers of the house were becoming my life. I'd hung out with a few friends before meeting David and the other members of the household, but every relationship always felt as if it were going nowhere. Finally, I had people in my life who were interested in investing in a friendship as much as I was.

Since Joe, no adult visitors had come to my classroom. Having Marlin spend the day with me and my students felt good. I was finally sensing I had found a new life past Joe.

I continued to dwell on this train of thought as I turned into my cobblestone alley. It was then that I saw him, sitting on my doorstep, wearing his black leather jacket and smoking a small, straight, black pipe. It was David.

All of the emotions of the last few days without him rushed to my senses. I collapsed into his waiting arms, as if I had been the one out in the woods alone. He took my weight as if expecting me to do so, traced my hair with his hand, and puffed a small cloud of smoke through his mustache.

"Oh, Mr. Wallace," he said. He held me there in the alley for what seemed like a very long time before letting me go and tracing my face with his woodworker hands. "I've missed you, too."

He pulled the pipe from his mouth and kissed me passionately. My briefcase fell to the street. We kissed again. He took my hand and led me to my doorstep where there were a couple of bags of groceries.

"I'm cooking tonight. I have a lot to explain," David said.

I unlocked the front door and we headed inside. After I hung up his coat, he paused and looked over at me with the softest look. His brown eyes were as vulnerable as ever. I walked over to him and rubbed the hair coming out of his shirt. Looking into my eyes, he reintroduced himself to me.

"Hello, love, my name is David; I've been away for a while, but I think all of me has returned. I missed you so much! I never want to be away from you that long again, hear me?"

"That, David, is the right thing to say." I reached out, took him in my arms, leaned in, and felt his breath as I sniffed his mustache. In that single moment, I wanted to be as close to David as I could.

In the small silences that ensued, we caught ourselves staring at one another. I just couldn't keep my eyes off of him. Even though I tried to act as if nothing had happened, as I watched him prepare our meal, he could read in my eyes that I had many questions about his quest; I was anxious to know everything.

"I have so much to tell you about my trip, Mr. Wallace, but let's do that after dinner. Tell me what you've been up to while I've been gone."

He turned to the counter as I moved in behind him. I nuzzled into his neck and peered over his shoulder to the contents he was emptying on the counter. He'd brought pasta and pesto sauce, vegetables, and chocolate ice cream. The pasta was quickly boiling as I told him about my days at the gym with Moose and Bear.

"Leave it to them to get you naked and all turned on in public, before I had a chance," he said, smiling.

In my excitement of seeing him, I momentarily forgot about his journey and babbled on and on about the men and the last few days. I told him about my evening with Tristan and how I thought I had misjudged him and about how Tristan had gone out of his way to apologize for his treatment of David. I admitted that each of his brothers in the house was finding ways to become part of my life. I told him about Marlin's visit to my classroom and how my kids had been delighted with him. He laughed and told me that Tristan had been even more delighted that Marlin had to clean himself up in order to look and smell so nice. We were soon sitting at my small table, enjoying the food, and I told him about my kids. I told him how they had talked about Thanksgiving and that we all were looking forward to the holiday. He smiled at me and kept hold of my hand on the table the entire time. We washed the dishes side by side. I poured us each a glass of wine, and we sat by the fireplace with the fire soon warming the small room.

"Mr. Wallace, it was the most amazing time. Marlin was right; this was indeed the place to go to find myself," he said, relaxing into my arms. His voice lowered as he told me about his quest.

"I came out of my room for dinner on Sunday, and they were all there. We ate quietly, as had become the custom, and as I got up to go back to my quarters, William spoke to me.

"'Don't you think it is time, David?'

"'Time for what?' I said, turning back to face him.

"Moose and Bear shifted their eyes from me and were obviously uncomfortable. Marlin looked at me from the kitchen where he was helping Tristan with the dishes. William stood facing me; as he spoke, everyone stopped in place.

"'Time to embrace the mahalet. We're all meaning well, David boy, we just can't sit around while your hurting resurfaces, not with Mr. Wallace here now. Not now, David,' Marlin said.

"'We are asking you to take your place in the circle again, David. To honor the master's last wishes,' spoke Tristan.

"'We love you, big guy,' said Bear, and I saw Moose nod in agreement.

"I stood there staring at my brothers, and it suddenly occurred to me that I had hurt them in unseen ways. They were hurting as much for me as for themselves. I knew it was time to relent. It was time to rejoin my brothers in the circle, to come out of my self-imposed exile.

"It was then that I asked William, 'What do you suggest we do?'

"'Follow me,' said William.

"For the first time since Richard had left, all the men stopped what they were doing and heeded the call of the house. William led us to the round meditation room. There, in the middle of the room, he set a small black pillow and lit incense. He asked us to come and sit in a circle around the center, and set my mahalet back on the black pillow.

"William then said to me, 'When I came into this house, I was mentored by See-He-Ahi. He was the spiritual master of my love, and the brother to Bear, Moose, and Marlin. But he was a mentor and father to you, David.' "William continued. 'As we approach the two-year anniversary of See-He-Ahi's transformation into spirit, it is time that you re-enter the circle. We, your brothers, ask that you take a retreat and wear the mahalet See-He-Ahi left for you on your person to see what healing and peace unfolds in your heart.'

"I gave them my answer by reaching into the center and picking up the mahalet."

David then showed me his mahalet, which was on his belt. It was dark red leather and designed very differently from the others, with braids of twine holding it closed and only a single mark on it, an eagle.

"I had feared the mahalet for so long, particularly since Richard had seen fit to mark it with his totem, the bald eagle. I knew the legends and the customs. It lay in the house with me for a year, even after William and I had taken the remainder of the ashes to Bowman Bay. That is why, Mr. Wallace, I reacted so strongly to your initial vision with the mahalet. William and I had never told anyone else in the household about that trip. So, when you clearly described it right down to prayers to Richard that I had said to myself and to nobody else, I didn't know what to do, and I ran from you.

"Then you show up at my room. Unlike the others, you were unable to let my denial and fear stand. Where the others, as much as they loved me, never had the power to stand up and ask me to do what was right, you showed them by example. You, Mr. Wallace, showed my brothers that I belonged in the circle. My time away from them, spiritually, had been highly destructive. I knew that more than anyone.

"So, I told them I'd go to the forests and see what they would say to me with the mahalet in hand. Marlin helped me gather my things, and then I packed my truck.

"I was soon off to the islands. I drove the same route you and I had taken just weeks earlier, but it was uncharacteristically free of fog. I crossed Deception Pass Bridge and pulled into the campsite, paid my fee, and set up on the water. I was starting a fire in my campsite. I'd purposely picked a campsite across the inlet from Bowman Bay.

"I sat there for a moment, staring across the narrow passage; there was the boat dock and the paths around in the woods.

"I sat perched over the campfire waiting. Waiting for the magic to begin. I knew I was in the right place. And nothing. Not a damn thing happened, Mr. Wallace. I began to pace around my campsite, growing restless. The sun began to fall beneath the horizon.

"I remembered when I first took Richard to Bowman Bay. We arrived there at the end of a long summer day, and the sunset lasted forever. I remember joyfully skipping rocks on the water and sitting with my feet in the water on that boat dock.

"I then recalled the emotions of my visit there with William, waist deep in the water, giving Richard back to nature.

"It was the first time in my life, Mr. Wallace, that those deep green forests brought me no solace. No peace whatsoever. In the darkness, beside myself with anger. Perhaps my brothers had been wrong; perhaps the mahalet had no magic for me after all. I sat in the darkness, considering what a waste of time my trip had been, and drifted off to sleep.

"When I woke the next morning, the first fingers of dawn were just touching my tent. I rose and wandered into the woods to pee, returned to my site, started a fire, and was brewing coffee when I heard a bird."

David stopped for a moment and looked at me as if to make sure I hadn't lost any of the details. He explained that he'd tried to remember it as clearly as possible. I assured him that he was doing fine.

"I heard a bird calling though the fog, and then I saw what was making that call. It burst from the fog just above my head and must've had a seven-foot wingspan. Crying out in the morning air with a call I'd never heard before, the bird flapped its giant wings and swooped down on a rock in the middle of the cove: a bald eagle.

"The eagle stood there for a second before I noticed a salmon in its talons. I watched this monstrous bird eat the fish while pinning it to the rocks. Occasionally, he would look up to make sure nobody was going to come take his breakfast. I smiled to myself. In all my years, I'd never seen one of these majestic creatures so close. He finished his meal and flew back into the fog by the bridge, the steep cliffs echoing with the sound of his call.

"Turning back toward my fire, I saw, standing by the fire, a small, white-and-gray wolf. I stood very still."

David stopped to explain that he'd heard they had reintroduced wolves to the islands but had never seen one. He'd actually understood that they hid from humanity. The Saanich said the wolves were so glad to have their homeland returned to them, they would hide so that the Molo could not take it from them again.

"So I stood there staring at a wolf. His dark eyes contrasting with his grayish white coat. He stared back at me, and I wondered if he was as fearful of me as I was of him.

"As if to answer my question, he growled a little and sniffed the sand at his feet, then looked back at me. He walked around my fire and sniffed around my tent and my food cooler. I was still frozen to my spot. He then looked up at me, seemingly content with the surroundings, and lifted his leg on my cooler. The damn wolf peed on my cooler!

"I was so scared I'd almost peed myself."

David was laughing and clearly excited.

"Then he looked back at me, obviously proud of marking my cooler as his and trotted off into the woods. I stood for a moment, still not wanting to make a move. I'd been in those woods all my life and had never been afraid of anything. But that wolf truly scared me.

"I sat there for a while, simply floored by the encounter with the wolf; but eventually I settled into my day, made breakfast, and went for a long hike through the park. I laughed to myself when I realized that I didn't need the mahalet bag to have magic happen to me. The wolf and eagle had visited me without any help or magic. I thought, 'I met you without the mahalet; perhaps I didn't need it.'

"I walked down through the woods and emerged on the ocean side of the park, past Deception Pass. The waves lapped at the pebbled northwestern beach, and the breeze was as salty as ever. I looked out across the ocean. To the north was Vancouver Island, shading the horizon, and straight ahead of me was the Strait of Juan de Fuca. I always felt that, standing here, I could stare across the ocean to Japan if I looked hard enough. To the southwest, the snowcapped Olympics loomed.

"The English explorers had named the tall and rugged Olympics after the Greek gods. The Saanich believed that the original spirits of the world came from there, making the mountains a great and sacred place.

"I spent the day on the rocks. Sketching in my pad, I was simply enjoying being alone in this favorite and sacred place. Soon I was greeting another sunset and my second night on the beach. I worried about how my brothers would react if I returned with no new feelings or having experienced nothing new. I was worried particularly for William and Tristan, who were so convinced that something magical and life–altering would happen to me. After writing a bit in my journal about my day, I rolled out my sleeping bag and called it a night.

"The next morning started identically to the last, with the early morning light filling my tent. It was cooler than the morning before, so I quickly had a warm fire going. I boiled water for oats and was stirring them in when, as if on cue, the small, white-pawed wolf stepped from the bushes. With me seated at his level, he seemed all the closer. He eyed me carefully. I don't know what came over me, but I spoke to him.

"'Oats?' I said, offering him my breakfast.

"He growled at me, sounding like Marlin when Tristan suggests sushi for dinner. "The wolf stared at me and then walked up the trail toward the woods. He then stopped, turned toward me, pawed the sand in front of him, whined, and yawned. I stayed seated and watched him. He then sauntered back down the path toward me, sniffed the sand near the fire, walked back up the trail, and turned back to me again, pawing the sand in the same manner.

"'Do you want something, Whitepaw?' I said.

"As if he'd actually recognized his name, he walked toward me, this time arriving within inches of my feet, sniffed, and pawed. Then he walked back up the path and again looked back. I set my oats down and walked toward him. He looked at me with anticipation, turned, and trotted farther up the trail. As I followed him, he kept looking back at me, making sure I was there.

"We climbed up toward the bridge, and the fog from the ocean began to dance around our feet like dry ice. We kept walking up the trail, and he stopped at a fork in the path. He looked up the path that led to the bridge, then back to me.

"The wolf stopped as if to say, 'This is where I leave you.' I looked at him and turned to keep on the lower trail. Immediately, he began to whine and paw at the trail leading up to the bridge. I walked past him and started up the final few feet to the bridge. When I turned, I saw Whitepaw slowly walk into the bushes. He looked back at me as if to say, 'Where you are going, I cannot follow. I brought you this far.' Then, as quietly as he appeared, he evaporated into the forest.

"I reached the top of the trail and the highway. The morning fog seemed to create an impenetrable barrier, engulfing anything in its path. It's frightened many a driver and petrified many pedestrians. I wondered to myself, in amazement, had the wolf really led me up here to cross the bridge?

"I knew that across the bridge was Bowman Bay, and I stood there for a moment. Was this the magic that William had wanted for me so much? Was this my fear representing itself?

"I walked toward the fog; the closer I got, I could see it churn through the narrow passage like the water below. I could hear the waves striking the rocks, and soon I was walking in a thick fog. The fog was so disorienting that I lost all perception of space. I was carefully holding to the railing with my hand and soon was completely enveloped.

"I walked slowly across the bridge and was soon at the trail-head down to Bowman Bay. I had walked these trails so many times, but it felt foreign—and suddenly very cold.

"However, as I started down, I was soon in touch with the trail's familiar cushion, and then I was in the small clearing by the boat dock. Just as it had during our visit there together, Mr. Wallace, the fog danced on the water but left a little clearing in the woods curiously alone. I stood there for a moment and realized this was the first time since Richard died that I'd been there alone. Then I realized I wasn't.

"On the edge of the dock was a man, sitting in a camp chair. Balding, with a white mustache, he sat reading a book and smoking a small black pipe. Looking up from his book, he noticed as I emerged from the woods.

"'Good morning!'

"'Good morning,' I said back to him. 'Beautiful place in the morning, eh? So peaceful.'

"'Yes,' said the stranger, peering over a pair of wire-rimmed reading glasses.

"'Have a good day, then.'

"As I turned to walk into the woods, the man looked down at his book, took a puff on his pipe, and began humming a tune that immediately made me stop in my tracks. The song was familiar to me and had been a favorite of Richard's. The man saw me turn, and spoke: 'Isn't that a beautiful tune?'

"I stood there scared and thrilled at the same time, remembering when Richard taught me that Shaker hymn, ''Tis a Gift to Be Simple.' I looked down at my belt and touched the mahalet, wondering to myself but deciding this was no coincidence.

"Walking toward the man, I asked if I could join him. As I got closer, there was something very familiar about him. I remembered how Richard loved to escape to nature, particularly toward the end of his time with us. He would go off to the woods to listen to the breeze in the trees, just to be alone with nature.

"The old man set his book down and looked at me with familiar eyes. He was smoking a burley blend like my own.

"I lit up my own pipe and puffed.

"The old man and I sat there for a while in comfortable silence. I stared out over the bay while he continued to read a tattered old book with a leather cover. I asked him what he was reading.

"'An old friend gave me this shortly after I met him, as a housewarming gift. It's an old copy of Emerson. I don't how many times I've read it, but it's always spoken to me, particularly now that I am alone. Emerson has this wonderful saying,' he added, pointing to a highlighted section in the battered text. He read it aloud: 'We but half express ourselves, and are ashamed of that divine idea which each of us represents. It may be safely trusted as proportionate and of good issues, so it be faithfully imparted, but God will not have his work made manifest by cowards.'

"Smiling, he said, 'I've always loved that statement—God will not have his work made manifest by cowards—brilliant! The world is not a place for cowards; we have to have the courage to live authentically. We have to break out of our fears and make overcoming them part of who we are.'

"He looked down at me with his soft eyes and wrinkled complexion, giving me time to ponder the quote. Then he continued speaking. 'So, why do you come to Bowman Bay, in the fogs of November, son. Do you have a fear you're looking to escape from?' He smiled softly.

"I was wondering to myself whether I was meeting the spirit of Richard. Had Whitepaw known Richard's spirit was here? I was completely at ease despite the odd possibilities. Answering him, I said, 'I guess so, and I am out here to do a little soul searching. I have ignored my spiritual side for a year or more, and I guess it's catching up with me. I lost a partner and have been grieving hard, but now I've also met someone new. I guess I am a little confused. So when I need to find clarity, I've always returned to this place, these woods I grew up in.'

"Just as when he was alive, the spirit of Richard was here, slowly coaxing my feelings out of me.

"'Well, then, we have that in common. My partner loved this place. So I return to it when I think of him.'

"'Your partner?'

"'Yes, he was a woodcarver. A brilliant artist. He carved the designs of the Indians that first settled these lands. I really shouldn't be out here; the cold affects my arthritis.' He paused while staring at his knuckles, flexing them. 'But I love it so much here. It brings me peace now that he's gone.'

"'He died?'

"'Yes, he made the transition about a year ago.'

"At the mention of the word transition, I suddenly looked up at him. My heart raced, but I slowly got up the courage to ask the man his name. He took a deep drag from his pipe and let the smoke dance in front of his face before answering. The old man looked over at me with those soft, aged eyes and said,

'My name is Roy. Roy Wallace.'"

David stopped speaking as I audibly gasped. I thought I'd been prepared for whatever he had to tell me about his trip, but meeting me as an older man? It was pretty overwhelming. David looked me in the eye, and I could tell he needed to continue.

"I was as shocked as you are, Roy. Here I was—on the pier at Bowman Bay—talking with you. You, I mean he, continued to talk to me: 'David was a proud man. In his older years, he'd lost his fear of death. We discovered powerful things together, with the others.'

"My mind was suddenly racing with questions. What did this spirit mean by 'the others'? Why would the spirit world show Roy as an old man? The old man went on to speak about the House of Wolves.

"'The house has been such a beautiful retreat for me over many decades. I've found an entirely new life. In my later years, I retired and took over for the others. I became the master, teaching the new members our ways. And now, look at me.' He paused with a chuckle. 'I'm the old man leading a new set of men to a new horizon.'

"He looked over at me, smiling. Before I could respond, the fog enveloped both of us, and I felt I was suddenly no longer on the dock at Bowman Bay. It was disorienting. Then I heard a different voice.

"Unmistakably, it was Richard. He said to me, in the fog, 'Oh, my love, my Seehotid. You have finally chosen Aquohiyu. You have chosen to complete the circle.'

"I called out to Richard. 'Why show me Roy as an old man? Why not let me see you, see your face? I have missed you, See-He-Ahi.'

"'Oh, my tender son, you must no longer grasp at the past. Wachdalehna is the Stegeyeai, your future; I am your past. Stegeyeai...he is but a catalyst to bring you back to the circle where you will join with him and make the circle complete once again; finding new paths, you will lead the House of Wolves into a new place. You, Seehotid, you will bring them, finally. You will make them believe what I have revealed to them. You will also make them believe what you will reveal further about them. Only when you return to the circle will all this be done, and it must be done without me. Go walk the red clay path with Stege-yeai. Bring your brothers, Aquohiyu!'

"I could feel him close to me, but he did not touch me. I yearned to be touched. "Then, suddenly, I was awake in my tent.

"I sat up quickly, wet with sweat. I realized the morning light was just now touching my tent and that the entire day had been a vision. I leapt out of my tent wearing nothing but sweatpants. The fog had cleared, and the brilliant sun of the morning flowed over the water. I stood across the channel from the pier.

"I felt myself trembling and my heart racing. As if it were the right thing to do, I lowered my sweats and ran for the surf. The water chilled me as I dove in. I felt a sudden freedom and power as I broke out of the surf and washed myself. I swam back to the shallows near the shore and stood there, waist deep, letting the water bead down my chest. I then I realized the bald eagle stood on the rocks a few feet from me.

"The eagle eyed me cautiously, the remnants of his breakfast at his feet. He looked right at me for a long moment, studying me. I am sure my sudden frolic in the morning waves had him considering what kind of silly animal I was. As I stood there, smiling at the thought of it, he bolted out over me, again displaying his immense wingspan. He called out in a loud screech and disappeared past the bridge. I returned to shore and got myself ready to return to the city.

"I was eager to get back to the library and find out what Stegeyeai meant. Richard had called you Stegeyeai. I made myself some oats to get me going and then quickly had camp dismantled. I was down on all fours rolling up the tent when Whitepaw emerged from the edge of the woods.

"'You again,' I said with a smile. He paused and looked at me as if he could hear and understand me, then approached, sniffed the half roll of tent in my hands, and stared me directly in the eyes. The softness of his eyes stopped me cold. It was like staring into the eyes of the spirit version of you. He whined and yawned, as if to say he was bored and had other places to go, and trotted back up the path. He looked back at me once before running into the bushes.

"I finished rolling the tent and was quickly on the road to town. I pulled the truck up into the driveway and found Tristan and William returning from a jog.

They greeted me enthusiastically, and I told them of the vision with you at Bowman Bay. "When I opened the door at home, I realized my brothers had been busy. They had been inside and cleaned up my little home, putting everything back where it belonged. The walls were freshly painted. All the rooms were orderly, to a level none of them had seen in months. Incense was in the air, smelling of William's trademark passion for eucalyptus. Fresh flowers stood in a vase by the bed.

"'Oh, how my brothers love me,' I thought to myself. Tristan appeared at the door I'd left open.

"'I hope you don't mind us cleaning up for you. We just felt perhaps you'd appreciate returning to some order and freshness.'

"I turned to him and said that it was perfect. I told him I loved him, and he said he loved me, too, and we embraced. I can't remember touching Tristan in such an authentic way previously. He pulled away, looked me in the eye, and told me I needed to come to you. He said you were in despair with me gone, that you needed me more than ever.

"And so I came. And here I am, Mr. Wallace."

Even as I looked into his eyes and knew that David had at last come back to me, I couldn't help but voice my curiosity about something. "But, David, you haven't told me…what does Stege-yeai mean?"

He smiled with that smile he had greeted me with that first day at the coffee shop and said, "The first thing I did after speaking to William and Tristan was go to the library." His smile became broader. "There, in the Saanich dictionary, I discovered that my hunch at the beach with Whitepaw had been correct. Stegeyeai is Saanich for wolf-spirit; Richard has named you and given you the totem of the wolf-spirit."

With that said, David leaned in and kissed me. I licked at his mustache and pulled him against me on the couch. He pulled back just long enough to touch my face with both of his hands and, with tears suddenly edging the contours of his eyes, he whispered, "Well, Mr. Wallace, you are the wolf-spirit. And now you belong with me."

10. Learning to Dance

FOR A FEW MINUTES, David and I did not speak; we just sat there on my couch, holding each other close. I could not tell which heartbeat was whose. When he finally did begin to tell me more about his visions at Bowman Bay, I could immediately sense a new clarity about him. He spoke with real emotional security and an intensity that was new and bold.

He wasn't sure where this new vision and zest would take him, but he was certain he had ground to make up with this brothers since he'd withdrawn from them. With deep conviction, David told me that he had finally realized that he'd stopped contributing to the household that meant so much to him. He left my apartment that night visually exhausted from his ordeal.

I got ready for bed and sat staring out over the bay. The moon stared back at me, full as a dinner plate. The soft moonlight filled my loft as I considered David and the rest of his brothers in the house. I lay down and was quickly in a sound sleep. In what felt like moments, I awoke suddenly to the phone ringing, bringing me out of the dream.

"Good morning, Mr. Wallace," said David.

"Good morning, David," I mumbled into the telephone.

"Oh, dammit, I woke you. I am so sorry!"

"Don't worry about it. What's going on, handsome?"

"Marlin's got the kitchen in a state, getting breakfast ready; could you be over in a few minutes? How soon can you get here? He and Bear are making eggs and waffles."

"I'm packed. All I need to do is shower, and I'm out of here," I said, waking up.

"Good! There's a place waiting for you. See you soon, Mr. Wallace."

I hung up the phone and sprang into action. I was quickly showered, dressed, and with a travel cup of hot coffee, I was on my way. I soon pulled up into the driveway of the house.

David was waiting outside and walked up to my truck. When I got out, he kissed me deeply, his breath already flavored with burley tobacco. I felt my body respond to him as he stared into my eyes, sucking on my mustache and lips. I reached around and pulled him against me, feeling his strong butt.

"Woof," he said, as he withdrew. Then, with my hand in his, he led me into the house.

The kitchen was a flurry of activity as Marlin greeted me with flour flying from his fingertips. Bear was cooking at the stove behind him. Tristan, Moose, and William sat at the counter drinking coffee.

"Mornin', boys!" I said. Everyone lit up as we entered the room.

"Roy!" said Marlin. "Good mornin'!"

Bear walked up and lifted me off the floor in a big, strong bear hug. Setting me back on the floor, he kissed me, then turned around and goosed Marlin from behind. Marlin let out a girlish shriek that made me laugh as I gave him a hug and kissed his neck.

"You'll get a better welcome when I'm less gooey," giggled Marlin.

"And when do you plan for that happen?" quipped Tristan from the bar.

"I'll never know what Richard was thinkin' bringing such a bitch into this house!" said Marlin, continuing his loud impersonation of an offended drag queen.

I looked over Marlin's shoulder.

"Bacon waffles!" Marlin exclaimed, like a four-year-old cooking for his parents.

"My favorite," I said, giving him another strong hug.

I walked around to the bar and greeted Moose with a hug. Then William gave me a strong hug and a polite, but affectionate, kiss. Tristan rose and gave me a strong hug and whispered in my ear, "It's so nice to have you here, Roy."

David raised his coffee cup. "A toast—to Chef Marlin and his bacon waffles!"

"It's nothing, really. Oh, stop!" Marlin said, faking being embarrassed, while our coffee mugs clanked away.

David and I joined the others at the half-moon-shaped bar. It was great fun seeing everyone so relaxed. Each of them in a casual morning outfits, from sweats to shorts.

"So, we hear you'll be spending a few days with us," said Moose.

"Woof!," said Bear, in a voice that had an underlying tone of a growl.

"Down, boy, down!" giggled David.

"I got the guest room all made up. I guess we'll be needing to protect you from more than just David!" said William.

"It's getting hard to keep my promise to ya'll with David around, though," I said.

Bear stepped up behind me and bit on my ear. "Not if we get you first, little man."

David beamed, but Tristan shot Bear and Moose a disapproving look.

"But it will mean more when you do get to be with David, much more," said William.

"Now, shut yer yappers, yer food's going to get cold," barked Marlin.

Marlin was quickly serving up waffles while Bear added eggs to each plate. I noticed that, by each serving, there was a small ceramic cup of pills. I even had a plain white cup with pills at my setting. Some cups had more than others. Tristan saw me notice and explained, in his matter-of-fact way, "These are the supplements designed for each individual. Each cup is different to suit the individual. See, Bear's is ginseng and some other herbs to help his joints after strong workouts. I gave you a similar set— just herbs and vitamins—to take if you want to.

"Many of the new HIV pills have to be taken with food, and, well, David needs acidophilus to help him digest dairy products; Bear and Moose take herbs to combat high blood pressure; and Marlin takes pills for his arthritis as well as his HIV regimen. Bear, Moose, David, and Marlin are HIV+; William and I take multivitamins and herbs to make sure our health stays strong."

As if on cue, the entire group took gulps of pills and water with Marlin barking, "Salute."

"Glad we've got Mr. Meds here tellin' us what ta take and such," said Marlin.

"We have taken a group approach and have all four men on the same regimen. I have researched some extra supplements for each of us to combat the side effects, and they do tai chi and yoga with the rest of us for balance," finished Tristan.

Because of this regimen of exercise, medicinal herbs, and medications, Tristan said he was proud that everyone in the house had a strong immune system. Tristan continued to explain that those who were HIV+ had immune systems almost indistinguishable from those who were not. You could see in his eyes and his manner that he felt this was a badge of honor.

To break the seriousness of the moment, William changed the subject.

"David, don't you think you should get our boy settled? Isn't there something you need to do today?"

"Well, yes, get the boy settled," said Marlin, shooting a parental look at David.

"Let me get your things," said David, walking out to the living room.

"It's like having a teenager who's having his first date. We've had to explain everything to—" Marlin started but stopped when David reappeared with my bag.

"Let me show you the guest quarters, and then I have a special surprise for you," said David.

"I bet you do!" Bear giggled.

"Oh, shut up," David giggled back.

Getting up from the table, I followed David out into the courtyard. "They seem to be enjoying picking on you," I said.

"Yes, they are making up for lost time; but I guess there are worse ways to show that they love me," he answered, as he put an arm around my neck, leaned in, and nipped at my neck.

David led me out of the main building into the courtyard. The inner courtyard of the household was peaceful in the calm overcast. A slight breeze contributed to the atmosphere, and everything seemed like another world. The house had an incredible calming effect on me as David led me past his little house to a small cottage.

As he opened the door and we entered, I discovered a pair of single beds and a round window, looking out through the trees onto the park, which brought to mind Tristan's tales of flying kites and long days spent together there. David caught me daydreaming.

"It's very simple, but it'll have to do till you are sleeping with me, I think," he said, as he stepped up to join me looking out the window. I could feel every curve of his body press against me as we stared into the forest.

He then led me back into the courtyard and back toward his workshop. The air smelled of linseed oil and wood chips as he opened the door into his home. I was astonished at how much work had been put into cleaning it up, remembering the disarray when I'd visited just days earlier. The futon was made up with fresh white linens, and fresh bouquets of iris sat in vases on both sides of the bed.

Captured in a wooden vice was a stunning Indian carving. The deep eyes and long nose of the caricature were very powerful. The carving was far from complete, but I felt I could follow the finished carving into the wood, as if the spirit within the raw materials had simply drawn itself.

"He's coming along well," David said, tracing his hand along the form of the creature. He touched it tenderly, like a father touching a child.

"It's going to be a crest," he continued. "Matching the wolves on the door out front. It is a design I started, or rather tried to start, after Richard died. This kind of design is called form line."

I watched David intently as he explained his carving. His eyes lit with joy as he explained that the creature is formed out of a single continuous line, usually painted black, which narrows and widens as it sweeps through an entire composition, outlining the most important shapes of the creatures the line represents. The abstract shapes that make up a crest creature are called ovoid.

He led my hand across the carving while continuing to explain that form line was supposed to have been a craft traded from craftsmen to their sons. A professor of his in art school had been a Tlingit Indian. The Tlingit Nation had lived on the Pacific Coast, in Washington and Oregon, and had been trading partners with the Saanich and Salish of Richard and Ben's origins.

"One day I was working on a carving, and just as it's been told to me, the form line presented itself in the piece. My professor came over to me and asked me where I'd been taught Native American form line. I explained to him I had never been taught, the creature was simply waiting in the wood for me to find him. I soon became his apprentice, and he taught me the real power behind form line carving, and I have been enamored by it ever since."

"It's very beautiful," I said, tracing its rough edges with my fingers as David had.

"I'll finish it one day and paint it and varnish it to its true beauty. But, pup, that is not why I brought you back here. Come out back and see my latest project."

Out the back door of David's cottage, on a pair of wooden sawhorses, was the most beautiful kayak I'd ever seen, glimmering even in the subtle light falling through the trees. The kayak was at least twenty feet long. Leather hides had been stretched and stitched together creating a patchwork across the frame of the craft.

The hides had been tanned and dyed a dark green, and on the tip of the front of the craft was a killer whale carved in David's familiar style. I ran my hand across the surface and looked back at David with awe and appreciation for his skill and patience.

"This is a badairka, an ocean-going kayak. Soon, you and I are going to test her. She is the only project I've been able to finish in the last year. I've taken her out a few times but nothing like a run in the ocean."

David took my hand and traced it along the rough hides and stitches. He explained that he'd started building it the previous spring.

"I was completely drawn to the design. You see, Mr. Wallace, I was always somewhat uncomfortable with Richard's choice of the killer whale as my totem. That is, until I spent a day with Jean up on the reservation and she told me a related Indian story: The translation of orca in Saanich means 'black spirit.' The orca is not a killer but a guardian of the sea; nature demands balance, and the orca is simply the guardian of balance in the sea.

"I spent a long time meditating on the concept until I realized I'd lost track of balance in my own life. When I was feeling alone, I let the isolation weigh me down. I'd finally figured out the key to getting out of my dark funk.

"New perspective brought me to study the wonderful creatures, and I read about a sea kayaker who told the story of running in the swells of the ocean with a pod of killer whales. So, I started drawing sketches of a badairka and was soon discussing it with

William after he saw me one day in the computer room working on designs and ideas. Everyone in the house became immediately excited when they learned that I'd found a personal project that I wanted to investigate.

Soon, we had the shell put together in the garage. You know, before we added the skins, it looked like a whale, the long shape covered with the ribs and timbers. Then, Ben and Jean's son, young Richard, showed up one day with the bow piece carved as an orca."

David saw from the look on my face that I'd had quite the experience with the boy.

"Yeah, that one is an amazing lad. The first son of Ben and Jean and the most intelligent child I've ever met. He's going to be growing into quite the young man.

"Along with the carving, Ben and Jean delivered three deer hides they'd preserved. Jean was overjoyed to hear I was building a badairka, which was the primary transportation for the Saanich. They helped me learn to tan and stretch the leather and stitch it together to create the skin of the craft.

"I spent many evenings out here stretching, scraping, and forming hide pieces together. Every single stitch on this craft is my hand. Every inch was part of my recovery and return to life.

"I took it out on the water below the house for its first test runs, and I couldn't take the smile off my face for days when I realized the craft was exactly as I'd planned it. Ya see, Mr. Wallace, this craft is my recovery. It brought me out of the hard darkness I'd fallen into and allowed me to notice you that day at the clinic. And you've brought me the rest of the way. Have you ever kayaked, Mr. Wallace?"

"No, but that is something I've always wanted to try."

"Well, today is your chance. I have wetsuits waiting inside, then we'll carry the badairka down to the pier."

"The pier?"

"Yes, there is a trail leading to a stairwell down to a pier on the base of the cliff by the driveway."

"I see something here each time I visit your home that makes it even more amazing.'"

We walked back into David's home. He laid two wetsuits out on the futon, then turned to me.

"Allow me," he said, as he started to undo my shirt, slowly, as if he were unwrapping a special present. He carefully put it on a hanger. Looking back at me from the closet, he removed his tank top, and then returned to me.

Taking my hands in his, David lifted them above my head and quickly brushed his nose and beard into my armpit. Sniffing deeply and growling approvingly, he lowered my hands and grabbed me in a hold that was strong and firm. He ran his hands down my back, then pulled me tightly to him.

As he breathed gently into my ear, I was lost in the feeling of his nakedness against mine. The room filled with his small grunting sounds as his hands found the hair on the small of my back. Calloused hands searched my waistband and dove past my belt as I whimpered and relaxed into his pulling embrace. Releasing me, David stared into my eyes as he unbuckled my belt and lowered my jeans. He let out a quiet sigh as he helped me from my pants. I stood in front of him wearing only a jockstrap.

"You simply are very beautiful, Mr. Wallace."

Continuing to stare into my eyes, he ran his hands along my thighs and traced at the side of my jockstrap. It was unavoidable for him not to see the incredible hard-on he'd given me.

David stepped back and took off his pants. He was not wearing any underwear. His legs were strong and muscular. The black hair from his chest made a complex pattern down his stomach. If it was possible, his thighs and legs were hairier than his chest. His nakedness revealed a beautiful uncut cock that was pierced with a bright stainless-steel ring. His black body hair covered his crotch and balls in a thick forest of masculinity. Just as Bear had when I'd seen his piercings in the shower, David caught me gawking.

"Stare all ya want, Mr. Wallace. It'll soon be all yours," he said, smiling, broadly approving of my lustful attention. I stepped forward, and he touched my chest, tracing his fingers in the hairs. He studied me closely and then ran his nose up my jaw and into my ear.

"Get dressed, pup," he whispered.

He handed me the wetsuit and we helped each other into our outfits. He explained they were necessary because, particularly in winter, the water of Elliot Bay was quite cold. Then he laced our dry clothes in a daypack and was turning to me when there was a knock at the door. David answered; it was William.

"Hello, you two. I see you are ready to take the badairka out for a run. What a treat for you to get to share that, Moose said to stop by the kitchen. I swear, that boy never stops cooking. He's made you bag lunches to take along on your trip. Marlin's ready with your map to Blake Island."

It was clearer than ever that the members of the house took care of one another. I was touched by William's checking in with us and how Moose had made sure we were fed.

"Where is Blake Island?" I asked David.

"It's across the bay from Seattle. It was an ancestral camping ground of the Suquamish Indian tribe, and legend has it Chief Seattle was born there. It's a state park but only accessible by boat. The island has no roads. The Saanich went there to potlatch with the surviving tribes of Native people every year. They'd make Totem Poles, smoke in the great house, and trade gifts. It was actually this time of year, so that makes our visit very special," David explained, as we headed for the library.

Marlin had a small map on the table and was drawing on it when we entered the room.

"Ah, my two adventurers." Marlin looked up and smiled.

He showed us the map; we had an eight-mile ride in the badairka across Elliott Bay, then across Puget Sound by Vashon Island. He showed us where the currents were stronger and we'd have to paddle strong and fast, and other places where we might explore. He wished us luck, and we headed back for the badairka. There we found Bear and Moose waiting to help us bring the kayak down to the pier. The four of us lifted the craft, and David guided us around the grounds of the house, down the stairwell to a pier that seemed to appear on the ocean suddenly and beautifully, reminding me of the solitary pier at Bowman Bay. We set the kayak in the water, and Bear handed David a watertight bag.

"Here are sandwiches, power bars, dried fruit, and three or four juice pouches. You're going to burn a bunch of energy out there, so make sure you eat, my loves. Moose and I can hardly wait for a turn out on the water in this fine little craft," said Bear.

I stepped up to him and tugged his beard; he pulled me to him in a strong hug that soon became a group hug with David and Bear included. David showed me how to climb into the badairka. He told me to take the forward station in front of him. Once I was settled in, he climbed in behind me. He explained that he'd steer with foot pedals he'd installed in his compartment in the back, and he relied on me to be the brawn, telling me to keep paddling nice and strong. Moose and Bear pushed us gently away from the pier, and we were off.

I was startled by how low in the water we were traveling. We glided across the surface as David talked me into the right rhythm with the double-sided paddles; the badairka was quickly zooming across the surface of Elliott Bay.

The first thing I noticed was how incredibly quiet and stealthy the kayak was. I expected the seams of stitching to creak and moan in motion, but the craft was making almost no sound. I glanced back at David with a smile.

"It's so wonderful!" I said to him. He smiled back at me.

We emerged from the cove and were suddenly part of a busy scene, ferryboats dashing in and out, and large cargo vessels that made us feel like tiny insects on the ocean. Any chance for conversation quickly disappeared in the task of navigating the waterway.

Downtown Seattle dominated with its green-glass skyscrapers as we paddled hard to get across the channel. We were soon running along the shore of West Seattle, waving at folks on the boardwalk as we curved around before taking on the strong currents of Puget Sound between the mainland and the islands.

"Now, Roybear, we're going to need to really go for it on this crossing. The current is strong heading south. We need to paddle hard, and I am going to aim for the north of the island; with the current, we'll probably hit the middle. Just start paddling deep and hard, and we'll make it fine," David said.

With that we started to churn and paddle our way across the passage to Blake Island. The current was amazingly strong. David steered to the right, and we'd drift to the left. I guess it was time to give him that muscle he'd asked for. I dug in my paddle and dove into the water with great effort.

"That's it, that's it," David bellowed.

The badairka won the battle against the current. The little orca carved into the bow leapt up, and the kayak shot out over the water. We broke into a rhythm, and the few miles of the straight flew by. Blake Island kept getting larger and larger as we left the city behind and headed into the waters of the Olympic Mountains. As Blake Island drew ever closer, I saw the totem poles peeking over the treetops. They stood like sentinels and stared us down. One had a birdlike figure at the top, with outstretched wings. Another stared across the channel with large eyes that seemed to dare us to cross into its presence. The third was broken off at the top as if the creature that had once been there had come to life and flown away, leaving a splintered snag in its place.

"How could I have lived here so long and never noticed them before?" I said in awe.

"They've just been there, waiting for us to come visit," David said behind me, matter-of-factly.

Denser trees and the rocky shoreline quickly hid the wooden sentinels. The shore was gnarled rock left by a volcano from the island's past. Seagulls chanted as we hugged the shore, and we rowed to the back of the island where the map told us the Indian village and state park waited.

David patted the leather hull and let out one of his trademark childlike laughs. He was clearly pleased with the baidarka's performance.

"God, it's a beautiful craft! Think of the places we'll discover in her, Mr. Wallace. Just think of it! The quiet places of nature we can escape to," David exclaimed.

We continued to travel around the island. You could see the waters calm, as if spirits had reached out and demanded their respect. Gone were the turbulent swells of the open inlet, replaced by an apparently docile ocean surrounded by breathtaking wilderness. The morning clouds were starting to clear, revealing the towering Olympic Mountains and the echo of the sun glowing through the clouds, begging to be released. We then came around a set of rocks, and there before us was Tillicum Village, just as Marlin's map predicted.

A uniformed state park ranger waved us into the dock. As we got closer, she threw me a rope and gently pulled us into shore.

"Good morning, guys! Great morning for a paddle! Beautiful craft!" she said, noticing David's handiwork. "You don't need to worry about leaving a beauty like this here; there's fine security."

"Thank you," David said.

David scooted himself up in his seat and leapt out onto the dock. He held the kayak steady as I tried to follow suit. I clumsily kicked and rolled out onto the dock, much to David's amusement.

He paid the ranger the fee for the dock space, opened a small compartment in the middle of the kayak, and pulled out a small daypack, which he quickly filled with Bear's lunch pack. We said our good-byes to the ranger and walked up on shore where we entered a small building with a men's changing room.

David produced dry clothes, and we quickly changed, locking up our wetsuits. All ready for a hike, we left the locker room and took in the island.

The longhouse for the park was in front of us with an array of totem poles of all shapes and sizes. A large banner-shaped carving with rounded corners sat above the doorway; David explained this was the crest of the Suquamish people. It was a pair of winged creatures, each with talons in a large salmon. I stood amazed as a voice spoke from behind me.

"It's the osprey. The mighty hunter. He is the totem of the Suquamish people."

I turned, and a man wearing a leather coat, feathers in long, braided hair—apparently of Native descent—stood there.

"It is very beautiful," I said to him. "Is it a religious statement of the Suquamish?"

"The totem poles of northwestern coast tribes were actually family crests rather than religious icons, denoting the owner's legendary descent from an animal such as the bear, raven, wolf, salmon, or killer whale. Coming into a village, a stranger would first look for a house with a totem of his own clan animal. Its owner was sure to receive him as a friend and offer him food and shelter. Totem poles also preserve ancient customs by making sure that, in every region within visiting distance, the old stories were repeated.

The old beliefs about the spirits, the origin of fire, and other myths were basically the same despite linguistic differences between main tribal groups. You'll have to come later and hear our legends and sit with us in the longhouse. We do presentations at 2:00 PM and 4:00 PM."

I looked at David expectantly, and he smiled. "We'll see you then."

Glancing at his watch, David ushered me past the longhouse and into the woods. The woods were thick with ferns and under-brush and smelled of the ocean. We followed the path that wound through old growth trees, down along the water, and then onto a small beach. Breaking through the clouds was Mount Rainier.

No wonder Rainier was considered a god by the Native people: it's only visible two or three weeks of the year, otherwise shrouded by clouds. Today it was breathtakingly clear and towered over the landscape.

Unfazed, David laid out a small picnic blanket and unpacked our lunch. He leaned forward and pulled me, turning me around till I was staring up at him from his lap. I reached up and tugged at his beard.

"You make me so happy, David," I said.

He traced my hair and played with my beard.

"You are going to be so handsome with a gray beard. Handsome and still mine," David said.

He fed me dried fruit while he spoke of different things. We talked about his latest projects and my upcoming studies with my kids, spent the morning laughing, and shared quality time in each other's arms. With lunch behind us, we walked through the forest hand in hand, emerging, on the other side of the longhouse. David glanced at his watch.

"Right on time."

We walked into the longhouse and purchased tickets for the Indian presentation. The sign read, "Dance on the Wind." We walked into a room lined with logs. The earthen-floored room was probably 100 feet deep, but narrow—leaving seating for about 20 people.

There was a fire in the middle of the room, and the sides were lined with logs for seating. We took our seats, joining the other tourists as the lights dimmed. The stage at the back of the room was lit with orange and yellow, and four dancers leapt out around the fire. They wore black-and-red robes with Native depictions of animals displayed in beautiful beadwork. They danced for a moment, then drew paddles from their costumes and pretended to paddle around the firelight.

They spun off in a row from the fire to be greeted by three other actors in similar garments, only in forest green and dark blue. A voice narration explained that we were witnessing the paddle dance, in which a canoe is paddled across the stage and the occupants disembark to join the gatherers to the potlatch. They moved right into a new dance as a tree was laid out and women worked to remove the bark. The narrator said they thanked the tree for its bark; in their dance around the tree, they honored it and brought it into their homes.

The lights dimmed, and a man walked out to the fire. He wore a mammoth headdress matching the winged creature from the highest totem outside in the trees.

"I am the thunderbird. I am the wind. You have danced on the wind, and I have heard you. I hear your ancestors singing on the breeze. I speak so you might remember. I dance so that you might learn to dance alongside me. I ride the wind so these might be immortal," he said, pointing at the ceremonial masks on the walls facing the fire.

"I speak to you today of your ancestor Wakiash. The great king of the peoples of the north, the Kwakiuti. Wakiash was a chief named after the river Wakiash because he was open-handed and flowing with gifts, as the river flowed with fish.

"It happened once that the whole tribe was holding a dance. Wakiash had never created a dance of his own, and he was unhappy because all the other chiefs had fine dances. So he thought, 'I will go up into the mountains to fast, and perhaps a dance will come to me.'

"Wakiash made himself ready and went to the mountains where he stayed, fasting and bathing, for four days. Early in the morning of the fourth day, he grew so weary that he lay upon his back and fell asleep. Then he felt something on his breast and woke to see a little green frog.

"'Lie still,' the frog said, 'because you are on the back of a raven who is going to fly you and me around the world. Then you can see what you want and take it.' The raven began to beat its wings, and they flew for four days, during which Wakiash saw many things. When they were on their way back, he spotted a house with a beautiful totem pole in front, and they heard the sound of singing inside the house. Thinking that these were fine things, he wished he could take them home.

"The frog, who knew his thoughts, told the raven to stop. As the bird coasted to the ground, the frog advised the chief to hide behind the door of the house.

"'Stay there until they begin to dance,' the frog said. 'Then leap out into the room.'

"The people tried to begin a dance but could do nothing—neither dance nor sing. One of them said, 'Something's the matter; there must be something near us that makes us feel like this.'

"And the chief said, 'Let one of us who can run faster than the flames of the fire rush around the house and find what it is.'

"So the little mouse said that she would go, for she could creep anywhere, even into a box, and if anyone were hiding, she would find him. The mouse had taken off her mouse-skin clothes and was presently appearing in the form of a woman. Indeed, all the people in the house were animals who looked like humans because they had taken off their animal-skin clothes to dance.

"When the mouse ran out, Wakiash caught her and said, 'Ha, my friend, I have a gift for you.'

"He gave her a piece of mountain goat's fat. The mouse was so pleased with Wakiash that she began talking to him.

"'What do you want?' she asked eventually.

"Wakiash said he wanted the totem pole, the house, and the dances and songs that belonged to them.

"The mouse said, 'Stay here; wait till I come again.'

"Wakiash stayed, and the mouse went in and told the dancers, 'I've been everywhere to see if there's a man around, but I couldn't find anybody.'

"The chief, who looked like a man but was really a beaver, said, 'Let's try again to dance.' They tried three times but couldn't do anything, and each time they sent the mouse to search.

"But each time the mouse only chatted with Wakiash and returned to report that no one was there. The third time she was sent, she said to him, 'Get ready, and when they begin to dance, leap into the room.'

"When the mouse told the animals again that no one was there, they began to dance. Then Wakiash sprang in, and at once they all dropped their heads in shame, because a man had seen them looking like men, whereas they were really animals.

"The dancers stood silent until at last the mouse said, 'Let's not waste time; let's ask our friend what he wants.'

"So they all lifted their heads, and the chief asked the man what he wanted. Wakiash thought he would like to have the dance, because he had never had one of his own. Also, he thought, he would like to have the house and the totem pole that he had seen outside. Though the man did not speak, the mouse divined his thoughts and told the dancers. And the chief said, 'Let our friend sit down. We'll show him how we dance, and he can pick out whatever dance he wants.'

"They began to dance, and when they finished, the chief asked Wakiash what kind of dance he would like. The dancers had been using all sorts of masks. Most of all, Wakiash wanted the Echo mask and the mask of Little Man, who goes about the house talking and talking, trying to quarrel with others. Wakiash only formed his wishes in his mind; the mouse told them to the chief. The animals taught Wakiash all their dances. The chief told him that he might take as many dances and masks as he wished, as well as the house and the totem pole.

"The beaver-chief promised Wakiash that all these things would go with him when he returned home and that he could use them all in one dance. The chief also gave him, for his own, the name of the totem pole, Kalakuyuwish, meaning sky pole, because the pole was so tall.

"The chief took the house and folded it into a little bundle. He put it into the headdress of one of the dancers and gave it to Wakiash, saying, 'When you reach home, throw down this bundle.

The house will become as it was when you first saw it, and then you can begin to perform a dance.'

"Wakiash went back to the raven, and the raven flew away with him toward the mountain from which they had set out. Before they arrived, Wakiash fell asleep; when he awoke, the raven and the frog were gone, and he was alone.

"It was night by the time Wakiash arrived home. He threw down the bundle that was in the headdress, and there was the house with its totem pole! The whale painted on the house was blowing, the animals carved on the totem pole were making their noises, and all the masks inside the house were crying aloud.

"At once, Wakiash's people awoke and came to see what was happening. Wakiash found that, instead of four days, he had been away for four years. They all went into the new house, and Wakiash began to dance. Then the Echo came, and whoever made a noise, Echo made the same by changing the mouthpiece of its mask.

"When they had finished dancing, the house was gone; it went back to the animals. And all the chiefs were ashamed because Wakiash now had the best dance.

"Then Wakiash made a house and masks and a totem pole out of wood, and when the totem pole was finished, the people composed a song for it. This pole was the first the tribe had ever had. The animals had named it Kalakuyuwish, "the pole that holds up the sky," and they said it made a creaking noise because the sky was so heavy. Wakiash took, for his own, the name of the totem pole, Kalakuyuwish."

The lights dimmed, and the audience applauded. I sat there overwhelmed by the experience. I could feel David looking over at me.

As most of the audience shuffled out, David called my attention to various features of the room, as only a carver would notice.

"See there," he said, pointing to a band of carving on a beam. "The carver has etched all the animal spirits of the tribe leading to the center of the room. There on the wall are runes and stories of the past of the tribe. It's a real trick to take this long room and give it that round feel. It's designed to make you feel like spirits and forefathers surround you. So, pup, notice anything familiar about this room?"

I paused for a moment, let my eyes wander, and walked over to the wall, running my hands over the etched carvings. Then it occurred to me where I'd seen this design before.

"It's the meditation room."

"Well, yes, and no. The one at the house is for our tribe, as Richard saw it, as we see it, as I hope you will come to see it."

"Richard must have been some man. I wish I could have known him," I said, speaking first without thinking.

David, taken aback, suddenly smiled and, with a twinkle, cupped his hand around my neck and said, "By knowing the household that Richard leaves behind, you will know him. Richard was very deliberate in designing the house as a place for us to celebrate our unique culture and never forget the basic teachings that brought us all there alongside him."

I could see in his eyes that I'd understood a core component of the house that he didn't need to explain to me. He looked around and ushered me out and back to the pier. If we wanted to be home before dark, we would need to hurry.

As we'd been guaranteed, his beautiful badairka was right where we'd left it. There was small note in the front seat, from another boater, telling us that, if we ever wanted to build another beautiful leather badairka, he'd like one; the fellow included his name and number.

"I never thought badairka-building would become part of my business," David said, smiling at the notion that his handiwork had garnered such an offer. We were quickly sitting back in the badairka and on our way. The trip back was with the current, so it was much easier, and we were quickly across the inlet and heading toward Discovery Park. It was twilight was we entered

Elliott Bay, and the sun bounced off the skyscrapers that had bid us farewell that morning.

I'm always amazed how Seattle seems perched right in the middle of nature. All of its metal and technology seems to give way to the surrounding beauty like no other city.

We'd have to get the others to haul the kayak up the stairs, so David pulled it up and tied it to the pier. Our bodies were aching from the strenuous work of paddling home. We entered the living room where Marlin was reading by the fire.

"Pup! David! Good! You are home safe! The others have gone to the movie house, some slasher thing with lots of gore. I skipped it. I have some soup on. Go shower, and I'll have it ready in a bit," said Marlin.

David and I walked back to his home and got out of the wet-suits. David grabbed two towels from his closet, and we walked to the shower building. He turned his back to me and said, "Un-braid my hair would you?"

"Absolutely," I said, reaching out and undoing the rubber ring at the end of his ponytail. I slowly unwound the tight weave, and his hair flowed freely down his back. I removed my underwear, put my arms around him, and pulled him to me.

"Thank you for today, David. It was perfect!"

He took my hands in his and held me to him.

"Yes, it was, Mr. Wallace; it was, indeed, perfect."

We were both clearly aroused and delighted at finally finding each other naked. He turned me under the cascading water and pulled me to him. Our cocks pressed against one another, and he hungrily sucked on my lips and chin.

"Oh, yes sir!" he said, shaking in his hold around me. He kissed me, rolling his tongue into my mouth, then took a sudden step back. I realized he was checking me out under the shower. I did the same. He reached down and took hold of my cock. I've never really considered it that big, just simply enough to get the job done.

"That's going to look so beautiful with a ring in it," David said.

The look of wonder and shock at his statement must have been immediately evident.

"Don't worry, pup. We'll start real small and work up. Nobody gets a ring like this first off."

It was now clear that everyone in the house had a similar Prince Albert piercing.

I was, at once, turned on at the thought of having a ring in me, like the one making David's cock look so beautiful, but afraid of getting such a great piercing.

"Now, before I get carried away with you, Mr. Wallace," he said, tapping the end of my cock, "shower up and let's get to dinner."

We showered and toweled each other off, then walked back to his home, naked except for the towels around our necks. I watched as he got dressed, taking in all the bending and the curves as if watching a moving sculpture.

"Can I keep you this way?" he asked, taking my hand and dancing his eyes across my nakedness, making me blush. Pulling me along, he walked to the guest room, where I got into my clothes.

"My beautiful boy," he said as he buttoned up my final dress-shirt button.

We walked across the courtyard and entered the kitchen. Marlin served hot tomato soup and grilled cheese sandwiches as we regaled him with stories of our trip across the sound, and the legend that we'd heard at the Tillicum Village. He sat and listened while staring through his round-rimmed glasses. He raised his water glass in a toast to our day, and I helped him clear the table. This was so comfortable, and I felt relaxed in the home.

We retired to the library and the fire.

"One of Richard's favorite ways to end days in the house was to read to us from a book he was fascinated with," Marlin suggested. "I thought perhaps tonight, while we sit here by the fire, you'd read to me 'n' David 'ere."

"Well, Mr. Wallace," David said, "why don't you?"

Marlin asked me to browse and pick out a book that perhaps I'd enjoy reading to them. I told them that it occurred to me that I already had such a book in my bag.

As I walked toward the guesthouse, I realized that the whole tone of my relationship with these men had changed. They'd called me "our boy," and they'd started to make me feel like one of their own instead of a visitor. I was now walking around the house as if I did, indeed, belong there with my new brothers.

It made sense to end the day with the same ritual Richard had introduced. I smiled to myself as I retrieved my book from my things. This was perfect: reading to David and Marlin for this first time. I entered the library and found David sitting between Marlin's legs as Marlin brushed and braided his hair.

I showed the book to Marlin. It was a copy of Thoreau's *Walden*.

"Excellent choice, 'ere, pup!"

We retired to the couch.

"Many years ago, I read this book; honestly, it changed my life. It showed me new ways of thinking and has always been a great inspiration to me." I opened the book and began:

I left the woods for as good a reason as I went there. Perhaps it seemed to me that I had several more lives to live, and could not spare any more time for that one. It is remarkable how easily and insensibly we fall into a particular route, and make a beaten track for ourselves. I had not lived there a week before my feet wore a path from my door to the pond-side; and though it is five or six years since I trod it, it is still quite distinct...

I read into the late hours of the night—to David and Marlin, by the fire in the House of Wolves—until I was yawning more than reading.

"Time for bed, eh, pup?" said Marlin.

"Yep, I think so."

I put the book down with my bookmark in place, and Marlin kissed us both good night and wandered up the stairway to his loft. David and I walked into the courtyard and to the door of the guesthouse.

"Thank you for reading to us, Roy. Thank you for being here."

"I love you, David," I said, kissing him good night. He walked away reluctantly, leaving me at? the small cottage on the edge of the compound. I undressed and sat staring out the window into the park. The moon was a slice of autumn heaven, and its pale light danced off the water. I smiled to myself and thought, "I was out on that water today. I was out there with the man I love."

Showered in moonlight, I got into bed under the crisp covers, lay on the pillow, and was almost immediately asleep.

11. Crumpets and Pipe Tobacco

     I AWOKE IN SILENCE the next morning, stretching out under the sheets and enjoying the opportunity to lounge in bed a little. I had slept soundly, uninterrupted. I had expected to have some great dream, considering I'd just spent my first night in the house amongst the spiritual men, but the night had been dreamless.

The sun played in the trees outside my window, leaving dancing shadows on the ceiling and walls around me. The branches shuffled in a morning breeze, and a few wisps of leftover fog moved through the treetops.

I got out of bed and looked out my window where I spied all six men in the courtyard. Despite the cool weather, they all wore loose workout pants and were shirtless.

David's dark, hairy back was toward me, as was the slender, muscular body of Marlin, who had traces of white fur on his shoulders. William stood with Bear and Moose; the three seemed to tower over the others. Tristan stood before them in pants of deep blue. Tristan would make a movement, and they would echo.

He spoke softly. Through the open window in my room, I could hear his soft voice as he led the members of the house in tai chi.

"Now, join and push hands," said Tristan. Almost as if he could feel me watching, without looking at me, he spoke louder.

"Pushing hands practice is not designed to train us to fight, though it does link the combat strategy and tactics with the practical application of the hand form. The sensitivity of our hands is such that our opponent's intentions are an open book to us while our intentions are a source of mystery to him. He will be completely frustrated, unable to attack or defend. Begin."

In pairs, the men faced one another in a classic martial arts stance, bowed, then leaned toward one another and simultaneously extended the palms of their hands, moving their fingers straight up.

"Hover."

Their hands never actually touched. They stayed "hovered" close, but not touching. Marlin stared into David's eyes with deep concentration. I watched as William, joined with Moose and Bear, towered over Tristan. Tristan stared down Bear like David vs. Goliath and was obviously the master in this situation.

"Sense."

The brothers continued their silent pose.

"Push."

The pairs touched hands, palm to palm, fingers to fingers. Eyes locked, the partners looked like statues, each echoing his partner's stance. It was almost like watching statues in a park.

"Hover."

The pairs released their touch and returned to the close awareness of the other.

"Relax."

I opened my door and stood in the doorway as the pairs relaxed. Tristan turned and addressed me. "Good morning, Roy, please join us. We were just finishing; your arrival could not have been better timed."

Turning to the others, Tristan said, "OK, let's shower, then, and get on with our day."

I was also shirtless but in a pair of pajama bottoms. I walked out in the courtyard, morning hair and all, and greeted the men. David and the others embraced me with strong hugs and warm kisses. We all walked as a group to the shower building.

The men nonchalantly undressed and headed for the shower stall. I hesitated for a moment. Being this close to the smells and physical bodies of all these men simultaneously was sensory overload.

"Don't worry, Roy, we won't hurt you," said William, smiling broadly. David shot a calming smile as the rest of them waved me into the shower.

They all started soaping up one another, giving me an opportunity to take a good honest look at everyone. Tristan was utterly breathtaking. His body was perfectly sculpted, from his incredibly defined abs to his strong legs. His hairless body stood in contrast to the men around him, his bright brass-colored Prince Albert extending from his body. It was obviously larger than the others I'd seen. To tell the truth, this was the largest Prince Albert I'd ever seen.

"Is your PA larger than a ought gauge?" I said, catching myself gawking.

"Yes, it is double-zero gauge. Once I got started with the piercing, it seemed to agree with me," Tristan replied.

"In English, what he means is, once they got the piercing needle in him, he turned into a little piglet for it. He kept asking for a bigger and bigger ring—and they can't make no bigger than that giant old ring," chimed in Marlin.

William stepped behind Tristan and put his powerful arms around him in the shower, smiling.

"It's beautiful, and Marlin is just jealous of the size," said William, reaching down and showing off Tristan's Prince Albert with his strong, darkly furred hand.

"It's so big!" Marlin squealed, like a schoolgirl, to the great amusement of all the other men.

While Marlin continued his antics, David leaned over and stroked my back, letting his hands rest on my butt.

"How'd you sleep, Mister Wallace?" said David.

"I slept deeply. I don't remember a single dream. I was, quite frankly, expecting one."

"Well, the dreams come when they are meant to, pup," said Marlin.

Bear and Moose walked up and started soaping each other amorously. Moose took a glance over at me at me as I stood under one of the showerheads.

"Boy, oh, isn't he pretty?" said Moose. I blushed, much to the amusement of all of them.

"I'm not used to such enthusiastic group nakedness," I said meekly.

"I used to be afraid to run around with my shirt off," said Moose, "but these guys cured me of that quickly enough. You'll get used to it, Roy; the more you are around us, the more natural it will feel. Besides, you keep popping a hard-on like that each time, and getting you naked will be a great treat."

I then blushed even deeper, realizing that I was, indeed, getting excited. Matching William's earlier embrace of Tristan, David reached around and grabbed hold of my cock.

"Who needs a shiny ring when you've got a thick cock like this to play with?" said David, biting my ear.

"Woof!" said Moose. "You got that right!"

"Can't wait to nibble on that treat," said Bear.

"OK. Leave the boy alone, will ya," said Marlin. "Remember when you were the pup and got all embarrassed at the slightest mention of cocks, so mind yer place." Marlin reached over and turned Bear and Moose's water to cold, making them both yelp and jump out of the way.

To my surprise, Marlin turned and joined David and me, close under the running water.

"You never mind those cock hounds, pup, they're just joshin' ya," he said, leaning in real close.

"Thank you, Mr. Emory," David said, as he leaned forward and kissed Marlin.

The kiss was touchingly gentle and honest. Marlin looked over at me and pulled me against him, and the three of us stood there for a moment, just letting the water flow down our bodies.

"You'll be used to this before ya know it, pup. And me and Moreau here'll make sure you are properly protected. Right, David?" He shot David a wide smile.

David pointed the showerheads at Marlin's back shoulders and ran his nose along Marlin's neck, making Marlin quietly groan. It was beautiful to watch and brought my cock to full attention.

"Ah, to be young again," said Marlin, admiring my persistent hard-on. "I need the little blue pill for my stuff to react like that anymore. Don't be ashamed; come 'ere and let me soap ya up."

As I stepped up to him, he got some gel from the pump on the wall and started soaping me slowly, starting with my legs and finding his way over my entire body to the tip of my cock.

"Hey! How come he gets to touch?" laughed Bear.

"Because he was a gentleman, perhaps?" quickly snapped Tristan.

"Turn around. Oh, my, aren't we fuzzy in the arse!" said Marlin, continuing to clean me by hand.

I then felt the familiar touch of David's hands on the small of my back as he ran the soap down into the crack of my butt. He stood forward, and I instinctively spread my legs as he soaped down my legs and toward my balls. David then stepped behind me and put his arms around me, letting his body rest against my back, and whispered in my ear,

"Indeed, Mr. Wallace. Woof!"

It was then Marlin's turn to get soaped up. I got my share of soap and worked the white hair on his chest into lather. I could feel the strength in his stomach muscles. I started to slow as my hands reached his pubes.

"Go 'ead, pup, it ain't gonna bite," Marlin said, as David grinned from behind him. I proceeded to soap up Marlin's cock and balls, our hands meeting in between Marlin's legs.

"Tug a whore?" laughed David.

"You are a cunt. You know that?" said Marlin to David. David leaned over Marlin's back and kissed him affectionately.

Getting back to the business of soaping Marlin, it was obvious he was enjoying the closeness as well. His cock had begun to harden.

"Isn't that good to see?" smiled Marlin. "The good ol' hydraulics still work occasionally," Marlin said, leaning in and kissing me.

This was different from the affectionate, polite kisses we'd share before. There was new urgency and masculinity in the kiss, as though, overnight, the affection from these men had gone to a new level where I was concerned.

"OK, break it up. We're wasting water, you two," William said, pretending to try to break in between us.

Marlin and I quickly turned to soaping David, and it was marvelous watching his body hair froth up. Marlin then helped him wash his long hair, and we were soon finished and drying off with the others. William announced that we were all headed to the market. He told everyone to get dressed and meet in the driveway.

David followed me back to my room. Removing my towel, he again embraced me from behind, giving me goose bumps…and a thrilling dance down my spine. He dried me off, toweling most of the dampness from my hair; watched me dress; and helped tuck my shirt in. Looking down, I saw he had a spectacular hard-on. I felt wonderful bringing out such a masculine reaction in him. I reached down, tracing the veins in the shaft, then held his erection. My fingers pushed against his piercing, and he let out a small grunt. I felt his cock pulse in my hand.

The strength I was using to grasp his cock had an obvious effect on David besides making him harder. He apparently enjoyed letting me take a little bit of control of the situation. I pulled again with my firm grip just to make sure it was a look of pleasure that crossed his face.

"That feels so good, Roy, grasping my cock like that. Woof!" David said, quietly, as he leaned in against me, letting me feel his entire weight in my arms. He relaxed and whimpered, totally giving in to the feeling of my holding him close.

It was the first time I'd seen David turn over control like that. I reached behind and held him to me by his butt cheeks with my other hand.

"I love you, David," I said, as I continued to slowly pull on his ever-harder cock.

Just as suddenly as he'd melted into my arms, he lifted his body up and took a small step backward, leaned forward, sniffed my beard, then step back farther, pulling his cock from my hand. My finger came away layered with glistening pre-cum.

Finding a way to bring David to that point of letting go and being with me was something I was eager to investigate. I liked the feeling that he was comfortable enough to let me bring out the pup in him, which he so enjoyed bringing out in me. Glancing at the clock, he suggested that we'd better get moving, and then led me to his house, his hard-on still raging and glistening. When we walked out into the courtyard, there were Bear and Moose, already dressed and talking.

"You'd think they were in love or something the way they keep causing giant stiffies in one another," Bear said, laughing.

David simply smiled ear to ear, his teeth showing through his beard. His pride in the erection I'd given him was obvious.

David was soon dressed in new blue jeans, his trademark solid-color T-shirt, and leather jacket, letting his black hair fall around his shoulders. He turned as if ready to leave and caught me staring at him with deep admiration. He looked at me with those penetrating eyes and simply studied me before saying, "You surprise me every time I touch you, Roy. I learn something new, and I let other things go. When we are free to be in one another, it's going to be a magical thing. I just know it. We'd better go join the others; they'll get impatient."

As we walked through the courtyard, he lit his pipe, soon puffing away on his customary burley blend. He and I walked out to the driveway to a red minivan.

"We call it Bear's Soccer-Mom-Mobile," David sneered.

It was actually quite amusing to see all of these burly men strapped in seatbelts in the extravagant vehicle. Bear had gone all out; the seats were leather, and there were separate temperature controls and earphone jacks for each member of the house. He also had a video screen in the ceiling between the front seats.

"You ain't watched porn till you've watched in my van goin' seventy-five on the freeway," Bear giggled, seeing me notice his setup.

"Like you really play porn on that thing," I quipped back.

"Ask and you shall receive," said Moose from the front passenger seat.

The screen lit up, and suddenly there were several men in a leather playroom gangbanging one another in spectacular fashion. The man in the sling was impaled on a spectacularly thick-cocked, gray-haired daddy bear, while others were working his tits and slapping his face with their cocks.

"I should have known better than to say that, huh?" I said, laughing at David, who shot me back a smile.

"Oh, this is the good part!" blurted out Marlin, as if he were a kid watching a rerun of his favorite Saturday morning cartoon.

"Please, Daddy, I need to cum," said the younger man in the video.

Speaking in rhythm along with the video daddy bear, everyone in the van chanted, "Not...until...Daddy...says...so!"

The entire minivan erupted in laughter.

"We wouldn't know anybody with those kinds of control issues, would we, William?" said Moose, laughing out loud.

I was sitting next to William and saw him react. He blushed, looking over at me as if some secret were out of the bag, but quickly shot right back at Moose:

"Well, if you didn't cum in two seconds when a real man fucks you, I wouldn't have to be such a dominator, now, would I?"

Tristan laughed out loud, and soon the entire van was laughing as the daddy and his friends continued to use the man in the sling on the video screen. We were soon downtown and looking for Pike Place Market, a public market in the most populist sense of the word. Located above Elliot Bay downtown, it spills over onto public sidewalks and covers several city blocks with vendors, shops, and booths. The place is a buzz of activity.

"Mary, Mary, full of Grace, find us a fabulous parking place! Mary, Mary, full of Grace, find us a fabulous parking place!" chanted Bear.

Just as requested, a perfect parking spot appeared. Thanking the parking goddess, we quickly disembarked. I asked Bear where he'd learned the parking chant.

"You can take the bear out of the Catholic Church, but you can't take the Catholic out of the bear. Besides, she's found some damn good parking spots in this town," laughed Bear.

We happened to park right next to my favorite little restaurant, "The Crumpet Shop."

"Let's stop here, eh?" I said, dashing ahead into the little store, with all of them following, a tiny bell on the door tinkling as if on cue. It should have come as no surprise that the shopkeeper knew Marlin. Besides being English, he was also a well-known member of Seattle's leather community.

The shopkeeper gave me an interesting smile when he realized I was with the boys from the House of Wolves, as I was also a regular customer. He only knew me as the schoolteacher with a taste for crumpets.

"Crumpet nutella, for you, Roy," he said, addressing me, "and crumpet butter and honey for you, Marlin?"

Marlin nodded.

"Nutella?" Tristan asked.

"Hazelnut butter with chocolate; it's divine," I said.

Tristan wrinkled up his face at the sound of it, but David and Moose each ordered one just like mine. We were soon getting the tasty buttery spread in our mustaches and making quite the scene.

"This is delicious!" said David, speaking with a mouthful. "I never thought of that on a crumpet. Yum!"

"One more benefit," I said, pulling hard on his leather lapel and licking his mustache free of butter.

"Woof!" said Bear.

"See you around, Gregory," Marlin said, as we all went to leave the shop.

Gregory signaled, "Call me," holding his hand up like a telephone at Marlin. As we headed out onto the sidewalk into the market, I asked Marlin if there was a story there, giving him a raised eyebrow.

"Nah, he's a prude. He wants to date and date and date and never let me in close enough for a kiss. He's all about foreplay – but no real intent. Blah! He's a big tease," said Marlin. "I'm hoping he'd turn into a nice friend to meet every once in a while, when I get sick of these hooligans."

"I represent that remark," laughed Bear.

We walked around the corner past a large, colorful florist shop and into the market. There was the famous Pike Place Market sign, and we passed right under it. On the right was the flying-fish counter where the salesmen hurled frozen fish at one another.

"Ick. Makes me think of a big lesbian orgy!" laughed Moose.

"You are so just foul!" said Marlin, shortly.

We walked into the fresh vegetable stands, and Tristan began busily studying produce. William dutifully bagged everything as it was purchased, following behind him.

The rest of us breezed through the produce as David stopped at a stand of fresh peaches.

"Richard loved taking us into eastern Washington for the first fresh peaches," David said, pausing to puff on his pipe. "Want some?"

"We could make pie!" I said.

"That is the magic word! Pie!" said Marlin.

David selected a few peaches, and we paid the shop owner. Tristan and William caught up with us, and I asked Tristan if we could put the peaches in his bag.

"Someone convinced you to make pie, didn't they?" said William.

"It was his idea. We didn't even have to bring it up!" barked Marlin.

Tristan smiled and took the peaches, putting them into his shopping bag.

"We have some herbs and spices to shop for. Shall we meet you at the tobacco shop in a few minutes?"

Without waiting for an answer, he was gone. I was starting to understand the dynamics of the various men, watching them run their various errands and shopping.

It was becoming clear who thought they were in charge; which one of them you had to keep an eye on because he wandered off, which one was the mischief maker always looking for a new target. The real, true, day-to-day dynamics of these men were starting to take shape.

As David and I continued to browse through the art booths, we agreed that, on the way back to the car, we'd get some fresh flowers. Various booths of photography, local artistry, and jewelry came and went. At our different paces, David and I finally caught up with Moose, Marlin, and Bear at a jewelry counter. It took me a moment to realize it was a body-piercing jewelry business.

The woman behind the counter looked as if she were wearing samples of most of her merchandise. She had large grommet piercings in her ears, elongating her ear lobes, and multiple piercings in the upper circle of each ear and eyebrows. She and Marlin were haggling over an elaborate earpiece. It attached in two places, the lobe and the top of the ear, and they were linked together by a muted brass chain.

Having agreed on a price with Marlin, she then looked at me with great intensity.

"This the pup you've been tellin' us about?" she said, with an accent identical to Marlin's. "Frank'll be pissed he missed meeting him."

"How you doin', young man, they treatin' ya right?" she said, studying me.

"Yes, Ma'am," I said, shyly. "I'm Roy, Roy Wallace."

I shook her hand and she winked at me.

"A pup with manners; now, that's good 'n' rare," she said, turning her attention to David. "Good thing you got to your senses fer this one, he's a rarity."

David put his arms around me and replied, "Yes, Marla, he's a rarity. That's true."

"It's great to see you boys so happy again!" Marla replied.

"Is he going to be needing some jewl'ry?" she said, glancing at my crotch.

"Um, not yet. But we're thinkin' 'bout it. Maybe next time. Don't want to shock our boy too soon!" giggled Marlin.

"These are good men, there, Roy. You can learn a lot from 'em. Particularly the old coot," she said, pointing at Marlin and laughing a ragged grin, missing a few teeth.

"I'll old coot you, woman!" Marlin said indignantly.

He then smiled and added, "Thanks for the ring, Marla. Be well," as he ushered us out the door. "We'd better be down to the tobacco shop before Tristan gets all huffy."

We all giggled despite ourselves and walked down the stairs into the lower market; there were Tristan and William, with a now-full shopping bag. David and I went inside to buy some tobacco as the others waited outside.

The smell of the shop alone was worth the visit. David perused the different pipes on display, then walked up to the counter. He told the shopkeeper that an order was waiting, and the shopkeeper went into the back.

While waiting, I picked up a pipe that caught my eye. It was a short, straight-stem, black pipe but with silver garnishments along the stem and bowl. I stood tracing my fingers around it.

While waiting for his order, David took some fresh tobacco out of the pouch and packed his pipe. He saw me look at him expectantly, and he blew the fresh smoke into my face, bringing out the reaction in me that I'd been bringing out in him earlier.

He stepped in closer and blew another thick cloud of smoke slowly over my face, then whispered, "Yet another thing you and I will spend long hours discovering: why this pipe makes you such a submissive little pig. Woof."

His eyes lit up with a fire and passion. He was clearly enjoying himself.

"Any time you'd like to get a move on, kids," barked Marlin into the smoke shop.

David smiled. I walked out of the shop as David turned to pay for his order. The rest of the boys were waiting impatiently outside.

"Perhaps you'll help us finally rid David of this bad habit, eh?" said William.

"Actually, I think his pipe is as much a part of him as his piercings; they are inseparable. I actually find it very hot when he's smoking around me. He's been so remarkable since he got back: affectionate, attentive, and intuitive. And he's so beautiful."

Bear shot me a friendly look as if he were considering the way I'd come to David's defense.

"That a boy, Roy! I knew there was a reason David liked you," said Bear. "You stand up for him. That's good and rough a ya, pup."

Tristan frowned at me. David walked out of the tobacco shop with his tight bags of tobacco.

"So, Roy here thinks you are beautiful," said Moose, goosing him in the cheek like a grandma at Christmas. "He's right. You are so cute!"

David shot me an embarrassed smile, and the group slowly walked through the rest of the market: Marlin, David, and I walking close; William and Tristan, Bear and Moose walking hand in hand. The open market was actually an apt analogy for the group of men. Raw ingredients in an open atmosphere, complementing each other yet completely different. Our appearances and affection caught the eye of a few wide-eyed tourists. Moose asked if we were all shopped out, and with agreement the group wound its way back to the van. When we'd seen all we wanted, Bear drove us back to the house.

The ride home was just as raucous, only we didn't have the television playing. Now it was the sounds of happy men, teasing, asking, and being comfortable with themselves. Upon arriving at the house, each of the men retreated to his routine. William wanted to spend some time in the garden; Marlin said he had some reading to do; Bear and Moose headed to the gym.

"Wanna come, pup?" said Bear.

"No!" said David, throwing his arms around me protectively. "I have other plans."

"Yeah, you get to have all the fun," chided Bear to David as they departed.

Tristan said he had some herb deliveries to make, and David wanted to go back to work on the wolf carving in his studio.

"Can I watch?" I asked.

"I was hoping you would. I'd enjoy the company for once."

He took me by the hand and led me out to the studio where he pulled out a tall stool near a table and said "Sit here," giving the seat a little pat. David walked over to the carving he had shown me, ran his hand along one edge, turned, smiled, and then stripped off his shirt. I let out a little woof, and he again winked at me.

David started running his hands across the wood as if he were reading Braille. He paused for a moment, decided where to go with the project, then picked up a tool and started in.

Slivers and chips fell away in silence. He was no longer in our world but his own. His body started to move like choreography as flesh, tool, and wood became one. I watched the muscles arch in his neck and shoulders as he worked with his tools. He'd glance over at me every once in a while, but mostly he studied the wood as if gazing intensely into a lover's eyes. His motions were slow and methodical. He'd work the tiniest area till a smile came on his face, as if the wood had agreed with him that the spot was complete for the time being.

We spent a quiet afternoon with classical music playing on the stereo, David carving, and me lying on his bed reading a book. It felt as if this was the way it had always been.

Marlin appeared at the door and said that Tristan had started dinner and perhaps David should get cleaned up.

"You know how he gets about you showing up all covered in sawdust at the dinner table," said Marlin, affectionately, looking to head off an argument. "My, don't you two look at home and perfect here." Marlin paused for a moment, looking at us, softly smiled, and returned to the kitchen.

I rose and walked toward David. His beard was, indeed, dusted and wood chips were scattered down his chest, catching in his hair. He continued to work, almost ignoring Marlin's words. His forehead beaded with sweat, and his musk—that mixture of sweat, the oils and wood of the shop—was overpowering. I reached out and picked a wood chip out of his frothy beard and suggested that he do as Marlin had asked and get cleaned up.

He turned to me, and I realized his eyes were full of tears. There is something incredibly sexy about a man who is capable of crying unapologetically. He trembled and stood there staring at me in all his vulnerability.

"Oh, Roy, you are just what Marlin said: absolutely perfect here."

I wiped a tear from his eye and tousled his mustache in my finger without answering. He took my hand and sucked my finger into his mouth, then pulled me to him, kissing me deeply and with great passion; I felt his arms connecting me to him. Breathless and totally loved, I kissed him back. His hands ran through my hair.

He stood back and started brushing himself off.

"You make me feel things I thought were dead," said David. "It's delightful having you here in my home, dreaming of the day when it's ours."

He held me close again, then led me hand in hand to the kitchen across the courtyard. The other men were already there, and Marlin was pouring wine. Tristan had made pasta with garlic pesto. We were soon laughing around the dinner table.

It's always fun to watch men with lots of facial hair try to eat saucy pasta politely. This group was no exception; as if on their best behavior, they were rolling up their pasta and eating like disciplined schoolboys. Sensing they were not relaxing, I deliberately took a length of pasta and sucked it loudly into my mouth.

David smiled, as he caught on to what I was doing, and noisily sucked on his pasta, also. Soon the entire table was eating with abandon. Even Tristan was slurping and smiling with the rest of us. After we'd wiped sauce from our beards, William tapped his glass to get our attention and spoke softly.

"Well, gentlemen, it's time we retired to the meditation room; I think it's time," he said.

Then he turned to me and continued: "I'm afraid, Roy, that tonight the brothers have something to do, and we just need some private time together as a group."

The others around the table looked at me fondly, then started to clear the dishes and move to the meditation room. David walked me into the library and sat with me on the couch.

"Is this about me being here?" I asked.

"Yes and no. It's just a private meeting that they've asked me to leave you out of. I don't want you worrying. I am sure you are capable of entertaining yourself, eh? There is a television in my room; why don't you go there and hang out? I'll come find you later. Don't worry yourself, Mr. Wallace," David said, tousling my hair, "I am confident that one day there will be no closed doors for you here; but until that time, you and I have to be respectful."

We stood, and he gave me a deep passionate kiss.

"Off you go, then, and I'll see you in a while."

I walked with him into the courtyard; he left for the meditation room, and I continued to his home, looking over my shoulder to watch him disappear into the door of the round room. Inside David's room, I dropped onto his bed and found a football game on television.

It was the last bastion of my father's influence on me that I enjoyed football. I'd been a long-suffering Seahawks fan, and, as usual, they were out of the playoffs. I propped up some pillows and watched the game. The softness of the bed did its job on my body, and I fell to sleep.

Richard appeared in my dream, sitting on the edge of the bed. He sat there as if he'd been watching me sleep the entire time and smiled when he realized I was awake.

"The tribe is considering you, Sagahlie. Considering your place in the House of Wolves. Now that it has been revealed that you are the wolf among wolves, there is a lot to prepare you for. We have a path to walk together, because at the end of that path, I will have to leave the House of Wolves. And, finally, leave David to you."

12. Red Clay Between Our Toes

I SAT UP IN the bed. Richard was there, clear as day, and spoke to me. I still found the intense reality of the dream unsettling. I could smell Richard and his earthiness but could also smell tobacco, on the bed sheets, from David. It was indeed a waking dream.

"The tribe is now meeting to consider you as one of their own, to start you down the path to becoming their brother, their soul-connected brother in the House of Wolves," he said.

After a long pause, his eyes searching me, he continued.

"If that scares you a little, Sagahlie, it should. Your place in the house is not set, and events are already in motion. Come, walk with me, Sagahlie," Richard said, rising.

As he rose and walked toward the door, he motioned to me and said, "Do not be afraid; come and see my world."

I pensively followed him. He opened the door, and we stepped out and into what I realized were the woods of the Indian reservation rather than the House of Wolves. The scene was so calming that I immediately found myself relaxing into the magical nature of the dream.

Richard and I walked silently for a moment. I looked around at the crisp and silent woods. Richard frequently glanced back over his shoulder, encouraging me to follow. The red earthen path we walked , the blue NW sky pierced through the tall evergreens all around us. I started to hear and smell everything around me with great intensity.

Richard bent down and scooped a handful of the earth.

"What color do you get if you blend black, brown, white, yellow, and red? Do you get clay-colored mud on a mossy river-bed?" he said, looking up at me, allowing the rich color to stain his fingers as the soil crumbled between them, falling back to where it had come.

"When I started this path," Richard said, motioning to his feet, "I was a child. I walked into these woods one day, and the spirit of the great tyee came to me and showed me a new way, showed me the path toward the brotherhood of wolves. He bonded me to Ben in a permanent and inescapable way. Ben and I grew up and, upon finding adulthood, walked our parallel paths of broth-erhood and love.

"He gave me the vision to recognize Marlin and Bear for who they were when they entered my life. The three of us were the nexus for something greater, something more. I remember when I first introduced them to these woods and to the deep spiritual meaning found within them. It was as if they were destined to understand, and we began our journey together without fear, without regret.

"Soon came Moose, Tristan, William, and our David," Richard said, motioning between us. "For a time, it seemed we'd found perfect harmony. Then the illness and it accompanying darkness stepped in, claimed me, and threatened all.

Richard stopped for a moment, and I was sure a silver tear had emerged from his eye, but with a breath he continued.

"The one thing we hadn't considered was one of us succumb-ing to illness. We all had dreams, much as you had of Joe, to live forever in that one moment in time. It was our mortality that kept us there.

"The house now has a new opportunity: to live in a time when the brothers will be more of a collective voice, rather than ral-lying around a single leader. My departure has brought out new beginnings in each of them, even more remarkable than when I was amongst them."

With a new energy and pride in his voice, he punctuated the moment by turning away from the forest and looking directly at me; a tiny smile creeping across his chin, he spoke of his brothers.

"Tristan has become a master of the art of concentration and order; he has begun to recognize the leader in himself. He came to us wandering, without controlled discipline, and is now the example of order and restraint. His wandering tempered, he now finds the freedom to share that focus and deep-rooted spirituality with others.

"Marlin, my playful Englishman. Oh, how I sometimes miss his touch and his immediate smile. I know of your closeness to him. Marlin doesn't let people in the way others do. You have shared a common passion for knowledge and have brought to him a sense of having a peer in his midst.

"David, oh, my David. He feels so powerfully, whether it be bliss or mournful sorrow. You have set a light in his soul; he knows you will be there with him. Yours will be the eyes he stares into when his time in this life is finished. He is now ready for the great love of a man who is not a mentor but an equal, someone to find new one-of-a-kind adventures with.

"Bear and Moose continue to celebrate every single moment of life, bringing a necessary childlike quality to the group. Voraciously sexual and masculine, the two of them find in you someone they covet and see as a source of joy. Hidden behind their bravado is a sense of admiration and pride that their household could attract a soul like yours. In them is the male energy, free to express itself nakedly.

"Then there is William. His quiet, brooding soul, like a violent passionate storm kept at bay. His eyes swirl like the eye of the storm. He will lead the house for these next few years as you take the path along with them, but he knows that you will eventually lead. He knew it from the day you joined him in the vision at Bowman Bay. He admires you and knows, as I do, the leader you will become. Follow his lead and let him show you the magic that can come from it.

"And you, Sagahlie, dearest Roy, you will be the teacher, the voice that brings peace to the household. They don't realize quite yet that the uncomfortable balance they've found will become their comfort. They are ready to move forward again with David back in the fold and being one in the circle again. I know they will find that, with you amongst them, they will reach for new goals and new ways to enrich the household.

"It has become clear that the collective now stands strong with my guidance. And you will bring them the completion: from transition of the household as a tribe with a chieftain into a collective of shaman. Rather than a tribe of wolves with a leader, they will evolve into a wiser group of peers walking together through the world.

"The spirits have named you Sagahlie, the wolf. You will be admired for your strength and powers of endurance, and you will teach the tribe many skills. In the years ahead, the men of the House of Wolves will learn to share their individual visions as never before.

"Now, there are things I must tell you that you would rather not hear, but hear you must. I see the transitions of you all. The strength needed comes from the brotherhood. You will live to see many of your current brothers make the transition to the spirit world. You will bury David and some of the others, and you will bring strength to those who survive. You know that from the vision journey David and I had together here.

"The strength of the wolf will guide you through these journeys as new tribal spirits enter your midst. You will mentor these new men as a wolf would his young, and your strength will forever change the house.

"Your future is part of the legacy of the house. You will know that the house will live, well beyond your years. Oh, how I wish I could join you on that journey."

He could see in my eyes that the thought of outliving David, as I had Joe, deeply troubled me. He turned and faced me, tracing my face with his dirt-stained hand.

"There is in you a man that you cannot see. I see that man, and in time you will grow into him and enjoy this bounty. I know, Sagahlie, the path you are destined for has deep challenges. You will have David with you into his twilight, and his transition will be peaceful and at the right time. You will have a household of new tribe members to mentor, and you will be deeply loved."

I turned to Richard, deep in the forest of the dream, and looked him straight in the eyes for a moment, considering all he'd said.

"It feels like so much responsibility, Richard," I said, realizing that this was the first time I could remember addressing him directly. "A terrifying burden. I'm unsure."

"Dearest Sagahlie, that is the beauty of your part in the house. You can share the impact of your burdens. This is no longer a singular vision; it's your contribution to the group. You have six kindred spirits along with you on the long journey of your life," said Richard.

"The life of the house will expand; and, Roy, the man that you will become is far beyond the man you can imagine at this juncture in your life. Rejoice in the new beginning and indulge yourself; with that, the others will be equally drawn to you and what you bring to the house. Open your body to the rewards of the brothers and explore the depths of what a man can do, with men. With this joining, all will enjoy the pleasures of your company, not the least of which is David. David has needed for so long to become vulnerable and naked, not of the flesh but of emotion; with your joining, the hurt, both his and yours, will heal.

"And with that, my dear Sagahlie, I will depart for new paths myself. It will no longer be about guiding the household on my path, but will encourage them to find new, strong, parallel paths to walk. Turn to the tribe when you yearn with questions; in the souls of the brotherhood of the wolves lie all of your answers.

Part of me is in all of them and in you. You will all soon depart with your mahalets. You will all walk into the new morning sun of renewed life, and I will walk the opposite way, into a new path."

He repeated, "There is in you a man, that as of yet you cannot see. I see that man, and in time you will grow into him and enjoy this bounty."

Richard traced my face with his hand, "You are a blessed man, Sagahlie. I know the house is also blessed to have you with them. The House of Wolves is your destiny. Good-bye, Sagahlie."

As if the mist had swallowed him, Richard simply vanished from the dream. I sat there alone in the woods and cried. It was such an overwhelming sense of joy and of loss. Richard had been instrumental in the lives of the men I now loved, and he was confident that I belonged.

That moment, I noticed the smells of the moss and wetness of the woods around me. I breathed in the breeze that danced through the evergreens.

I was suddenly awake, and gasped for air as if startled. I was lying on the bed, David sitting next to me, tracing my face with his hand. He smiled and stroked my hair as I regained my calm, as one does when waking suddenly from a deep sleep.

"Hello, Mr. Wallace," he said, looking down at me softly. "I've been sitting here for a while watching you, mumbling under your breath. So calmly, so quietly."

David was sitting on the edge of the bed, exactly where Richard had just appeared. I wanted to tell him all about my walk with Richard, but it was clear that David wanted to share what the group had talked about in the meditation room.

"Many things have happened to all of us over the last few weeks," David began. "My dreams at Bowman Bay, your coming to us, to me. I have some things to tell you that I hope will continue this journey. Please just listen, and when you have heard my question, save your questions, as I think all will get answered in time.

"The men of the house have decided that the mourning period is over. When Richard spoke to me in my vision at Bowman Bay, he showed me finally that he was my past, and you, my dear Mr. Wallace, are my future. And oh, what a future I have in mind for you: the collective, the men of the house, have decided to ask you to join us. Now, that means so many things to each of us, and our emotions are running strongly around you right now.

"The house wants you to come be part of us, to live amongst us and take us all on as your brothers. You need to seriously consider that offer—that idea. I know you realize it is not something to take lightly. So, I am not looking for you to answer right now."

We sat there for a moment staring into one another's eyes. All of our time together as a pair of men had built up to this very moment. While I was clearly complimented by being asked to join, I wondered what would be involved in joining the household.

Finally, I told David about the dream and how I felt I'd actually been in the woods. I told him how Richard had described each member of the house and his contribution to the spiritual circle the house represented.

"And you, Mr. Wallace, how did Richard say you fit?"

"He said I'd grow into a leader. That I'd be the mentor for others as the house grows and moves on to new things."

"I love you, Roy...my special Roy," David said. "I know," he continued, "that you will enjoy the rituals of the house: learning tai chi with Tristan, learning the meditations that William leads us through in the roundhouse. Beyond the great man you are to me, it seems you fit here amongst us...quite naturally."

He leaned in, sucked my upper lip into his mouth, and kissed me passionately.

"What would happen if I joined you, if I decided to move into the house to be with you?" I asked, softly.

With a deep breath and a little smile, David went on to tell me: "We would go through a series of rituals. These are things we have fashioned over time and yet are individual to the broth-

er and his initiation. They are, as we believe, rites of men, before
men, with men, your brothers. They will do nothing but enjoy
you with us as our brother, so there is nothing to be afraid of. It
is about you knowing us and about us knowing you. Something I
have wanted to do for weeks now…

But the first task we ask of you is to spend time with each
member discussing what it means to be a member of the house;
you will exchange tokens of bonding, small gifts that are from
each other's hearts."

I sat listening to David, realizing the intense conversation he'd
just come from. How to include me? How to make me part of
the group? Despite the rich emotions we all shared, I am sure
they took such an offer extremely seriously. I felt truly desired by
these men. I loved each of them more strongly than I'd realized.

"Then, after time to consider, we'd ask for your answer. Should
you choose to join the household, we would mark you with your
totem: Sagahlie, the wolf.

"Tristan would do research and find out the right location
for such a marking, and you'd work with him for a design that
was both respectful to the origins of the totem and for your own
comfort since it will become a permanent part of you. I would
hold your hand and Tristan would mark you as a member of the
House of Wolves.

"Still wearing a bandage over your tattoo, you'd be physically
tagged by the tribe in the inclusion rite. We'd bring you into
the meditation room and ritually join you with our bodies. We'd
mark you with temporary henna and with our cum, sweat, blood,
and urine. Then, finally, that first night as a brother, we would
give you the steel of the tribe, a Prince Albert, whereupon you'd
be locked with us."

He watched my face and body react to the description. I'd assumed that joining the house might include some sort of ceremony or ritual, but one including sweat and piss? It was all very
earthy and, frankly, powerfully erotic. I'd always found erotic
power in sweat and cum, and I'd considered piss. I'd never had it

offered, but had thought and read about it. Strangely, it wasn't making me uncomfortable but was filling my mind with visions of being approached in that fashion by the six other men in the household. I was thinking of Bear and Moose being let loose erotically, the beauty of Tristan and William, the earthy muscular Marlin, and, of course, my beautiful bear, David.

I moved into him and let his arms wrap around me as he spoke softly into my ear. With his breath on my neck as he spoke, he could feel me pushing in against him, honestly aroused by his closeness and the visions of the men in the house in such a sexual rite. The tone of his voice told me he was smiling as he continued to speak.

"You'd be bonded to all of us in a unique way that only feted members of the house can understand. And once you accept, there is no turning back; this is a one-way decision."

David explained the path to inclusion in the home so clearly and so strongly I honestly found myself breathless. Even if I had wanted to respond, there was no way I could. He spoke again after pausing to give me time to take it all in, as if he knew exactly what I was thinking.

"The first time I heard of all this, about the inclusion rite path, I was a bit frightened and taken aback. It took me a few days to digest and understand. I urge you to take that time as well, discuss it with the others as they suggest.

"We all love you, Roy, but this needs to be the right choice for you as a man."

I reached up and pulled David down on top of me, sucked his beard into my mouth, and chewed on his chin. He growled and smiled as I grunted and kept chewing my way up his jaw. He put his hand behind my head as my tongue found his neck. The mixture of sweat and pipe smoke in his beard and neck was the perfect erotic scent.

He gently pulled my head back and kissed me deeply, our tongues exploring each other's mouths as he moved in between my legs, encouraging me to wrap them around his waist. Our beards meshed together in deep, wet kisses. His hands found my butt, and I could feel him press his hardness against me.

My mind escaped into the thought of soon having this man strip me down with his brothers and claim me as his lover. We were both soon grunting and kissing desperately. I reached up, unbuttoned his shirt, and cuddled my face into his chest. He let out a gasp and held the back of my head, leading me around his chest. My mouth soon found his pierced nipple; taking the small killer whale ornament in my mouth, I sucked on his tattooed nipple.

"Oh, yes, pup, that's it, boy," he said, as I could feel his hardness growing more intense against my own. "Now, bite it. Gently bite it."

I did as I was told and felt a shiver explode across his body. He kissed the top of my head and began thrusting against me.

"That's it, pup, oh, god, yes sir."

I continued to bite and suck on his nipple. The musk from all the deep black hair and the sweat on his skin was intoxicating. He suddenly withdrew and stared down at me with a fiery look in his eye, unbuttoned my shirt, and ran his hands down my chest.

"You are my pup...Mr. Wallace."

He found both of my nipples with his strong hands and pinched them hard, smiling broadly as I whimpered and bucked underneath him.

"You are mine." He leaned over and kissed me furiously, licking my beard and my neck. We were both letting it go much further than we'd ever dared before.

"I will make you so happy, Roy," he said, rising again and staring down at me.

"But it's late, and Tristan will pitch a fit if you sleep here tonight instead of the guest quarters. Mind you, it's a tempting sight, you sitting here in my bed."

David started to move off me; but he suddenly smiled, leaned down, and loudly sniffed my crotch. He grabbed my thighs and purposefully sniffed my aching cock through my jeans. Rubbing his nose on my crotch, sniffing, he stopped for a moment and peered up at me. He licked my crotch but then pulled back and stood up.

I glanced at the clock. It was 1:30 AM.

"Let me walk you to the guesthouse. We all love you, but right now we both need rest."

We got up, and he led me from his little house. With crickets singing and bright moonlight, he walked with me hand in hand to the guest quarters.

"Things are going to be intense around here for a while—considering someone new in the tribe is taken very seriously by everyone. So their feelings for you and their intentions are going to be raw and open for you to experience. You have clearly captured our hearts, and now it's going to be the process of bringing you to us as a member of the household."

He kissed me gently. "Sleep well, Mr. Wallace, and we'll talk much more in the morning."

He walked away. I stood still for a moment, enjoying the quiet of the courtyard as it glowed in the sparkle of a bright harvest moon. That was the first time I remember considering the house my home. I entered the guest room and was quickly asleep, resting for the day ahead.

13. Totem against the Night Sky

I AWOKE THE NEXT morning to an overcast day, its dark, moody light filling the windows and the doorway. The silence of the night before was replaced by the sounds of the city awake beyond the walls of the house.

"Ah, you are awake. Good. Moose has almost finished preparing breakfast. Get showered and join us, eh?" said Marlin, appearing at my doorway.

Draping my towel across my shoulders, I walked, otherwise naked, across the courtyard and had just turned down the path to the shower room when I came face to face with Jean. Completely flustered, I dropped my shower bag and quickly covered myself with the towel. Jean laughed at my embarrassment.

"Sagahlie, please, I've seen all the men here naked once or twice. Nothing shocks me with these boys any longer."

I smiled nervously and said, "Good morning, Jean."

"William invited us into town for Thanksgiving. Ben and David had things to discuss, so we came early. Sorry if I embarrassed you, dear one."

I excused myself and dashed into the shower room. As I allowed the hot water to ease away the last traces of sleep from my body, I began to reflect about all that David had told me about the ritual of becoming a member of the house. I looked around the shower room remembering the camaraderie here the day before and realized how happy and safe I felt. How could I tell these men I loved them without sounding flip or corny?

After I showered, I wrapped the towel around my waist and returned to my quarters. Dressed, I walked across the courtyard to the dining room and entered to find that all the members were already there along with Ben, Jean, and their son, Richard.

"Roybear!" bellowed Moose from the kitchen. "You are just in time."

The meals presented at the house made all the exercise necessary. Breakfast included piles of sausage and eggs, and potatoes steaming in giant trays.

David hugged me. He leaned in and whispered, "Woof, woof," loud enough that only I could hear. He told me he loved me and sealed it with a deep sniff and a gentle kiss on my neck.

Tristan handed me a cup of coffee, and I joined the noisy communion of the room. William and Ben sat at one end of the table talking to each other, while the young Richard sat giggling and chatting with Marlin.

Soon we were all eating breakfast, and it wasn't long before the noise level in the room, with everyone talking or eating, was near to overwhelming. Tristan and I sat observing the scene.

"Sometimes the constant noise and need for commotion just gets too crazy for me. I am glad that there will be someone else who doesn't get all loud and boisterous," said Tristan. He turned to me and, after a moment, asked if I was OK. Apparently, one look at my face told him there was something on my mind, something that had little to do with the clamor in the room.

I told him that David had explained to me the night before all that was involved in joining the house. I needed to declare whether I really wanted to belong to the house, but I didn't know how.

He took my hand in his, looked me in the eye, and said, "With these men, just show a bit of control, and they'll simply come to you naturally."

Tristan picked up his fork, tapped it against his glass, and everyone very quickly became silent. Their attention focused on Tristan, who looked over at me, encouraging me with a soft look, to speak to them. Each of the men turned and concentrated on me, at the end of the table.

Taking advantage of the quiet Tristan had created, I stood and spoke: "David told me how coming to you is a one-way path. When I met you all a few weeks ago, I had no idea how you lived, or what was involved or the complexity of your lives here. I can't remember a time in my life when I felt safer, more a part of something special.

The closeness you all share is something I'd like to experience for myself rather than watch as a spectator. I'd like to start the path toward becoming a member of this house, and am truly humbled by your gesture of faith and love toward me.

That you make it on Thanksgiving, a time to be thankful for what we all have in our lives, makes it even more special. I love you all very much."

The men all rose, came to me, and showered me with touches and hugs. David held me tightly from behind as the room erupted in celebratory chatter.

Marlin immediately became flustered with all the things to plan, and William spoke of what a wonderful gift it was for all of them to bring in a new brother.

"Well, my brothers and friends, happy Thanksgiving. This is a special day, truly," he said. "Lots to learn from one another and lots to share. We will, indeed, walk with Mr. Wallace down the path." The table erupted in cheers and everyone clanking coffee cups together.

David touched my leg under the table as William continued: "Jean has finished the totem—so we will be raising it in the courtyard this afternoon."

Everyone's faces lit up around the table. Except for the three of us who had visited Jean up at the reservation, none of the others had seen the totem. When Marlin, David, and I saw the totem, the work was unfinished. William continued to explain that we needed to complete the foundation before setting and raising the totem.

"Can we see it?" asked David, excitedly.

"After this fine meal," said Jean, "it will be waiting for us."

Marlin regaled the others with the story of going to the Indian reservation a few weeks earlier and seeing the carving. Conversation at the breakfast table was filled with anticipation of seeing the finished form.

We sat in the dining room, loudly working our way through it all. Afterward, as we were cleaning the dishes, I overheard young Richard speaking with David about the totem pole.

"Mother says that the wood simply wouldn't speak to you, See-Ho-Tid," said Jean's son, softly, "because you did not know Segahlie was coming." He smiled over at me with a big, toothy grin. "The spirits of the totem have been impatient to arrive here; the voices in the wood have been calling to be brought home to you, See-Ho-Tid."

Jean reached out and combed back his black hair. "Indeed, the spirits have been calling to be brought home to you all," she said, motioning around the room at all of us.

"It's waiting out front," said Jean.

Everyone stood and followed her out to the front porch. There, lying on the ground in several pieces, was the finished totem. All of the totems were represented: the bear, the moose, the hummingbird, the moon, the eagle, the owl, the killer whale, and, finally, the top of the totem pole, the carving of a wolf.

I'd never seen the completed wolf totem. The form was quite powerful and overwhelming. It reached skyward—claws bared— eyes set on the heavens. In the totem design, the legs wrapped around the eagle, which held the killer whale in its claws.

All the characters in the totem pole were painted in a deep gray, red, and black and was the most beautiful carving I'd ever seen.

David knelt and traced the carvings with his hands in a reverent quiet. He'd started the carving for Richard, and Jean had finished it. I knelt behind David and put my arms around him.

He kept his hands on the finished carving as we all surrounded him and touched it respectfully.

"It's so beautiful, Jean, exactly as Richard imagined it," said David, his speech broken as he fought back tears.

I nuzzled his neck and kissed him gently. The group sat in the driveway, studying Jean's creation, almost like one single being embracing another. It was the perfect reunion of the totem with David, as well as the perfect unveiling of its beauty to the rest of his brothers in the house.

Marlin finally broke the silence by gently instructing us on how to get the different lengths into the backyard. He split us into two groups. One would mix cement to pour into the base while others would help Jean raise the totem by placing the separate carved pieces on top of each other.

The base's form was already shaped. It was in the center of the courtyard according to Richard's design. Jean asked me to help her clear the fallen leaves from the hole that had been dug for the totem's resting place.

"Richard designed this perfectly," commented Jean. "The totem will tower over this yard, visible from every window. His spirit may be walking a new path, but his memory is in every brick of this place."

I thought to myself that she surely had been in touch with Richard the same way the rest of us had been. How else could she know that Richard had moved on? Jean turned to me, as if I were the only one there to speak to.

"You know that you are the influence that's brought real peace to this home again? When See-He-Ahi left, I feared that the sense of peace and serenity would never return. This had become a house of grief and sorrow. Their dependence on See-He-Ahi kept his spirit here too long. Then, the spirits guided David to you, the wolf amongst wolves.

"I am glad the men finally asked you; I was wondering what was taking so much time. You know that you belong here, don't you?"

Without pausing, I replied, "Somehow, yes. I have felt comfortable here from the very beginning.

"I felt that comfort when we met that cloudy day and I gave you the mahalet," she said. "You reacted so quickly! It was exactly as if Richard had come into your life as a living spirit. I hope, as you consider a life with the men of Richard's household, that you take it seriously. You surely realize that destiny has stepped in and revealed the magic here."

She was interrupted as the others started arriving with the pieces of the totem. Each large piece was set carefully around the base. The busy scene of the men working in every direction quickly stopped as Jean asked all present to come to her as she knelt next to the hole the totem would rest in.

"We now need the mahalets for the base," she said softly.

Her proclamation clearly took the men by surprise.

"In raising this totem, your mourning of See-He-Ahi is over. You should surrender the mahalets to the earth."

Ben stepped forward and placed his small leather pouch into the deep hole. With only a moment's hesitation, each man untied his mahalet from his belt and set it in the resting place.

David paused for a moment, studying the mahalet in his hand. He traced the symbols. I stood next to him, untied the mahalet from my belt, and handed it to him. David stared into the ground quietly, as Ben and Jean's son then knelt next to us and set his in with the others.

Young Richard looked up at David as a small child's tear ran down his face.

"I do not want See-He-Ahi to go away," he said softly. "Who will walk with me in the woods?"

David said softly, "I will, and the brothers of the house. I will walk with you in the moss-filled forests. We will remember your See-He-Ahi together."

Richard leaned over, and I took him in my arms and kissed the top of his head. He hugged me softly, then rose and returned to his parents. Ben smiled at me warmly, and Jean looked at her son with great kindness.

David then set his mahalet into the ground and, with all them in place, Bear and Moose lifted the owl totem down into the hole as William and Tristan started pouring cement. The cement quickly began setting, sealing everything into the earth.

Marlin found great satisfaction that his totem was the foundation for the rest of the pieces.

"Don't go getting a big head, you old perv; it's not all about you," laughed Moose.

Bear helped David lift the Moose totem into position. The bear, the moon, and the hummingbird soon followed. With each piece being about three or four feet tall, the totem was quickly growing above its surroundings.

Perched on a ladder, David placed his own totem, the killer whale. The rest of us looked on as he worked with Bear to complete his section.

The eagle, with its broad wings and towering presence, in the embrace of the wolf almost making the two glyphs appear as one. The eagle looked forward as the wolf looked straight up into the heavens.

Seeing the wolf staring off into the swirling gray Seattle sky, the trees swaying in the wind, I was suddenly caught up in the overwhelming beauty of the scene. The totem pole gestured to its surroundings as if to say that it had always owned that spot.

The seven of us, along with Jean, Ben, and Richard, stared with a sense of accomplishment and quiet awe at the finished totem pole. Bear held Moose in his arms. William held Tristan tightly, whispering softly in his ear. Ben and Jean held their son close as Marlin, David, and I stood in a silent triad.

Jean broke the silence, finally, with a song. Her words, soft but clear, filled the courtyard:

My grandfather is the fire.
My grandmother is the wind.

The earth is my mother.
The Great Spirit is my father.
The world stopped at my birth and laid itself at my feet,
and I shall swallow the earth whole when I die,
and the earth and I will be one.
Hail the Great Spirit, my father!
Without him no one could exist
because there would be no will to live.
Hail the earth, my mother!
Without which no food could be grown
and so cause the will to live to starve.
Hail the wind, my grandmother!
For she brings loving, life-giving rain,
nourishing us as she nourishes our crops.
Hail the fire, my grandfather!
For the light, the warmth, the comfort he brings
without which we be animals, not men.
Hail my parent and grandparents!
Without which not I nor you nor anyone else could have
  existed;
life gives life which gives unto itself a promise of new
  life.
Hail the Great Spirit!
The earth.
The wind.
The fire.
Praise my parents loudly for they are your parents, too.

Jean followed her song with a prayer: "Oh, Great Spirit, Giver of my life, please accept this humble offering from these the brothers of the House of Wolves on their special day, this offering of praise, this honest reverence of my love for you. Teach us to walk the earth as relatives to all that live."

When she finished, she walked up to the wooden spirits, took a handful of earth, and rubbed it gently into the exposed base. She motioned for the others to follow her lead and, one by one, we did. Each member of the house silently walked forward and took a handful of dirt rubbing it against the base of the totem. David was the last of the others to take his turn. After he had finished, I knelt down and, taking a fistful of earth, I completed the ritual. Joining the others as we finished, I looked around at everyone and noticed that I wasn't the only one who had shed a tear.

Before the moment was gone, Moose remembered that a photo should mark the event, and emerged from the house with a camera and tripod. We collected around the base of the totem as the timer whirred away atop Moose's camera. With a snap of the flash, the scene was immortalized.

We started cleaning the supplies that had been brought out to erect the totem pole. The clang and noise of the procedure brought us all back to reality, and the work gave us something to do while our emotions returned to their normal levels.

Marlin and I stood for a while admiring the transformation of the totem as the sun set and the lights around the compound lit up.

"Richard always did have a thing about lighting," David said, as he came up to us.

He continued to explain that the flood lights would automatically come on at dark. I helped him position each of the lamps so that they illuminated the carving in a spectacular fashion. He then installed one with a brighter bulb that pointed straight up into the sky.

"A bright testimonial to those who are no longer with us, don't you think?"

"I do. This is such a beautiful memorial to both life and death. I will never again see a totem pole the same way," I said to him.

David and I worked silently, finishing the lighting. We walked into the kitchen to clean up. David moved in behind me, and we washed our hands together under the water while he nuzzled into my neck.

"You should go see Marlin, Mr. Wallace," he said to me, softly. "Keep in mind what I said last night, pup. Spend some good time with each of us and learn the depth of our care for you. He loves you, Roy. I think I shall be sharing you with him often. He's a good man and was the first to say to me that you were going to change us all. Marlin's wisdom is beyond all the rest of us. He's waiting in the loft."

David then kissed my neck and let me go. I turned around and gave him a kiss. He then turned me toward the library and smacked me on the butt. I realized, starting up the stairs into Marlin's loft, that it was one of the few places I hadn't been in the house. The stairs led into an impressive space. The walls were lined with bookshelves, all curving toward a desk built into the wall.

An old-fashioned wax candle burned on the desktop, which was covered with handwritten notes and drawings. There was a small opening in the wall by a desk made from old wood, cut in the shape of an oval.

I poked my head inside. Built into the attic was a small sleeping area where Marlin sat reading. He was shirtless, his white body hair glistening in the light of the windows as he smiled at me.

"Come in 'ere, pup."

I walked over and kneeled next to near him, and he reached and pulled me down in a strong hug. It felt so comforting and natural to lie there with him, feeling his strong body wrap around me.

"It's been so long since we've had a pup around like you. I'm glad you'll be joining us, Roy; I've been wanting ya in our midst," Marlin leaned in and whispered in my ear, "We'll take real good care a ya, pup, real good care."

He kissed my neck and ran his beard across my neck. I let myself relax into his arms and let out a little grunt of pleasure. God, these men knew exactly how to turn me on and bring me to a point of physical contentment. Marlin was clearly aroused as he pulled me against him. We relaxed in a spoon position, and I could feel his cock press against my butt.

"Real good care," he whispered, again running his hands up under my shirt.

He fingers found my nipples and the rings there.

I let out a whimper as his nipple play now had me in a state of complete arousal. It'd been such a struggle to be around these men without being able to act out sexually. Marlin's play had me squirming in his arms as if this were the first time a man turned me on.

"You'll come visit me up here sometimes, I hope," he said, letting go of my nipples and moving his hands outside my shirt. I twisted around to face him and licked his beard.

"Absolutely."

"There is so much we'll share together, sweet one," Marlin continued, "from long talks into the night about books to learning to let go physically and let the men of this house share their knowledge with you," he said, reaching down into his jeans to adjust his cock.

"Let me start with this," he said, reaching over me and pulling a small leather-clad book from a shelf.

I instantly recognized this small black book as the one David had described being read to by 'me' in his vision.

"This is Emerson's *Self-Reliance*. It's been a short book that has spoken to me for years. This copy has always been my token to share with new members. David read this copy, and now it is yours. Everybody has a book in their life that really changes who they are. This is that book for me. I knew the other day, when you picked out Thoreau to read to us, that you would love this work.

"Emerson celebrated the diversity and freedom he found in American life, and he demanded that his fellow citizens be worthy of their freedom by daring to be independent in their individual lives. In *Self-Reliance*, he declared, 'Nothing is sacred but the integrity of your own mind.' The quest for self-reliance was really a search for harmony in the universe, which could only be achieved by each person seeking his or her own unique means of self-fulfillment. Such truth!

"When Richard, Bear, and I first discussed the idea of the House of Wolves we agreed that it had to be founded upon a set of values that meant more than what your normal gay men seek. We set out to create a household where honor and ritual still had a place, and where love meant many different things."

"I love you, Marlin," I said, without really thinking about it. I knew instantly that it was true.

I ran my fingers through the thick white hair on his chest as we shared a quiet moment staring into one another's eyes. We could have sat there for hours like that, but Tristan called to us from the library.

"Marlin, Bear's looking for help in the kitchen. Ya up there?"

"Yes, I'll be there in a jiffy," Marlin bellowed back at him.

"My disorganization and little getaway up here weird that man upward and downward. 'He doesn't get up 'ere ever." He giggled, reaching for his shirt. His strong arm arched toward a shelf.

I leaned forward and sniffed his armpit. It was ripe and strong. He let out a surprised grunt that turned into a growl as I leaned in and pulled at his armpit hairs with my teeth.

"Ah, fuck, pup, yes sir,' he said, pushing up with his body and pushing his pit into my face.

I quickly withdrew, both blushing and radiating with lust. I licked my lips as I realized Marlin's thick scent was still in my mustache. He shot me a playful grin and pulled his T-shirt on.

"You, Mr. Wallace, are gonna get yourself in trouble doin' shenanigans like that." He laughed and then reached out and pinched my nipples hard. I let out a yelp, and he laughed again.

He ran his hands slowly over me, stopping over my hard cock, grabbed it firmly, grasping it with his fingers. He pulsed his hands and tugged on it through my trousers.

"Lotsa trouble," he said, gently tapping my balls. I relaxed back into the warmth of his bed as he tucked in his shirt and got ready to head downstairs.

"Yes, Marlin, you'll see me up here often." I said, with a gentle Cheshire smile.

"Good," he said, "You best go get ready for Thanksgiving dinner."

With that, Marlin was down the stairs and into the rest of the house. I sat there for a moment considering how everyone's level of intensity had increased, how David had warned me that emotions were running high.

I loved this house and the men in it. Holding my new book close, I headed for the guest quarters to get ready for dinner. I walked out into the abandoned courtyard. The winds had started picking up, and the last fall leaves danced around on the stone paths leading from room to room. The totem pole stared down at me.

Just a couple of months before, David had paid for coffee and brought me into his life. After my encounter with Marlin, I was more confident than ever that this truly is where I belonged. This would become my home. Back in the guest quarters, I dressed in a white oxford and brand new blue jeans, a detail I knew David would appreciate.

I thought somehow it was time to release the pain on this day of days, a day of Thanksgiving, and had planned to wear something special for the occasion. I pulled out of the closet a rolled-up garment bag and set it on the bed. Unzipping the bag, I paused for a moment and just stared at something I hadn't the courage to look at in months: a biker jacket. A vest had been custom-made to fit under the shoulder snaps. I picked it up and laid it down.

The words "ursus major" were written in Celtic script, and a bear paw was drawn there, grasping a length of barbed wire. It was Joseph's biker jacket, which I'd pulled out of storage.

"It's beautiful, Roy," I heard some someone say behind me.

I turned to see Tristan standing in the doorway.

"It was Joseph's. I just figured I'd start wearing it," I said, with a quiet reverence.

"It's a perfect idea," he said, picking up the jacket and helping me into it. I felt as if I'd always worn it.

"You're going to make David crazy wearing a leather jacket, but that's good for him." He turned me around, smiled, and straightened my collar like a father getting his daughter ready to walk down the aisle. He paused as if he were going to say more but, instead, let his eyes finish the conversation.

"We'd better get you inside before they wonder what I am doing with you," said Tristan.

I walked with Tristan into the dining room, and there were the men of the house, all dressed up for dinner. Bear and Jean fussed with each other in the kitchen. The table was set, with a space reserved in the center for a turkey.

Tristan poured wine as William placed the napkins at each spot. All the men with long hair had their hair braided, and each wore a black leather vest. I watched each of them, realizing that the vests had the wolf pattern from the doorway emblazoned in red on the back. Each setting at the table had a blue candle on the plate.

"Tadaa!" said Bear, walking into the room with a giant turkey on a platter so large that Jean had to hold up the other side of it. Everyone sat down. I looked at the men at the table, their faces reflected in the sparkling candlelight.

David appeared behind me, his arms wrapping around me. I felt his beard brush my ear. When he took his seat next to me at the table, his bright smile told me he had seen Joe's weathered leather jacket.

William asked David to say grace and bless the table. David held up the blue candle, displaying it for everyone at the table.

"I create sacred space in time that is not time; a place not a place; today is a day that is not a day; all malice and worry, now away, so all within here is right and just; this is a place of brotherhood, love, and trust. We light these blue candles in remembrance of those who are no longer with us—and in thankfulness for our continued health and fellowship," said David.

He lit the candle and then motioned to have me light my candle off his; Marlin lit his candle from mine and so forth, until all the candles around the table were lit.

Then David continued: "May we never thirst; may we never hunger. We gaze into the flame of what is to become; our lives are to be renewed with energy and strength. The land green and blossoming with life, joy to all—peace be on all of you."

"Peace," responded the others around the table.

David leaned forward and set his candle in the centerpiece, and the rest of us followed suit. He then rose from his seat to kneel at the side of my chair. His braid draped over his shoulder down his chest, the black of his hair matching his vest. He was so very beautiful.

"I am honored, Mr. Wallace, to be your love in this house. To be the man you will share a bed with and with whom I'll share everything openly."

He produced a small wooden box, which he handed to me. I opened the box with all the others looking on. Red felt lined the inside and held a thick silver ring whose engraving featured delicate runes and a brilliant, emerald-green stone at the center.

I still wore the ring Joseph gave me when we're together. I traced David's beard gently with my right hand, then reached down to remove the ring from my finger, laying it on the table. David gently placed the shiny silver Celtic ring on my finger and admired it; without looking up, he spoke: "This is my ring for you, your totem to me, and I wear its mate," David said, bringing his left hand up to mine. He wore a shiny ring that was identical to mine.

David had caught me totally off guard, and I started to cry. He leaned in, kissed me softly, then licked the tears off my face as the emotion poured out of me.

Holding me close, David whispered, "I love you, Roy. You are my beautiful bear."

I hugged him back with the same strength and ferocity. The entire room was silent for a moment as they watched the two of us touch and hold one another.

David leaned back and took Joe's ring and put it on the ring finger on Roy's opposite hand. He then put the bright silver-green ring on my wedding finger. We hugged again, and the men around the table broke out in applause.

"Richard always said you were a drama queen," quipped Moose, and laughter broke out around the table. David returned to his seat next to me as I cleared my eyes.

"Some things never change," chimed in Marlin..

After David wiped his own tears away, the laughter died down, and we all dove into dinner with all the trimmings. Bear's turkey was spectacular; he'd worked very hard on all the traditional Thanksgiving favorites. The group of us laughed and talked and drank wine through dinner. We could have stayed there together for the entire night.

When dinner was almost finished, Ben and Jean announced that they were retiring to their rooms and bid us all good night. Young Richard tried to complain but was soon ushered off with his parents.

Moose suggested we retreat to the library and drink some port, so we all got up. Moose poured the wine from a decanter, and we soon were all cozied up next to the fire.

Bear entered with a pair of photo albums under his arm.

"Perhaps a nice history of the house in pictures, eh, pup?" said Bear.

He sat down next to me, everyone else snuggled in, crowded around so that they could see. As he turned page after page in the first album, stopping at particularly special photos as if they were magic windows to the past. We drank wine and laughed at photos of Marlin with a red 'fro' haircut in the early 1970s. I saw some of my first photos of Richard when he was healthy and didn't know about HIV. He was breathtaking. His tribal tattoo

ran up his neck into his hair, clearly the most visible of all the
tattoos in the group.

We worked through pictures of the house construction, complete with photos labeled "the contractor" and featuring David.
It was fun to watch the pictures go from David, as a visitor, to
David, Richard's lover and son. The romance seemed to leap out
of the photos and fill the room.

We saw pictures of William's first days in the house and of
the famed kite flying trips on the windy bluffs. Finally, I saw pictures of Richard resting on the futon, his growing illness clearly
evident on his face. It was so comfortable sitting with all these
men as we laughed by the fire that I could have stayed in that
moment forever. Then the men started to yawn, and we decided
that it was time for bed.

As we untangled ourselves from the couches, David suggested
we see how the totem pole looked at night, lit by the flood lamps.
Several of us let out a gasp as we moved out into the courtyard.
The lights danced their way up the face of the carving, bringing
it to life in a particularly powerful way. The faces shadowed upon
one another, leaving the wolf to reach skyward, carrying the rest
of the characters in its claws.

We stood there for a moment before moving off to our rooms.
David walked me to the guest room. He told me that he was
growing weary of sleeping across the compound from me. We
came together in a tight hug and shared a leisurely rubbing of
beards and deep, true kisses. I watched him walk quietly to what
would soon be my home.

I returned to my quarters and sat there with thoughts of the
evening swimming in my mind. That's when I noticed an oblong,
jade-colored box sitting on my pillow. I opened it to find a rolled-
up parchment. Undoing the ribbon, I discovered a beautiful
Native American drawing of a wolf. Soft, perfect handwriting
below said: "To be marked with this wolf will make you my soul
mate—my confidant—my equal. To be marked with this wolf
means completion. We are cups, constantly and quietly being

filled, and you have shown us all the way to tip ourselves over and let the beautiful stuff out."

I smiled suddenly at Tristan's use of an altered form of the Bradbury quotation here; it brought back all the memories of that day at the sushi bar, when I first knew that he and I would be friends.

I looked at the wolf design again. The drawing on the parchment reached upward with its claws, much like Jean's carving. I studied every inch. In the bottom right corner of the parchment was a small drawing of a man's shoulder, with the design from the parchment leading from his shoulder down the center of his back. It was then I realized that he was drawing where he wanted to tattoo my body. I would wake the next day and begin my journey to become permanently bonded with my brothers. I would become, finally, a member of the House of Wolves.

14. Completing the Circle

I WOKE IN THE dark to the sound of the wind as it howled through the trees and across the roof. I lay under the covers, warm, awake, and preoccupied with what the day had in store for me. It felt to me that this single day would be like the blank page that waits impatiently for the first words of a new story. I stared over at the bedside table at the drawing Tristan had left for me.

I'd seen the tribal markings of the other men in the tribe and known that, with my decision to join them, I would be marked in a similar way. The reality of it all suddenly came over me in a very intense way. I wondered about the pain involved in being tattooed. There was a part of me that wanted, in fact needed, to prove its physical self. The desire to beat the pain and withstand the ordeal of being marked was overwhelming to me.

I could not sleep, so I decided to go to the kitchen, thinking that perhaps a cup of tea would help. I pulled on my sweats and wandered across the courtyard. Even in the darkness I could still make out the outline of the totem pole, almost as if it glowed from within with an otherworldly light. Though I could not see them, I looked up and saw, in my mind's eye, the claws of the wolf spirit atop the pole as they reached up into the night sky. Somehow, that image did little to calm my unsettled mood.

Finally stumbling my way to the kitchen in the dark, I turned on the light and searched the cupboards for a kettle, filled it, and lit the stove.

"Whatcha up to, pup? Can't sleep?" said someone from the darkness.

The voice startled me; I turned and greeted a very naked Marlin. His small amount of white hair on his head was tousled into a bee's nest.

"Oh, you frightened me!"

He flashed his furry grin as he caught me "taking a glance."

"Lying awake; guess I'm a bit excited about tomorrow," I said.

He walked toward me and traced my beard with his hand.

"I've got da best trick for slow nights," he said, walking me to the fridge.

He pulled a pitcher out and poured me a cup of what looked like the makings of hot chocolate.

"Tristan's chai. Ever had chai?" Marlin asked. "Tea with vanilla, cinnamon, cardamom, ginger, cloves. Mixed with soy milk, it's like pumpkn' pie in a cup." He set the cup in the microwave and turned the flame off under the kettle.

"So what's got ya all worried, pup?"

"Before I met you guys, I would have never considered any of this. Although it's now been a few weeks, it still feels like everything is happening so quickly." I smiled nervously. "I mean, to go from no boyfriend to six! I knew that David would be my partner shortly after I met him, but now I've fallen in love with the rest of you. And on top of it all, I would have never considered a tattoo or a piercing—and here I am considering both. It's just a lot…"

"All of us love you, pup, 'n' we'd do nothing to hurt ya; heart and soul, you don't have to do anything you don't want. But I assure you, you will have fun," he said, closing his statement with a wink.

"I know that, Marlin. I know that."

The microwave beeped, and he handed me the steaming cup of tea. It was just as he'd described—wonderful. He took the cup out of my hand, leaned down, and kissed me, licking the tea froth from my mustache.

"I'm heading back to bed," he said, his body feeling warm and wonderful next to mine, "as you should, pup."

He licked my chin and, this time, took a glance at my crotch, then gave me that trademark smile of his and walked out of the kitchen toward his loft in the library, as if this was the most natural thing to do.

I smiled to myself. The men of this house always seemed to know the right amount of affection that would melt my heart and make me relax.

With every sip of the tea, I felt my mind relax. Still, with the cup half gone and what was left grown lukewarm, I knew that sleep was simply not going to be rewarded to me. When the tea was finished, I sat there and began to experience a quiet, curious level of meditation. How many minutes or hours I remained in that state of mind, I wasn't sure; but as the light from the new moon lost its battle with the rising sun, I knew that my mind and my body were prepared for the day ahead.

The sun peeked over the horizon and lit the courtyard outside the guesthouse with a warm glow. I sat up in bed and noticed one of the men out in the yard—doing the tai chi exercises alone. It was William. Here it was November, and William was in loose white linen pants and nothing else.

His breath steamed in the cool morning air. The dark hair on his body, starkly contrasting with his light complexion, was a masculine, beautiful sight. He repeated the slowness of the day before, but they seemed all the more intense when watching him alone.

I got out of bed, pulled on my sweats, and continued to watch William; then I walked out and quietly approached him from behind. I paused, not sure if he'd seen me. I felt drawn to join him. As Jean had told me the day before, it was now my time to become an active member of the household. I could no longer simply observe.

William gently motioned me to his side, gave me a warm smile, but did not say a word. He set his hands at his side, then ever so slowly raised them to shoulder height and brought his hands forward as if pushing an invisible weight. William confidently melted into the movement, slowly reversing the motion and moving his hands back to his side. As he repeated the motion, I joined him, duplicating each of the moves he made.

Watching someone do taichi is beautiful. Watching someone move so slowly and meditatively as the movements take time to complete, almost feeling every joint contributing to the forward motion is like nothing else.

Before I knew it, the exercise was over, and William turned to me slowly, the same calming smile on his face.

"This move is called 'Grasp Sparrow's Tail,'" William said softly. "You will learn them all eventually. I was just going to come wake you. You have a curious and remarkable day ahead of you, and I wanted you to start out right."

He reached for my hand and led me into the shower building. The air smelled of eucalyptus, and the showerheads were soon running, filling the room with steam. William stepped toward me, gently undressed me, and led me into the showers.

He opened a cabinet in the wall and took out a sponge and a bottle of liquid soap, poured the soap into the sponge, and began to wash me slowly, beginning with my fingers and working his way up my arms.

The slow, concentrated bathing was powerfully erotic; as we stared into each other's eyes, our cocks quickly responded. Undistracted, he moved with slow circular motions across my chest, down my stomach, and between my legs.

He took me completely by surprise when he stood and pressed me against the wall, making our cocks press against one another, delivering a deep, passionate kiss. My body relaxed around him as he nibbled on my beard and chin. I let out a little grunt as the incredible feeling of this massive man against me turned me on.

"We are so lucky to have been found by you, Roy," said William, as he stepped back a little to make eye contact. "Today we will all spend the day demonstrating our love for you and making you our brother in the household."

Leaning in, he pulled me to his chest and proceeded to wash my back. I turned around slowly as his hands moved down my back. I felt his hands explore the furry patch at the small of my back and then descend toward my butt. The sponge continued its circular pattern until it was caressing my butt. I let out a whimper that encouraged William to continue at the same spot. Pouring more oily soap into the sponge, he moved it from there to the base of my balls.

He then knelt, proceeding down my legs with the sponge with slow attention to detail, then asked me to turn and face him. Washing up my legs and my front, William paused and looked contentedly at my hard-on. He leaned forward and sniffed at it, slowly and carefully. My cock leapt and throbbed at the attention—and the feeling of William's beard. I pushed forward gently; William smiled and retreated as if to say that actually being sexual was still not quite OK. Moving up my stomach and chest with the sponge, he stood to face me once more.

"We have to make sure you are clean and ready for everything today. Tristan is waiting for you in the other room for a massage; then you'll meet with David for breakfast."

He rinsed the soapy oil bubbles from my skin, walked me out of the showers, and attentively dried me with a thick towel. Then he scooped up my clothes and the towel and motioned me into the other room. Just as he'd told me, Tristan was waiting for me with a massage table.

"Good morning!" he said, uncharacteristically cheerful. He wore a white gown and had his hair tied back in a tight knot.

"Good morning Tristan, "I said, smiling broadly.

Next to the table were several bowls with colored dyes and a stylus. The massage table was laid out with linens, and incense was burning.

"It is my duty, Roy, to map your body and relax you to start your journey. Lie down on your back and we'll begin," he said softly.

He picked up scented oil and rubbed it into my skin. In complete silence, he gave me a careful massage—touching every part of my body—but began to speak as he dipped the stylus in ink from the tray of ink bowls.

"Chakra is a Sanskrit word meaning wheel, or vortex, and it refers to each of the six energy centers of which our consciousness, our energy system, is composed. The chakra represents not only particular parts of your physical body, but also particular parts of your consciousness," Tristan said.

He dipped a stylus in the red ink and moved toward the center of my forehead. I could feel him writing there.

"The forehead chakra is the home of the 'inner sound,' or the sound one hears inside that does not depend upon events outside. The inner sound speaks to our spirituality and the spiritual perspective, the point of view from that deeper part of our being that western traditions consider the subconscious or unconscious."

He dipped a new stylus in the green ink and moved to write on the base of my throat, near my Adam's apple.

"The base chakra is the home of the 'ether,' the crossover between the physical world and the world of spirit. On the physical level, it corresponds to deep space as the subtlest physical element."

He dipped a stylus in the blue ink and moved to write on the center of my chest.

"The heart is the home of the 'air' and the perceptions of love relationships. When we are close to someone, we are aware of what the person inside the other body feels, and that person is aware of what we feel inside our bodies. We can sense we are relating to the person inside the body."

He dipped a stylus in the maroon ink and moved to write on my solar plexus, right below my rib cage.

"The fire chakra is the home of the fire within and perceptions concerned with power, control, freedom, the ease with which one is able to be oneself."

He dipped a stylus in the lavender ink and moved to write on my abdomen.

"The sacral chakra is the home of the elemental within and perceptions about the body's communication to the being inside, about what the body wants and needs, and what it finds pleasurable."

He dipped a stylus finally in the brown ink, moved to my crotch, and took my cock in his hand.

"The earth chakra," Tristan said, writing a symbol on the head of my cock," is linked to survival instincts and our ability to ground ourselves in the physical world. It governs perceptions about personal vigor, security, passion, and trust."

"Vigor, security, passion," he repeated.

He studied my half-hard cock in his hand for a moment. I felt myself becoming comfortable intimately with each of these men. The urgent intimacy I'd sought from David, initially, now became something I wanted with all of them.

Tristan leaned over and kissed the tip of my cock and swirled his tongue on it. Pausing for a moment, he stared up at me with a soft intensity in his eyes. He stayed there for a long moment—the tip of my cock in his mouth.

Gently releasing my cock, he spoke softly. "In order to draw the tattoo, and make it part of you, I will need to shave your shoulder," he said, taking an old-fashioned barber razor out of its leather sheath and deftly holding it.

There is something uniquely erotic about the physical sensation of a straight razor against bare skin. The momentary scraping resistance as it peels the hair away has always struck me as a one-of-a-kind feeling. Methodically shaving the thick body hair from my shoulder, Tristan moved my arm forward and let it dangle off the massage table. He seemed to be studying the way my body moved to decide how to draw the tattoo.

"The chakra marks will shower off, and now I am simply drawing the wolf onto your shoulder. Then I will clothe you."

He reached for the stylus, and I could feel him begin the native drawing on my shoulder, creating the wolf claws. Despite the intensity of the situation, my mind wandered back to the fear of the tattooing. I experienced a flood of adrenaline, and my heart began to pound. Tristan, sensing this distraction, laid his hands on my back and spoke, softly and calmly.

"I will never hurt you, Roy. Never. Do not fear today, but let yourself free to feel all of it to its fullest."

He felt me relax with his comforting words, and he resumed drawing the outline of the wolf on my shoulder. I let myself return to the peaceful meditative state of the early morning hours alone in my room. Tristan continued to trace the stylus across my shoulder, and soon he was finished. Producing a clean white robe for me to wear, he sat me up on the table. Tristan leaned in closer to me and looked deep into my eyes.

"Welcome amongst us, teacher," he said softly, helping me off the table.

"David is waiting in the library."

I walked out of the shower building, the cool winter air shocking my body in the thin robe. Out in the courtyard, the sight of the totem pole again confronted me.

The bright morning sunshine striking its face gave it a unique shimmer. No longer the looming specter it had been at night, the totem seemed to beam and be proud of its new home.

This whole day was becoming a series of moments I didn't want to forget. Would I remember them all? I felt the newness of the dye on my shoulder and the softness of the silk robe Tristan had dressed me in. A shiver ran up my spine from the cold, and I entered the doorway into the library.

David was waiting for me, seated on the floor next to a roaring fireplace in a matching white robe. His long black hair came down over the robe and his chest, his black orca tattoo showing through the open robe. He was otherwise naked as he rose to

greet me, touching the chakra marks on my forehead and throat
before moving in and kissing me deeply.

"Good morning, Mr. Wallace," he said.

He took me by the hand and led me into the kitchen.

"Hungry yet?" he said, pulling pots from the cupboard.

"Yes, thank you," I said, smiling.

He started working over the stove, quickly stirring together a
pot of hot oats. I was actually surprised by how hungry I found
myself.

"The bread will be ready in a minute, then it'll all be ready to
eat."

David pulled the bread out of the oven; he served the oats,
buttered my bread, and slid in next to me at the kitchen counter. David and I sat there eating and touching each other softly.
So many times we'd had reasons to keep talking and working
toward each other, but this time together over was filled with a
fulfilling and touching silence.

I stepped up to him, staring him in the eyes, reached inside
his open robe, and traced the tattoo through the thick hair on
his chest, his bone killer whale ornament glowing a contrasting
white against his dark marking. He pulled me to him forcefully;
I could feel his hand run down my back and grab hold of my
body.

"Let's get dressed. I want…no…I need to take you to the
park," said David.

He led me back to his room where our clothes had been laid
out on his freshly made bed. The choreography of the day was
continuing with the unseen shadows of the other performers. It
was all unfolding in front of me like a magic spell.

The wind continued to whip through the trees as we walked
closely down the street toward the park. I told David about
Tristan and the story of meeting William in the park.

"The park is truly one of the best parts of having the house
up here on the bluff. Richard made everything so perfect," he
said, sighing. He leaned on me when we were on a trail in the

park woods. We walked quietly, and then the trail gave way to an expanse of grass atop the bluff. I knew at once I was at the place Tristan had described. The wind teased the tips of the tall grasses, running ripples across them like a body of water.

David stepped in behind me and spoke softly. He grabbed my belt loops and pulled me tight against him, just as he had that first day that I met him.

"Tristan tells us a story about the hummingbird floor. An old legend tells of emperors who designed floors in their rooms that made sounds at the slightest pressure, warning the ancient rulers of would-be assassins. He always called this field Richard's hummingbird floor. Only a man's true love could walk into this field and not make his presence known until he captured his heart."

Images of the Richard I never knew filled my mind. I realized that David was loving Richard and letting go of him at the same time. David loved this man, and maybe I should also, since it was he who gave David to me.

"Three years ago, Richard brought me here and told me that story. He set me on a blanket on a bright summer day and told me how I'd crept across the floor of his soul and captured his heart.

"I've hated the last year in my life, Roy. I haven't smiled; I haven't laughed—until three months ago, when you nearly fell over sneaking a look at me as I was walking out of the AIDS clinic," David said.

Even though I was not facing him, I could sense his smiling and feel his beard moving against my neck. He made me feel content and wanted.

"In my vision at Bowman Bay, Richard let me go. It was surreal to be having our first council about a new member of the household without Richard, so close to the anniversary of his transition.

"To be considering you, oh, pup..." David said, stopping to rub his beard on my neck. We continued to walk into the field. He pulled his pipe out of his jacket and was soon puffing along.

"So, no matter the other men in our commune, our tribe—I want you to know that, from the very beginning, I've considered myself yours. I am married to you in the deepest sense of the word. This afternoon I will take you as mine in the company of our brothers, and you and I will become one."

He took a puff on his pipe, then leaned forward to kiss me. The smoke swirled into my mouth along with his tongue. He pulled me close to him, licking up the side of my face as he finished the kiss.

"You are mine, Mr. Wallace, and I am yours."

I'd always eroticized pipe smoke as an extension of a man; the association now was even stronger. The aroma was David, as much part of him as a sweaty musk on another man.

I turned and sniffed loudly on the side of his beard. David smiled as he turned to me and then gently blew a mouthful of smoke on my face. He pulled his pipe out of his mouth and kissed me gently.

"So, Mr. Wallace, tell me about your morning."

I told him how the morning had gone with William and Tristan. As much as Tristan and David disagreed, David admitted to loving him and respecting him very much. I told him that, just as Marlin had done earlier, the others had started to show a lot more physical attention to me.

"Well, maybe Bear and Moose beat Marlin," I said, giggling.

"Bear and Moose would beat anyone to playtime," David said, joining me in a laugh.

The trail led into a clearing and down the bluff toward the ocean. Our conversation ended as the wind hit us hard, knocking us both back a step. It stopped us cold with its ferocity and bitterness. I had underestimated how much the trees had been sheltering us from the elements.

We stood there for a second, wind whipping in our hair, and looked across Puget Sound. The trees buckled to the wind, and the whitecaps frothed madly across the waterway. The darkness of some distant clouds moving rapidly in our direction convinced David that we'd better turn back toward the house.

As we reentered the canopy of the trees, I let out a sudden, huge, dramatic yawn. It was unintentional, but it made David giggle.

"And a nap," he added.

We were soon crossing back over the hummingbird meadow when David stopped to kiss me. We continued to walk hand in hand, back to the house, up the driveway to the door. The smells of the moist evergreens mingled with the aroma of David's pipe as he traced his fingers over the carving.

"Seven wolves tied together in brotherhood. After tonight, the number will be complete again," he said. He then hugged me for a long time, squeezing tight, as if I were never going to be with him again. It was, I think, his way of making sure that I was really there.

We walked into the house and found Marlin in a chair by the fire, reading. He was wearing a white silk robe, as everyone else had been that day.

"Well, 'ello, you two," he said, rising to meet us. He hugged me and kissed my neck, then hugged David and kissed him lightly, pausing to smell some of the tobacco smoke on his mustache.

"So, it's done, yes?" he said to David.

"Yes, I am ready to be his as he's ready to be mine," David said, his smile turning into a giggle. "But what the boy needs first is a nap. We want him to be awake and alert for what's to come."

"Yes, a nap does sound like a fine idea," Marlin said, smiling widely. "Perhaps 'e should go nap in a pile up in da loft. Eh, pup?"

Not reading any disagreement on my face, Marlin led David and me up into his loft. David moved in behind me and pulled off my shirt. Marlin took off the silk robe and lay naked on his bed. He ushered us both down onto his bed. It was wonderfully playful as we sat tracing the fur on each other's chest. Marlin was enjoying the deep red color of my chest hair.

"Enjoy all this auburn fur, pup, as it'll soon enough turn white as mine."

I leaned forward and kissed Marlin deeply. He responded by kissing me back with strong passion. I felt David's hands on my nipples as he began to chew on my ear. I was soon moaning, and my moans grew louder as I surrendered to the intensity of being loved by two men whom I adored.

Marlin leaned over my body and kissed David. To be close to such real intimacy between them was thrilling. David licked Marlin's beard, and his spit sprayed across my chest.

Remembering my last time up there with Marlin, I turned my head and chewed on his armpit. The thick scent of his body filled my nose as he let out a grunt and started grinding his cock against my thigh. I felt David's hand come over my body and take hold of Marlin's cock. Marlin continued grunting loudly as I continued to suck and chew on his armpit.

"No, no, not yet," Marlin said, withdrawing.

He recoiled slightly but with a mischievous smile on his face.

"Tristan 'd have a fit if I came all over you and ruined the ritual. Dammit, pup, you are a sexy boy. David and I will have many a night up here in da loft loving on you. For now, let's take that nap we talked about."

Marlin turned on his side and took me in his arms, and I instinctively took David in mine; soon we were all fast asleep. Surrounded by the smells of David and Marlin, I slept with a sense of security I hadn't known in a long while. When I woke it was just David and me. Somehow Marlin had vanished without disturbing my sleep. I realized that David had gently awakened me by drawing his finger across my chest and nipples. He was again dressed in the white silk robe.

"It's time we got up, sweet one, and got ready," he said with a calm grin.

We walked down the stairs from the loft. There on the couch was the white silk white robe Tristan had dressed me in earlier. David helped me out of my jeans, and I stood before him naked.

Smiling, he held the robe up and let me slide into it. He led me out through the library to the meditation room.

We entered, and I saw that all the other members of the house were there, waiting for us. The room was draped in green fabric; in the center was a round bed, covered by large pillows.

Candles were lit, and I could smell the odor of incense burning. The light from the candles flickered off the naked bodies of each of the men of the household. Their bodies were marked exactly as Tristan had marked me earlier. Their nakedness let their masculine scents fill the room. The soft colors and surroundings were contrasted by the smell of sex and masculinity in the room.

From behind me, David pulled off my white robe and let it fall at my feet; I heard his do the same. And with that, it began.

David's confident tone took command of the room.

"Having made the decision to join us, I bring you Sagahlie. I bring him to you naked as a man, to become one in our spirit. As See-He-Ahi taught us to do when the house began, I now bring him to you marked and ready to receive the gifts of the collective soul that is the House of Wolves. As the leader of this new house, I bring you Sagahlie, my love—my completion—who now will be yours."

The men moved forward and touched their hands to my chest. Marlin was teary-eyed. Bear and Moose moved in, ran their hands beneath my armpits, and carried me to the bed.

Laying me on my back, David knelt behind me. I could feel his PA rub against the hair on the top of my head. It was an overpowering feeling to see all the men as they stood around me. Tristan placed a small black bowl on my stomach and poured in dark charcoal, which he turned it into a paste with oil.

David touched my shoulders. William knelt to the right of David; he dipped his finger in the charcoal and marked my forehead.

"I bring to you, Sagahlie, the blessing of inner sight. I bring you peace; once you are bonded to the brotherhood of wolves, you will be blessed with a spiritual connection like no other. Even with the magic of the mahalets behind us, the magic this household will bring to your life is like no other."

In a bowl on my chest, he set a pile of eucalyptus leaves, then broke a stem and allowed the sap to weep into the bowl.

Bear took up the second position. He dipped his finger in the charcoal and marked my throat.

"I bring to you, Sagahlie, the blessing of physical love. I will always remind you that, by being bonded to the brotherhood of wolves, you will celebrate your physical body in our circle and with your beloved David. I will teach you to work harder at personal fitness and to remain centered, for health in this household is more important than any other principle."

Bear stepped around to each man and wiped the sweat from their brow, for the rising warmth in the room was already leaving its mark on each man's face and body. He then wrung the cloth out in the black bowl.

Moose then moved in next to Bear. For a moment, he stared down at my body. He then dipped his finger in the charcoal mixture and marked the center of my chest.

"I bring to you, Sagahlie, the blessing of safety. I will be your protector and your shield in time of need. I will be the strong powerful embrace in time of trouble and in time of great joy. I will remind you that protecting the sanctity of our bond is a daily commitment—and one that will change your life like no other."

Marlin then moved in next to me in the circle, gently closing around me. He poured what was obviously urine from a small jar into the bowl on my chest. Stirring the mixture with his finger, he then marked the base of my ribcage.

"I bring to you, Sagahlie, the blessing of knowledge. I will be your sage and your debate partner in things intellectual. I will stoke the fires of original thought and refresh your mind and the obligation to teach. My dream for you is that your intellect never grows weary or feels unused, and that your mind and your spirit will enter the House of Wolves and make it like no other."

He leaned down and kissed my cheek, which was wet from tears.

Tristan moved in next to David on the left, completing the circle. Picking up a needle, he pierced his thumb and let the blood drip into the charcoal then reached forward and marked my abdomen.

"I bring to you, Sagahlie, the blessing of spirit. We will meditate in this room and enrich ourselves with a deeper spirituality. The mixture of our histories and passions will become one in the spiritual bond that brings us to this place. To this spiritual sanctuary, to the place where all bonds fall, we will be as one."

As the ceremony progressed, I could clearly see that every man in the circle was becoming quite aroused, and the smell of sweat, already in the room, was now joined by the scent of pre-cum. The circle became closer, and each of the men traced his cock on my body, each staring down at me with lust in his eyes.

Then, each took the cock of the man next to him in his hand, arousing the entire circle of men. David then moved into my sight, to the other side of the bed, by my feet. I could tell that the other men of the house were closer to the marking of me with their cum. Bear and Moose were already grunting softly, and I could hear Tristan whimper.

I stared down my chest and saw Marlin move in behind David. David let out a grunt as Marlin pushed up inside him from behind. David looked up my body with an intense look and struggling to speak, said, "I bring to you, Sagahlie, the blessing of unbreakable love and partnership. We will share a bed and a life and become a new force within the house of the wolves. I will remind you daily that love and partnership and the demonstration of that love form our duty to one another as spiritual partners. It will shine within the love of our brothers, which is like no other."

David dipped his fingertips in the charcoal mixture and took the head of my cock in his hands, tracing it with the charcoal.

"I love you, Sagahlie," he said, reaching forward and wiping my cock free of the charcoal. He then leaned down and took my entire hard-on into his throat. Nothing had prepared me for the feeling as David swallowed my cock completely.

The warmth and lust were startling and overwhelming. The other men started to move their hands over my body. I let out a gasp and a grunt as David kept my entire cock in his mouth, working around it with his lips and tongue.

The smell of masculine sex filled the room as Marlin slowly fucked David—even as he continued to suck on my cock. Sweat beaded across Marlin's face as he pushed David's body toward me with each thrust.

Moose lay down next to me, and Bear was quick to follow, pushing Moose's legs up and mounting him with great force. Moose let out a grunt as Bear began fucking him with animal intensity. All the men were letting out grunts, groans, and whimpers of growing pleasure. Withdrawing from David, Marlin moved toward me, his cock frothing with pre-cum as he stroked it wildly.

His PA quivered as his cum exploded across my chest onto Moose's face. David was concentrating so much on sucking my cock that he did not seem to notice when Marlin shot his load. He was now taking my entire cock into his throat on each thrust and was grunting and sucking like an animal.

William continued to moan, stopping only to tell Tristan how good his mouth felt on his cock. Bear told Moose how warm his butt was, before giving out a loud grunt. Never had I been sur-rounded with such honest lust in my life; it was incredibly thrill-ing. Moose started to whimper and warn Bear that he was going to cum. Still connected by Bear's cock, they changed positions, and Moose began to be beat off over my chest. Bear continued to fuck him hard. I could hear his balls and belly slamming into Moose's furry body.

"Oh, yes, that's it, yeah," said Moose.

Bear reached up and twisted his nipples. Moose exploded, shooting great streams of cum into David's hair and face as he continued to suck my cock.

Without warning, I felt William shudder, his warm cum exploding across my right shoulder. I looked up and saw Tristan sucking on his balls as he continued to drench my shoulder with his cum. Moose relaxed onto me, he head lying on my chest. After Moose moved off of him, Bear got up and moved around to Tristan.

Tristan had not stopped sucking on William's balls, even when Bear entered his butt just inches from my face. Tristan bucked back on Bear, but he made no sound, his mouth still enclosed on his lover's balls.

Bear's enormous cock slammed into Tristan's butt without mercy. Bear's grunts and moans got louder, and he withdrew from Tristan, slapping his ass as he did so. Staring down at me, Bear was drenched in sweat. Bear's cock exploded as cum splattered across my chin and up my cheeks; it was a huge load. I moved in, sucked the shaft of Bear's cock, and sucked and bit and feverishly fed on the sweat from his having fucked Moose and Tristan.

"That's it, pup, yes sir," said Bear.

"Yeah," said Moose, looking up at me, still lying on my chest. Bear pulled his cock from my mouth and smeared its saliva-covered hardness against my face.

I was then suddenly picked up by the legs and pulled downward. I felt my legs move up against David's body as he was moving into position to fuck me. The lust was clear in his eyes; he needed to fuck me and to finally cum inside me. David stared down my body and into my eyes. Holding my legs against his torso, he spit into his hand and worked his cock.

"Here I come, boy," he said, as he lifted my legs higher and entered me in one strong motion. I grunted and yelped. My legs pinned between us, he remained entirely inside me as he kissed my beard.

I heard Bear say "thatta boy" as David started to slowly fuck me. He let out these quiet, gentle whimpers as his balls slowly bounced against my butt. His eyes read of urgency as his body moved in against mine.

"Oh, Mr. Wallace, yes sir," he said, as he continued to slowly fuck me.

I licked his face and trembled as his lover. I took hold of his nipples. His entire manner changed. As I pulled on his nipples, the calm, slow fucking became faster and deeper.

"I love you, David," I said, as I pulled harder and harder on his nipples.

I could feel the orgasm building in his body; his legs begin to shake with spasms, and his breathing became short.

"Oh, Roy, oh God," he said. Then I felt it happen; his body arched and bucked from a shockingly intense orgasm. He pounded away with his cock as he came deep inside of me.

William moved in behind me and lifted up my shoulders. Moose started sucking on my nipple as the others began again to trace their cocks on my body. David reached down and started to beat me off, remaining as close as two men can be.

"Yes, pup, that's a good man," said Marlin.

The sight of David lustfully playing with my cock was beautiful. My masculine man was finally allowed, in the sight of his brothers, to make me cum. I was hardly about to disappoint the man I loved so much. My body lurched forward, and my cum exploded up my belly and my chest. David looked down at me, his cock still inside me, with tears in his eyes. I cannot remember at any other time being more in love with a man. Sweat poured from every inch of his thick, hairy body.

Withdrawing from my butt, he moved around and set his cock level with my face. He was becoming aroused again. He traced my beard and hair with his semi-hard cock. I felt his Prince Albert slowly trace my features. I then turned to him and stared up at his beautiful chest and into his chestnut eyes, taking his cock into my mouth.

I'd dreamed so long of this moment. With my brothers watching, I savored the position of staring up at my David while he slowly pumped his reawakening cock into my throat. The lust between us was the most intense I'd ever experienced.

Cradled in William's lap, I felt David's PA enter my throat. I could see that all of his brothers were touching him and playing with him.

"Oh, Mr. Wallace," he exclaimed. To my amazement, soon after cumming inside my butt, his cock exploded in my mouth. The feeling of the PA quivering in my throat as he came—I'd never experienced that before. He shuddered as his cock pulsed again and sprayed more cum to the back of my throat.

I didn't want it to end. I bore down until his spent cock was down my throat. I could hear Moose and Bear voicing approval. David reluctantly pulled his cock from my throat, and the groups of men were quickly curled up around me. It was bliss!

I felt the hands and body of each of them touching me. We lay there smiling and touching and tracing one another. The group of men slowly swarmed together, sniffing each other, kissing one another, and showing such powerful affection.

David rolled over on me and kissed me deeply and powerfully. He sucked on my beard and then rolled back off me.

"Now it's time to get inked, pup; we'll all be here for you," said David. "But Now you must wear the mark of a brother, the mark of Sagahlie."

Tristan excused himself to retrieve the tattooing gear; the others cleaned up and then helped me get ready. Five men worked quickly to wash the cum and sweat from my body and, just as efficiently, towel me off. I felt their hands on me, slowly exploring as Tristan came into the room pushing a small cart.

"It has always felt right that brothers get their initial tattoo in the arms of everyone else," said Moose.

"Makes it something you'll always remember as a collective act. Something we all witnessed," said William.

As Tristan sorted through his supplies on the cart, I rolled over on my stomach. Each of my new brothers was now very close to me.

"OK, Roy, today we are simply outlining the design on your shoulder; we'll come back to this and fill it in over time. I'll first need to sterilize the site of the inking. Move your arm up, the way you did today on the massage table."

I lifted my arm above my head.

"The best way to endure this is to breathe in rhythm with the tool. I will dip the tool in the ink, then trace, and repeat. Try and not flinch—simply breathe and relax into the sensation," said Tristan.

I gripped David's hand as Tristan wiped my shoulder with an alcohol swab. As I heard the sound of the tattoo gun kick on, my panic set in. Tristan then started outlining the design on my shoulder blade.

The first pain was mild but bearable. It was exactly as Tristan had explained; the procedure carried its own deep rhythm. Among the words, the breathing, and the focus, there was the buzz, the line of pain that swirled and shifted because I didn't know where the needles were. The silence, as the hand skimmed over to the ink, dipped, shook, and slipped back to the buzz and the needle in the skin, then a line, pausing to wipe away the blood so he could see where to continue. Each moment the needle was up, a part of me would ask, over and over, "Where is that pain?" because it vanished without the needle. But it returned. Then vanished, overwhelming me. I lost the world beyond the sounds, the voices, and the small room of pain I was in. I could hear David and Marlin speaking to me as the tattooing proceeded, but their voices were ghostly, like something I could not respond to.

After a solid hour of inking my shoulder, Tristan finished. The tension and angst fled. It was over. I felt tremendous relief, a surge of pride, and the oddly masculine thump of "I fucking did it!"

David held up two mirrors so I could see my new tattoo. The dark curves of the wolf spirit were now part of my body. Tristan's brushstrokes were now lines across my skin. At this point, it didn't hurt or, for that matter, even sting. It just, well, moved and breathed along with me.

Tristan then covered the marks with white gauze dressing to allow healing. I sat back, surrounded by my new, loving brothers, all of us touching and caressing one another. I had never experienced such unconditional closeness with a group of men before.

Marlin spoke softly: "We need to give this pup a rest and some water! He still has his first night to endure."

The men slowly let go of the pile. The group felt reluctant to release me from our newfound intimacy. After some final touches, kisses, and caresses, we all moved from the meditation room. We walked out into the courtyard to find our clothes had been laid out, and we were soon dressed and heading into the main house where we spent the afternoon sitting around the library, talking and relaxing in each other's company.

The grandfather clock against the wall in the library struck six, and David suggested it was time we retired privately to what was now our bedroom. Bear and Moose teased David for wanting me all to himself. After another loud eruption of jeering and laughs, each of them kissed me good night, and David led me, hand in hand to our room.

He opened the door, and I noticed immediately that my belongings had been moved from the guest quarters. Fresh flowers filled the vases Tristan had put in David's house after his trip to Bowman Bay.

"Welcome home, pup," David said.

He gently touched my left shoulder and asked me how my ink was feeling. I honestly hadn't thought about it. I told him it ached a little but was not causing any serious discomfort.

David then moved to the bedside table and pulled out a black box, beautifully wrapped with a red ribbon, handed it to me, and led me to sit on the bed with him. I slowly untied the ribbon, took the cover off the box, and discovered, carefully wrapped in tissue, a scarf made of luminescent wool in rainbow stripes. I lifted the gift out of the box and admired it, suddenly realizing where I'd seen it before.

"It was Richard's most prized possession. I am so happy for you to have it, and wear it as your own," said David.

Nothing surprised me anymore in this household. I held in my hands the scarf I'd admired in visions and dreams with Richard.

"Thank you, David; thank you so much. It's beautiful! I love it."

David leaned over and wrapped the scarf around my shoulders, then gently set me back on the bed. He kissed me gently, and we lay there for a moment in an embrace. We sat up and cuddled on the bed while watching television. David lit up his pipe, playfully blowing smoke my direction. He knew it was a turn-on for me and loved exploiting it. He'd purposefully take in a deep breath of his pipe smoke, then kiss me, letting the smoke swirl in our beards and into my mouth.

Unbuttoning my shirt, slowly, he said, "They are absolutely right. I want you all for myself."

David ran his hand up into my shirt and played with my nipples as he continued to blow pipe smoke over my face. This man knew exactly what he was doing. Seeing my eyes melt into his, and feeling my body reacting to his affections, he reached down into my pants and took hold of my now very hard cock.

"You are so beautiful, Roy, so fun to touch."

David started kissing me and continued to grasp my cock in his hand. We were both soon kissing deeply and enjoying each other. He took his shirt off, revealing his dark, furry chest, and he rolled over on top of me. He undid my pants, and then his own, and brought our cocks together as he stared down at me. His pierced cock rubbed erotically against my own. He blew a thick cloud of pipe smoke in my face. I let out a desperate whimper; he was turning me on much more than I think he knew.

"So much to explore with you, pup, so much," he said, smiling.

I reached down and grasped his cock, pulling on it gently. It was so sensitive to touch; the more I pulled on it, the harder he became. I started to aggressively beat him off, both of our cocks in my hand. I could see in his eyes it wouldn't take much, that our passionate kissing and his imagination had him almost to the point of cumming. He clenched his pipe between his teeth, furiously puffing away, and pulled on his nipples. Intent on shooting, he started to sweat, and I could feel his balls retreating.

"That's it. Yes," I said.

He arched his back and stared down at me with surprise and lust as his cum erupted across my belly and up into my beard. I kept pumping his cock, and it throbbed and leaked in my hand. He lurched and grunted in his unique, masculine way. He set his hand down on our cocks, signaling me to stop. He grinned and growled at me.

"Let me up to get a towel, will you?" I said smiling.

David moved to the side, and I got up from the bed. I surprised him by turning around and going for his crotch. I took his sensitive cock into my mouth and sucked on it deep and hard. He yelped and jumped around.

"Oh, god, stop, oh shit!" He said, giggling with me, seeing the smile on my face. I kept sucking until every shiver had been wrung out of him.

"You, Mr. Wallace, are evil," said David.

Licking the tip of his PA, I smiled again and said, "You have no idea, David, you have no idea."

With that, I got up and headed to the bathroom to get a towel. Returning to the bed, I mopped his crotch and chest and settled in for a serious cuddle. David traced my chest and laid me gingerly down on my inked shoulder.

We got back to watching the television, all the while remaining in a wonderful embrace. This room felt so comfortable; I knew that I was finally relaxed here and that it was, indeed, my home.

In the back of my mind, I knew that the evening would end with me receiving a PA like the rest of the members of the household. David said he'd picked out a ten-gauge, curved barbell for me, which was the largest Marlin had recommended.

Marlin knocked on the door. He had a small leather bag with him. "Are we ready, gents, for the jewelry?" Marlin asked, cautiously.

"I think so," I said tentatively.

"Remember what I told you last night, pup; I'll never make ya do anythin' you don't want. But this will hurt…it's not easy."

He set the bag down on the bed. Opening it, Marlin pulled out a small, sealed, plastic bag containing the piercing jewelry.

"Go wash your cock carefully, Roy, and come back," said Marlin, handing me some iodine soap.

I walked into the small bathroom; then my emotions hit hard. This was now our room, David's and mine. So much had happened that day, from the beginning, with the intimacy with the brothers, followed by the tattooing. I started wondering if I were a complete nut for wanting to have this done.

Tears welled up in my eyes as I looked in the mirror. I was about to ask Marlin to put a metal ring in my cock. I sat there staring at myself in the bathroom mirror, trembling as David came up behind me. He wrapped his arms around me and looked into the mirror with me for a moment.

"I know this is intense for you, pup. We don't have to do this now if you don't want to."

I shook my head, telling him no, that I wanted to go through with it. He pulled a tissue from the box and wiped my face. Becoming a part of the House of Wolves meant committing to their customs and rituals. I was now completely committed.

"You aren't human if you don't think twice about piercings. It'll all be fine," David said to me, "Now get washed up. If I do it for you, we'll give you another stiffy, and that's not good in this setup. Get to it!"

After a thorough washing, I returned to David and Marlin. Marlin had removed his shirt, and my two furry companions waited for me. Marlin placed a towel over the center of the bed and asked me to lie down. I have to admit that I was so scared, my cock had shrunk to the smallest it had been in my adult life.

He put on a pair of latex gloves, then casually lifted my cock so he could examine the head. It was almost humorous as he studied with such obvious intensity.

He then took a marker and placed a small dot just below the crown and asked David if he thought that looked OK. David agreed, and they discussed the imminent procedure matter-of-factly. Marlin then asked me if I would like to look, just to make sure.

"I trust your judgment; you'll have more of a personal view of it in the future, I quipped.

They both smiled and, in unison said, "He's ready!"

My tone of humor set all of us at ease, and I relaxed. Marlin then told me that I would feel a little pressure as he inserted the needle guide. He manipulated my cock and the steel tube until satisfied.

"Now," Marlin said, "when I tell you, I want you to take a deep breath."

With that, he said, "Now."

I sucked in a huge breath of air just as the needle punctured my flesh. Completely unprepared for the pain, I gritted my teeth but didn't make a sound. I thought we were finished but suddenly felt the jewelry being pushed through. A second wave of pain ran through my body as that hurt as much as the needle.

Marlin complimented me on my patience and self-control. He told me he was almost finished. I could hear him screwing the ball on the end of the barbell, and then he asked me to take a look.

"There ya are Roy boy, it is all finished," he said, snapping off his rubber gloves.

Both men had wide smiles as they waited for my approval.
David was holding up my now-expanding cock. Much to my surprise, there was some discoloration from the sterilizing solution
but almost no bleeding.

Marlin wrapped a piece of gauze around my cock and very
carefully helped me pull on a pair of underwear. He said to sleep
in these overnight so my cock didn't move around excessively.

"For the first couple of days, there is some discomfort," said
Marlin, "as the urine flushes the wound, pushing out all the
white cells that may have dried up. Then we'll have David make
sure you do a saltwater soak four times a day to keep it clean."

Marlin stepped up and kissed me softly.

"Enjoy your first night at home, Roy. I always remember mine,"
he said, leaving David and me alone in the room. David gave me
a good, strong hug.

"You must be exhausted, Mr. Wallace. It's been a long day."

He felt me relax into him.

"Why don't you lie down here and put the music on, and I'll
go get us something to eat from the kitchen. Then we'll make it
an early night," he said.

David kissed me tenderly. I cared for this man profoundly, and
he clearly reciprocated. After David left, I turned on the television, crawled into bed, and pulled the warm flannel sheets up
around me. He returned with a tray of food, and we cuddled.
His warm body against me, I was quickly nodding off, despite the
aches in my shoulder and my pierced cock.

I'd taken the first step into my new life today, and there would
be many more days, turning into months, into years, to discover new dimensions within myself. With David's muscular arms
around me, I felt my soul relax into this world that was now
mine. I turned under the sheets, placing my face in his chest, the
smell of sweat, burley tobacco, and his skin surrounding me just
before I finally was lost in peaceful sleep.

Epilogue

I CLOSED THE LEATHER diary and looked up at the younger man. His dark hair was braided and curled around into the center of his chest.

"David would be so proud of you," he said to me, smiling.

"I'd like to think so," I said. "I really miss him sometimes."

"He'd be proud of the new brothers and the way they keep the stories alive—and keep reaching to new places," he said softly, tracing his fingers along my face.

We rose from the bench we'd been sitting on while I read. As we walked along the beach, I watched the springtime sun reflect on the water. I was now in the twilight of my life, my own white hair on my collar. The sea salt in the air reminded me of countless other spring days sitting in this small cove.

The young trees bent themselves before Mother Nature's wind as if in prayer to her against the sky.

Strange how places like the peaceful waters of Bowman Bay call out to you over the years and bring you peace and solace. When my David brought me to this place long ago, it became intertwined with our love for one another.

Living on the bluff in Seattle with the men of the household was as natural to me now as anything had ever been in my life. Over the years we'd brought six other men into the household, and we'd softly watched the passing of three of those who had welcomed me long ago.

Marlin passed quietly in David's arms in his loft over the library. A few years later, Bear passed on and this past October, my David. We'd lived together in love for an amazing forty-one years. In that time, we'd both become new men and learned that the loss of our first partners was simply the beginning of another adventure. We'd spent years discovering ways to love one another, as well as all the brothers in the house.

The ragged rainbow scarf wrapped around my coat and trailing down my back, I pulled out my pipe and tapped it gently, lighting it in a poof of gray smoke. The younger man told me about his day. He was a teacher, as I had been.

He taught high school biology. I knew he'd always been brilliant, and his students learned to have a relationship with nature, understanding that, in studying it, they were, in fact, studying themselves.

He reached over and tapped the mahalet, now honoring David, on my waistband.

"You honor him so strongly," he said to me.

We turned the corner along the water and saw several kids playing and laughing in the springtime sun.

"They remind me of Marlin; you know that," I said smiling, "Even in his nineties, that man could laugh and make people giggle like children."

I stopped for a second and somberly stared out to sea. His hand touched my shoulder, knowing instinctively that I needed that touch so badly these short days after David's transition.

"Whenever I remember Marlin I think about the kites in the park…"

I turned and looked at him with love. His Native features showed themselves sharply.

"The winter snows had given way to clear blue skies and windy afternoons," I began telling Richard as we stood there watching the children play.

"The trees showed the first green leaves of early March. I'd sold my little home on the hill and moved entirely into the House of

Wolves. My days were full of after-school workouts with Bear and Moose, learning cooking with Tristan, and long nights talking in the library with William. Marlin had become a regular visitor to my classroom. Tristan had long finished filling in the beautiful red-and-black wolf tattoo on my shoulder.

"I was walking into the park with my brothers. We'd spent the morning working on a beautiful, paper box kite that Tristan designed. It was adorned in several different colors of paper as well as several runes.

"As was the custom of the house, we all had written quotes on the kite. David then added beautiful characters, Native drawings, one for each of the totems in the house; now it was ready to fly.

"Marlin held it as we moved into the park. All seven of us were soon standing knee deep in grass in Hummingbird Field. Bear tied string to both sides of the box kite, tying it to a single roll of string. David held me from behind as Marlin and Moose gently lifted the kite up. You could already see the wind tug at its frame. Bear handed me the roll of string; David reached around me, and we held it together. Marlin let out a loud yell as they let go of the kite. Grown men's laughter echoed through the ancient evergreens, across the quivering field of grass and out to sea.

"Tugging on the string in our hands, the kite bolted forward, showing off its tail in the whipping wind. It soared skyward, dancing and swaying side to side on its way into the heavens."

The End

About the Author

A self-described disciple of Henry David Thoreau, ROBERT B. MCDIARMID is both a writer and activist. Robert lives in Palo Alto, CA with his husband, David, and Miss Kate, their terrier. As an avid cyclist, he has participated in AIDS Lifecycle, a 550-mile bike ride from San Francisco to Los Angeles. In the spirit of his activism and giving back to the community, royalties from *The House of Wolves* will be donated to HIV/AIDS charities.

Made in the USA
Las Vegas, NV
05 April 2022